His hands and his mouth moved possessively against her body.

Sebastian lifted his head. Pilar felt the slow breath he released, sighing out over the moisture his lips had left on her skin. She shivered again, uncontrollably, and his hand soothed across her back, holding her gently against his chest.

"There's nothing to be afraid of," he whispered, his mouth moving now against the thin, fragile skin of her temple. The words were as soft as the breath he had taken.

"I'm not afraid," she said. "Not of you. Not of this."

He held her a moment more. And then, putting his hands on her shoulders, he set her away from him so that he could look down into her face. In his eyes were promise and hunger. And she wanted them both.

Acclaim for RITA® Award winner Gayle Wilson

"Rich historical detail, intriguing mystery, romance that touches the heart. These are the elements that keep me waiting impatiently for Gayle Wilson's next book."
—*USA Today* bestselling author BJ James

Anne's Perfect Husband
"The author excels in creating compelling characters who behave intelligently and honorably. Gayle Wilson never disappoints."
—The Romance Reader (theromancereader.com)

My Lady's Dare
"...three-dimensional characters and intriguing plot twists kept this reader glued to the pages."
—*Romantic Times*

Lady Sarah's Son
"...a moving tale of love overcoming great obstacles, of promises kept and trust restored."
—*Romantic Times*

HER *Dearest* SIN

GAYLE WILSON

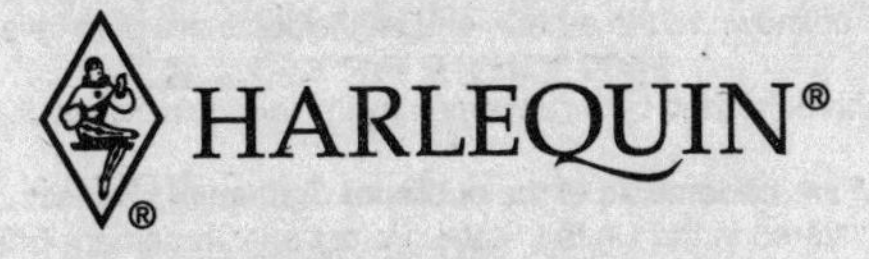

TORONTO • NEW YORK • LONDON
AMSTERDAM • PARIS • SYDNEY • HAMBURG
STOCKHOLM • ATHENS • TOKYO • MILAN • MADRID
PRAGUE • WARSAW • BUDAPEST • AUCKLAND

ISBN 0-373-29207-4

HER DEAREST SIN

This edition published by arrangement with Harlequin Books S.A.

Visit us at www.eHarlequin.com

Printed in U.S.A.

Available from Harlequin Historicals and GAYLE WILSON

The Heart's Desire #211
The Heart's Wager #263
The Gambler's Heart #299
Raven's Vow #349
His Secret Duchess #393
Honor's Bride #432
Lady Sarah's Son #483
My Lady's Dare #516
Anne's Perfect Husband #552
Her Dearest Sin #607

Other works include:

Harlequin Intrigue

Echoes in the Dark #344
Only a Whisper #376
The Redemption of Deke Summers #414
Heart of the Night #442
**Ransom My Heart* #461
**Whisper My Love* #466
**Remember My Touch* #469
Never Let Her Go #490
***The Bride's Protector* #509
***The Stranger She Knew* #513
***Her Baby, His Secret* #517
Each Precious Hour #541
†*Her Private Bodyguard* #561
†*Renegade Heart* #578
†*Midnight Remembered* #591

* Home to Texas series
**Men of Mystery series
†More Men of Mystery series

Please address questions and book requests to:
Harlequin Reader Service
U.S.: 3010 Walden Ave., P.O. Box 1325, Buffalo, NY 14269
Canadian: P.O. Box 609, Fort Erie, Ont. L2A 5X3

Dedication

To Melissa, with my admiration and affection

Acknowledgment

A multitude of thanks to Olivia Ouijano for answering innumerable questions concerning names and titles for this book. Any mistakes are mine or were deliberately written to be made by my English-speaking characters. Olivia, I love you!

Prologue

Spain, 1813

"Did you say *bathe?*" Lord Wetherly drawled, never stirring from his comfortable occupancy of his host's only chair. His booted feet, dusty of course, but elegantly crossed at the ankle, were propped on the edge of the cot, the other major furnishing of the tent.

"Bathe," Captain the Honorable Sebastian Sinclair reiterated. "As in to become clean again."

"I think you've had too much sun, my dear. Likely prove fatal to venture out in your condition. Best lie down and rest until the fit passes."

"Would you care to be seen in London in our present state?"

"The thing of it is, Sin, we ain't *in* London," the viscount remonstrated with a grin. "Just in case you hadn't noticed."

"I've noticed," Sinclair said shortly.

With his knee, he pushed Wetherly's boots off the cot to allow himself passage across the tent. Once there Sebastian began to rummage in the trunk he'd brought out from England two years ago.

"Frankly, it's damned impossible not to notice," Sinclair went on, "when one is forced to sit down to dinner with gentlemen who haven't had more than a rudimentary spit and polish in months. And in case *you* hadn't noticed, there's a perfectly good river within a quarter mile of camp. I see no reason not to avail ourselves of the opportunity."

"The Beau's orders seem reason enough for me," the viscount said mildly, watching his friend lay clean clothes on the end of the cot. "The presence of a few bands of French deserters and the occasional Spanish bandit in the area might provide another. Not that I expect either to make the slightest difference to your plans, of course."

"Good," Sinclair said, lifting the breeches of his spare uniform out of the trunk and holding them up for inspection. "What the hell did they clean these with?" he muttered. "Mud, do you suppose?"

Wetherly recognized the observation as rhetorical and not requiring an answer.

"Boredom," the viscount said instead. "That's all that's wrong with you. Our collective stench hasn't bothered you before. Now, all of a sudden things have quieted down, no Frenchies to kill, and you damn well can't stand it. So you plan this little adventure into enemy territory—"

"The enemy is a dozen miles away," Sinclair said absently, brushing at the suspicious brown smear on the otherwise spotless white linen. "The rabble that's out there..." He gestured outside the tent with a tilt of his head. "*They* want nothing to do with soldiers. Attacking old men and girls is more their style.''

''If you're taken, and they demand ransom, Wellington won't pay it,'' Wetherly warned. ''Not after that last harebrained episode he was forced to extricate you from. And if no one pays the ransom, Sin, my lad, you'll be sold to the highest bidder. Probably end up in a harem somewhere. Spend the rest of your days as a rich old woman's lapdog.''

The famous Sinclair eyes, deep blue and surrounded by a sweep of long black lashes, lifted from their consideration of the uniform.

''Do you think so?'' Sinclair asked. For the first time he seemed genuinely interested in his friend's opinion. ''How exciting. Of course, Dare would be displeased to have me disappear into Spain. Family feeling and all that. Never forgive me, I suspect. *Or* the Beau.''

Despite the seeming arrogance of that last phrase, everyone in camp was aware that Sebastian Sinclair, who had been affectionately and rather accurately known as Sin since his school days, never sought to trade on Wellington's well-known friendship with his oldest brother. And because the viscount knew him so well, he understood that Sebastian would never dream of doing so. To Sinclair that would be a far worse offense than sneaking off for a dip in the nearby river.

After all, Wellington's order hadn't applied to his officers. They were simply charged with seeing that it was carried out. In leaving camp Sebastian would not be disobeying the letter of his commander's directive, only its spirit. That was exactly the kind of moral hair-splitting at which the youngest Sinclair had always excelled.

"Oh, yes. Lapdog or a harem. I have it on the best authority," Wetherly said solemnly. "And if your reputation with the ladies has in the least preceded you, I can guarantee there will be a spirited bidding for your services."

Laughing, Sinclair aimed one of his extra pair of boots at his friend, who warded it off with a practiced twist of his wrist.

"There are, I suppose, worse fates than becoming a love slave," Sebastian said.

"I'm not sure. Have you seen the women in the market?"

The long war had caused endless deprivations among the civilian populations of the Peninsula. The Spanish were as determined as the English to free their country from the domination of the French puppet who occupied the throne. Unhappily, however, it was the women and children who had seemingly borne the brunt of those efforts.

"Poor creatures," Sebastian agreed. "However, they don't represent the aristocratic women of this country. Anyone capable of joining in your 'spirited bidding' would surely be one of those. Beautifully pampered and cosseted."

"Thank God," Wetherly said. And then, his tone changing from the familiar raillery in which they had been conversing, he added, "Still have to say you're making a mistake, Sin. Too dangerous, my boy, even for you."

"You may be right, Harry, but at least I shall meet my fate smelling like a man and not a horse."

"Is *that* what that is? Been trying to identify exactly what it is you smell like for a month or more. Glad to have the riddle solved."

The other boot followed, thrown over Sebastian's shoulder at a target he could not see. It was characteristic of Sinclair's luck that this careless toss accomplished what the first had not. In spite of the viscount's belated attempt to knock it away, the boot landed squarely on top of Wetherly's head.

Laughing, he threw it back, striking his friend on the shoulder. Sinclair ignored the blow, continuing to arrange his selected change of clothing into a neat bundle.

On his way to the opening of the tent, he bent to pick up both boots, rolling the supple leather of their high tops around the clothes. When he reached the tent flap, he stopped to sketch the viscount a quick salute.

"Tell my brothers I not only died bravely, but cleanly. More than any of you will be able to say."

"Never had any desire to become a love slave," Wetherly retorted. "You run along now, Sin, and have your bath. But if you get into trouble out there, don't expect any gallant rescues. Quite beyond my skills. You're the damned dashing one."

"If I go missing, just send for the cavalry. They never met a fight they didn't like."

"Now if that don't sound familiar," Wetherly said. "Always wondered why *you* wasn't cavalry."

"Dare couldn't afford the commission," Sinclair said cheerfully.

Which, as the viscount was certainly aware, was blatantly ridiculous. There were few fortunes in England larger than that of the Sinclairs. And despite the long war, the present earl had, unlike so many of his fellow peers, managed to increase the vast sums he had inherited.

"Saving it for the ransom?" the viscount suggested.

"No doubt. See that Dare pays up, will you? While I may be perfectly willing to bleed in the service of my country—"

The rest was cut off as Sinclair let the flap of the tent fall. Left alone and still smiling, Viscount Wetherly rose, the movement characteristically languid, and walked over to the opening. He lifted the edge of the canvas and watched the figure of his friend cross the compound.

His were not the only eyes that followed the captain's progress through camp. Sinclair's dark good looks were compelling enough that they always garnered attention. Among the troops, however, it was his reputation for a reckless and selfless bravery that had won their admiration. More than one trooper's eyes also lifted to watch the passage of the most popular officer on Wellington's staff.

As was his custom, Sin stopped to exchange greetings with those who spoke to him. Although the distance between them was now too great for Wetherly to be sure, perhaps he even chose to disclose to a few his destination.

What was certain was that none of those who watched that charming and graceful progression through camp could possibly imagine how this day's adventure would irrevocably, and forever, change the man they had grown to love.

Sebastian Sinclair had already finished his bath. He had even managed to coax enough lather from the sliver of lye soap he'd bought from one of the women in the village to allow him to wash his hair. Now he was floating lazily on his back, enjoying the warmth of the water and remembering long summer days back in the peaceful England of his boyhood.

Then, in the midst of those pleasant daydreams, he felt an indefinable prickle of unease along the back of his neck. Too long accustomed to living with danger to ignore such a premonition, he raised his head, slowly allowing his feet to sink until they touched the sandy bottom.

His eyes scanned the rock-cluttered slope he had descended. Finding nothing there to alarm him, he turned to consider the opposite bank of the river, the slope there far steeper and more treacherous than the side held by the English.

There were a dozen places among its ledges and escarpments where someone might hide. Given the loose rock, he believed he would surely have heard them moving into position. His gaze traveled the length of the ridge overlooking the river before he turned his head, again focusing on the English-held side. There was nothing there. No movement. No noise. And yet…

Moving carefully so that no telltale splash would be created by his passage, Sinclair began to make his way back to the spot where he had laid his clothing and his weapons. He could see the small pile they made, its color darker than the tans and yellows of the surrounding rocks.

He had hidden his pistol at the bottom of the stack of garments, but he had placed his sword in the open beside his boots. And he would feel infinitely better when one—or both—was in his hands.

He stepped onto the bank, water streaming down his calves and ankles from the knit drawers he wore. He had debated taking them off during his bath, but in the end he had decided he would feel too vulnerable if completely nude. He was perfectly willing to fight his way out of any manner of tricky situations, but he preferred to do so at least partially clothed.

Which was why, as soon as he reached the heap of clothing, the first thing he reached for was the clean pair of breeches he had taken from the trunk. As his fingers closed around them, something sharp was pressed against the side of his throat, right above the pulsing artery.

Obeying that unspoken command, Sinclair froze. Bent forward in order to reach for his clothing, he was in the perfect position to examine his possessions—the ones that were where he had left them. As well as the one that wasn't.

It took him less than a fraction of a second to conclude that he was being held captive with his own sword. Out of the corner of his eye, he followed the length of it to the hand on the hilt. And beyond that—

"Stand back, if you please."

The voice was soft. And it was unmistakably feminine. Although the English in which the order had been given was impeccable, it was also accented.

Sebastian hesitated a heartbeat, wondering what would happen if he allowed his hand to close around the blade and tried to wrest it away from his throat. Since he was aware how fine an edge the tempered steel held, he understood what the immediate consequence of that action would be. If his assailant were quick enough, and courageous enough, that particular consequence might well be followed by other, more serious ones.

Besides, Harry was right. He *was* bored. And this attempt to rob him—for he had no doubt that's what was afoot—was less dangerous than the other scenarios that had been running through his brain when he'd left the water.

Despite the fact that the woman was pressing the point of his sword against his throat, he believed that at any time he chose he could take the weapon away from her. And, more important, that he could do it before she managed to inflict any lasting harm.

The desire to see how this played out, or perhaps the urge to get a look at the face that went with that intriguing voice, won out over his first inclination. Moving very slowly, he began to straighten.

The blade followed. As it did, the woman who held it moved in front of him, so that by the time Sebastian was upright, the point of the sword was firmly lodged against his larynx. The line it had traced over his skin burned as if his valet had shaved him too closely.

Face-to-face with his captor, awareness of that discomfort faded to a secondary consideration. *Extremely* secondary.

In spite of the unusual timbre of her voice, he could never have imagined anyone like the girl—for she seemed little more than that—who stood before him. She was dressed very simply, in the same garments worn by every peasant woman he had encountered in the district. On her, their effect was nothing short of remarkable.

The tail of the dark skirt had been caught up in

its own waistband, revealing a froth of embroidered petticoats, two slender ankles covered with white stockings and neat black slippers. An embroidery pattern, which matched that on the petticoats, had been stitched along the neckline of her off-the-shoulder blouse, its fabric only a shade or two lighter than the cream of her skin. Its paleness was in marked contrast to the midnight hair, held away from an oval face by two silver combs.

Her eyes were as black as the curls that tangled over her shoulders. And they were deadly serious.

"In fairness I should warn you that my comrades are just beyond that hill," Sebastian began.

"But your comrades don't bathe. You would have been wiser had you followed their example."

Sebastian controlled his amusement, meeting the dark eyes steadily. "I'm afraid I don't have much of value."

She made a quick downward survey. The point of the blade, pressed hard against his throat, never wavered. When her eyes lifted again, they were amused.

"So I see," she said.

As his gaze followed hers, Sebastian discovered that the wet knit underdrawers clung revealingly to his anatomy, exposing his body as clearly as if he had been wearing nothing at all. And incredibly, Sebastian Sinclair, who had bedded more than his share of opera dancers and actresses, felt a rush of blood stain his cheeks.

The women he knew would have been embarrassed by his state of undress. Or they would have pretended to be. Certainly none of them would have been able to deliver that set-down with such poise.

"Don't worry," she went on. "I'm interested only in your clothes."

"My clothes," he repeated, feeling at a distinct disadvantage as the exchange unfolded.

"The clean ones," she clarified. "If you would be so kind as to lay them out for me in a separate stack..."

"Perhaps you believe that I have an unlimited wardrobe," he said, thinking that this demand was outside of enough.

She was welcome to his money, but he'd be damned if he'd hand over his only decent change of clothing. Even as he reached that decision, he acknowledged that his reluctance to do so was probably as much a matter of pride as necessity.

"But I assure you I do not," he continued before she had a chance to speak. "Everything that has not been lost to swollen rivers, thieves or bloodstains during the last two years lies before you."

"And I wish it to be in a separate stack, if you please," she said again, obviously unmoved by that recital of disaster.

It seemed to Sebastian that as she said it, the point of the blade bit more deeply into the small dimpled depression it was creating at the base of his throat.

"*I* assure *you,*" she went on, "that I have more need of them than you. If you will give me your name and your regiment, perhaps I can arrange to have them returned to you when I have finished with them. Would that be satisfactory?"

He was struck again by her command of the language. Despite the accent, the words themselves might have been exchanged in any London drawing room. If one were to divorce them, of course, from the highly unusual nature of the subject they were discussing.

"I believe I prefer to keep them with me. It's so difficult to know where one will be in...?" He hesitated, inviting her confidence about when she believed she would be finished with his clothing.

The smile that had almost broken through her control before twitched again at her lips. "Perhaps you are right. My plans are unsettled as well, so I should not lead you to expect the return of your garments. And now, if you please..."

There was no doubt about the increased pressure of the point this time. He felt the tip pierce the skin of his throat. Warm blood trickled downward over flesh chilled by his recent immersion in the water.

Clearly that prick was a warning. One he stubbornly didn't heed. For several long seconds they continued to stand, frozen in their adversarial positions, eyes locked in challenge, each refusing to give in.

And then, the sound distinct above the rush of the river, they heard the ring of horses' hooves on the rocks high above them. She glanced up, her eyes widening. Whether from shock or by design, the point of the sword was moved back a fraction of an inch. Away from his throat. Freed from its imprisonment, he turned his head, moving very slowly so as not to provoke retaliation.

His eyes were drawn to the top of the ridge behind him. He was hoping Wetherly or one of the others he had spoken to about his intent to bathe had finally realized how long he'd been gone and mounted a search party. Although why they should approach from the opposite bank...

And of course, they were not. Search party this might be, but the men lining the top of that slope were not looking for him.

He estimated that the man riding at their head was perhaps a decade older than his own twenty-nine years. Old enough, then, to be the girl's father. *Or her husband.*

He had time to feel an inexplicable jolt of disappointment at that thought. Then the rider gave a sharp command to the others and sent his horse down the incline, seemingly without regard for its safety. Or for his own.

As skilled a horseman as Sebastian was acknowledged to be, he would have been reluctant to try his mount on that precipitous descent. He would certainly not have dared it at this speed.

Apparently the other riders in the party felt the same way. They remained along the crest of the ridge, their horses held near the edge as they watched their comrade's headlong plunge. And whoever the horseman was, Sebastian thought in quick admiration, he was a superb rider.

"Run," the girl said.

Surprised, Sebastian pulled his eyes from that astonishing feat of horsemanship and back to her face. It was absolutely colorless. The dark eyes were still wide and, although there had been not a trace of fear in them when she had held him prisoner with his own sword, it was there now. For some reason, he found he didn't like seeing it.

"Your husband?" he asked, his gaze flicking back to the madman, who was now almost halfway down the slope.

"No."

She had managed to inject bitterness into the single syllable, the emotion strong enough that it brought his eyes again to her face.

"But he *is* coming down here for you?"

"He'll kill you," she warned. "I never meant for this to happen." Her eyes considered horse and rider briefly before they focused earnestly on his face. "If you run, I'll try to distract him long enough to give you a chance to get away."

Not surprisingly, Sebastian found he didn't relish the idea of running back into camp clad only in his drawers. If he were killed here, no one would ever know exactly what had happened to him. If he fled in his underwear, like some hotly pursued virgin, he might live, but his fellow officers would dine out on the story for the next twenty years. Not only here, but in London as well.

He could imagine Dare's face when he heard the tale. The thought of his older brother's sardonic enjoyment of his predicament was quite enough to ensure the choice Sebastian Sinclair would ultimately make.

He dove toward the pile of garments, throwing articles of his clothing aside until his fingers closed around the pistol he'd concealed beneath them. At any moment, he expected shots to rain down around him. After all, the muskets that the horsemen carried had been in plain sight the entire time.

He rolled away from the scattered clothing and then scrambled, crouching, to his feet, his gaze sweeping the top of the ridge. The men who had lined it seconds before had disappeared. Only the leader was still visible, now guiding his horse into the river on the opposite bank.

Sebastian closed the distance between him and the girl, his fingers fastening around her upper arm. He drew her with him toward the pile of boulders she must have hidden behind to launch her ambush. They would offer some protection until he could figure out where the other riders had gone.

Still holding his sword, she allowed herself to be carried along with him for a few feet. Then, with a twist of her arm, she jerked away from his hold. He had already taken a step toward her when he realized what she was doing.

She ran back to the scattered pile of clothing, stooping to grab the pair of breeches he had been reaching for when she'd stopped him. And then she turned, hurrying toward him.

She threw them over his arm, the one that was outstretched to hold the pistol pointed at the horse and rider, who were now swimming across the current. In a matter of seconds—

"Go," she demanded.

"Not bloody likely," Sebastian said.

He threw the breeches over his shoulder and took her arm again. He dragged her with him as he retreated, never taking his eyes off the approaching horseman. As far as he could tell, the man wasn't armed, which made her repeated requests that he run ridiculous. Armed and with sufficient cover—

"You fool," she said, the words low and intense.

Surprised by the vehemence of her tone, which had been almost as bitter as that with which she'd answered his inquiry about the identity of her pursuer, he glanced toward her. And saw what she must have known from the beginning.

The line of horsemen who had disappeared from

the top of the opposite ridge were now riding at a canter along the bank on this side. Obviously, they had crossed the river at some nearby ford, which they must have been aware of all along. As had the girl, he realized. That knowledge made the action of their leader in risking life and limb in that treacherous plunge even less fathomable.

It hardly mattered now. Both methods of reaching this side of the river had been successful. Too damn successful from Sebastian's point of view, since they were closing in on him from two directions. A highly efficient tactic that had afforded Wellington's forces more victories than Sinclair cared to remember.

The rapidly dwindling options ran through his mind like lightning. His soldier's instinct, honed by two years of hard fighting, discarded them all.

Of course, the first shot in would arouse the camp. Whether his friends would understand its significance and respond in time was another question.

"Release her."

The command was in Spanish. Sebastian had picked up the language quickly in his time on the Peninsula, certainly enough to understand the order he'd just been given. Instead of obeying it, he leveled his pistol at the chest of the man who had pulled up his exhausted mount, its heaving sides still streaming water, in front of them.

Close enough that Sebastian could see the rider's features quite clearly, despite the wide-brimmed black hat he wore pulled low over his eyes. They were as dark as the girl's, but somehow this was a different black, cold and opaque. Almost soulless.

Looking into them, Sebastian Sinclair, who had

been said to possess the steadiest nerve on the staff, shivered involuntarily. A chill from his recent swim, he told himself, denying that uncanny wave of apprehension.

"She's under my protection," Sebastian said in English, hoping that something of the claim would translate.

For an instant, the rage in those black eyes was clearly visible. And then the man on the back of the trembling, exhausted steed laughed, the sound far more chilling than his anger had been.

"*Your* protection?" he mocked in the language Sebastian had used, his gaze raking the Englishman from head to toe. "Then she is more foolish than I had imagined."

"Let him go," the girl said. "He has nothing to do with this."

"And I wonder why I don't believe you, my dear?" the man on horseback said.

Behind them, Sebastian could hear the other riders beginning to descend the slope. He held his pistol high so the fact that the muzzle was pointed at their leader's heart would be obvious. Its warning didn't slow their approach. The man before him had never glanced their way.

"I was stealing his clothes," the girl said. "He knows nothing, I tell you."

"He knows enough to recognize that he is in danger."

"He's no threat to you," she said, pulling her arm from Sebastian's hold.

She held out the sword so he could take it from her hand. Holding both the sword and the pistol would, however, leave him without any way to control her if she tried to surrender to the horsemen. It had become clear she believed it was her duty to save Sebastian rather than the other way around. Since he had never before been in the position of hiding behind a woman's skirts, however, he was unwilling to begin that practice now.

"Despite *her* opinion of the situation," Sebastian said. "I assure you that I fully intend to be a threat, sir. This lady is under my protection. She has no wish to go with you."

"Do not make yourself more foolish than you already are," the man said. "What she wishes is of no concern to me. Nor are you. Come, Pilar. You have wasted enough of my time."

There was a long hesitation. No one moved, but it seemed to Sebastian that he could feel the muskets behind him drawing a bead on his naked back. There was an unpleasant crawling sensation along his spine, as if the nerves were preparing themselves for the impact of a ball.

He was near enough that he could hear the breath she drew before the girl said, "Your sword, sir." Again she offered him the hilt.

"Don't be afraid," he said. "I won't let him take you."

He was well aware that claim was sheer bravado. He was outnumbered and outgunned. However, it was not in his training nor his background, and decidedly not in his nature, to do less than try to make good on the vow he'd just given, no matter the odds.

"A dozen of the best marksmen in Spain are behind you," the horseman said. "Their guns are trained on your back. I should hate for one of them to miss and hit the girl you are trying to protect."

"I think you should remind them that *my* gun is trained on your heart. If they shoot me, my finger will still apply enough pressure to this particularly sensitive trigger to cause it to fire. It seems we have reached checkmate, my friend."

The man laughed, and Sebastian again felt that cold finger of apprehension along his spine. He had known innumerable men who were willing to face death on a daily basis for love of their country. Few of them laughed at its threat. Few who were sane, he qualified.

"I want your word," the girl said unexpectedly.

His word? In the context of his exchange with the horseman, the phrase made no sense. Sebastian resisted the urge to look at her, unwilling to take his attention, even briefly, from the commander of those men at his back.

"Of course," the horseman said, his voice still mocking.

His gaze lifted to some spot over Sebastian's head, and the English soldier knew in that instant the signal for whatever was about to happen had just been given. Almost before the thought could form, the girl beside him brought the hilt of the sword she'd offered him down on top of his wrist. The heavy guard cracked audibly against bone, knocking his hand and the pistol it held downward. Just as he'd threatened, the hair trigger caused the gun to discharge.

When it did, it was no longer pointed at the chest of the horseman. The horse reared instead, screaming in pain and fear. Then it sank on its withers, staggering sideways before it toppled to the ground. The rider leaped away from the stricken animal, realizing even before Sebastian had, what was happening.

Shocked, Sinclair turned toward the girl who had betrayed him. Her eyes, washed with moisture, held on his for the split second before he was struck on the back of the head from behind. And her face was the last thing he remembered before he lost consciousness.

He would realize only later that it had been the shot that awakened him. At the time, he was aware of little beyond the warmth of the rock beneath his cheek and the ache at the back of his skull. He tried to open his eyes, but the sunlight reflected off the water dazzled them, creating dancing spots that obscured his vision.

When it began to clear, the first thing he saw was a pair of boots, directly in front of his nose. Their fine-grained leather was polished to a high gloss that rivaled that reflected off the surface of the water.

Too disoriented at first to understand what was going on, Sebastian gradually became aware that he was lying on the ground, his hands bound together at the wrists. The leather thong with which they had been tied was tight enough that his fingers were growing numb.

A number of men and horses seemed to be milling around him. He watched with disinterest as one of the men crossed his limited field of vision carrying a smoking musket. It was only then that Sebastian realized what had awakened him.

They had killed the horse he'd shot, putting the animal out of its agony. The noise the dying stallion had been making seemed to echo still off the rocky slopes. Although Sebastian had not been conscious of what had caused those sounds as he came awake, the resulting silence was a relief.

Before he had time to relish it, the point of his own sword was again pressed against his throat. This time the tip had been placed just beneath his chin, the point exerting an upward pressure.

"Look at me, you English bastard."

More in obedience to the urging of the blade than to the command, Sebastian turned his head, looking up into the eyes of the man standing over him. The man whose boots he'd been facing when he'd awakened. The man who'd ridden the stallion down that rocky incline and then jumped agilely from the dying animal's back.

Sebastian had thought before how soulless these eyes were. Now they were filled with a hatred that was palpable, and for the first time he was truly afraid.

Not to die. He had never really been afraid of dying. Not if the death were clean and honorable. In the two long years he had spent at war, however, he had become aware that there were many things worse than dying. All of them were reflected in this man's eyes.

"You killed my stallion," the Spaniard said.

If Sebastian had believed an apology might make a difference, he would willingly have framed one. He had never intended to harm the horse, of course. This bastard, on the other hand—

"With my own hands, I pulled him from his mother and blew into his nostrils," the horseman continued, his voice low, each word intense. "And you, you worthless piece of offal, have slaughtered him.''

The milling men and their horses had stilled. Only the rush of the river and the malice of the horseman's voice disturbed the afternoon heat. And the same ominous quiet that settles over the countryside before a storm seemed to surround them.

''You gave me your word,'' the girl reminded.

Pilar.

She had been the one who had knocked his hand aside. With that gesture, she had delivered him into the hands of his enemy.

The black eyes of the horseman lifted from their focus on his face to find that of the girl, and Sebastian realized she was standing on the other side of him. Despite the threat of the sword, he turned his head far enough that he could see her. Her eyes were on the man who held the sword against his throat—and with it, held his life.

''My word?'' the Spaniard questioned, mocking the soft determination of her reminder. ''And what do you suppose that is worth now, considering what he has done?''

''Your word was once worth a great deal. Is it no longer?''

''The situation has changed.''

''And so your word is no longer your word?''

''He killed El Cid.''

''That was not his intent. If you wish to blame someone for the death of the stallion, then you must blame me,'' she said.

Sebastian opened his mouth to protest and a sudden pressure of the sword against the thin skin under his chin pushed it closed. The eyes of the horseman had never moved from the girl's face.

As it had been from the first, the real struggle of will was between the two of them. Sebastian had simply gotten in the way. He was someone who had no part in this quarrel, but who might very well pay the price of it with his blood.

"I wonder why you are so interested in saving the life of an English soldier. A man you profess not to know."

"I *don't* know him. I never saw him before today. I needed his clothing, and so I tried to steal it."

"His clothing?"

The sword moved away from his chin, but before Sebastian could react to its release, the point lowered again, this time to score quickly down his breastbone. The pressure was enough to split the skin, leaving a thin line of welling blood from his collarbone to his navel.

The shock of what the horseman had just done was enough that he didn't feel the sting from the shallow cut. Not immediately.

"He doesn't seem to be wearing any," his captor gibed.

"Exactly," said the girl, her voice perfectly calm. "Making that which he'd taken off in order to bathe available."

"Clothing," the horseman mused as if he were considering the possibility. "Your only interest was in his clothing. You had none in the man himself, I take it?"

The sword had moved again. The point rested now on the most vulnerable part of Sebastian's masculinity. The threat was as effective as when the tip had been placed at his throat. Furious—and helpless—he tried to express his rage with his eyes, but neither of them was looking at him.

"I had no use for the man," she said.

The thin lips of the Spaniard curved, the expression more sneer than smile. "Then I take it you would have no objection if he were...no longer a man," he suggested.

Sebastian's blood ran cold through his veins, but he fought to control any outward revelation of that. He had known men like this, men who enjoyed inflicting pain, either mentally or physically. Their cruelty always fed on their victim's terror.

"You gave me your word that he would be unharmed," Pilar said again.

Her voice had not changed, despite the nature of that threat. Sebastian found himself clinging to the hope represented by her calmness. She knew this man, far better than he could. It was evident that she believed this argument would have some weight on his decision.

"I promised you his life," the man said.

"That was not the promise I sought."

"It was the one you were given."

There was a small pause, and Sebastian held his breath as it lengthened.

"You have won," she said. "You can afford to be magnanimous."

"I can afford a great number of things. I value only those that give me pleasure."

Sebastian wondered if she gave him pleasure, and again the unpleasantness of the thought disturbed even the fear and the fury at his helplessness.

The girl said nothing in response, but her chin

lifted. An unspoken challenge? Or simply an expression of pride?

"I hold you to your word, Julián. You are bound by the oath you gave me, no matter the circumstances."

The Spaniard's smile was as soulless as his eyes. Almost before it formed, the sword moved—one flick of his wrist and then another. With the point, he had drawn an X on Sebastian's chest, directly over his heart.

Before the Englishman could think of trying to respond, the point of the blade was pressed against the very center of that mark. All the horseman needed to do was lean forward, putting a downward pressure on the hilt...

"I hope you are telling me the truth, my dear. I do so hate liars and cheats."

"I never saw him before today," she affirmed.

"And you care nothing for him."

"Only as I care for any fellow creature. I do not wish to see him hurt for some groundless suspicion that he has given me aid. Or for your jealousy."

The point of the sword lifted again, settling this time very near the place where it had been resting when Sebastian had regained consciousness. The horseman's eyes fell to his face. Lips pursed, he seemed to study Sebastian's features as if he were memorizing them.

"Very well," the Spaniard said finally. "Since I gave you my word..."

Again his lips tilted upward and, with another flick of his wrist, so did the sword. It slashed across Sebastian Sinclair's face, a much deeper cut than the one it had drawn along his chest.

The blade had sliced diagonally, moving across the flesh of his chin and missing the corner of his mouth by a hair's breadth. Then it had continued on that same path, straight as a die, laying open his cheek. The point lifted only when it reached the hairline at his temple.

The horseman's eyes had followed the lightning-quick movement of the sword. When it reached its apex, his strong swordsman's wrist straightened, snapping the tip of the blade upward, straight at the girl's face. A droplet of blood was flung from the flexing steel onto her cheek.

"Unharmed. As promised," the horseman said, smiling. And then, as he turned to mount one of the other horses, which was being held for him by its rider, he threw a brusque order over his shoulder. "Bring her."

Two of the men stepped forward and took the girl by the elbows. She offered no resistance, but before she moved, she looked down into Sebastian's eyes.

"I'm sorry," she said.

Then, with one quick, decisive movement she freed her arms. As if she were a queen approaching her courtier, she walked across the rocks to the man who had slashed open Sebastian's face. When she reached the horseman, who had already vaulted into the saddle, he lowered his hand, holding it out to her.

She put her fingers in his and her foot on the toe of the boot he offered. With a movement as smooth as that with which he had mounted, she was pulled up onto the horse and settled behind the Spaniard.

Without looking at Sebastian again, the horseman put his booted foot back into the stirrup and used his heels to urge the gelding up the slope that led to the English-held side of the river. The other riders streamed behind them, heading back toward the ford they had crossed before.

Stunned by what had just occurred, Sinclair lifted his bound hands, trembling fingers touching the cut that marred his face. His eyes filled with tears, not of pain or anguish, but of sheer, unadulterated rage as he listened to the sound of their horses' hooves fade away on the rocks.

He lay where they had left him. And looking up blindly into the heat of the summer sky, he swore that he would find and kill the Spanish bastard who had ruined his face if it were the last thing he ever did in this life.

Chapter One

Madrid, 1814

"And finally, I would remind you that we are here as representatives of the Prince Regent," the Duke of Wellington concluded, his piercing eyes examining each of his officers in turn. "I need not tell you what an honor—and a responsibility—that is."

He inclined his head, almost a bow, before he turned. As if on parade, his staff followed him through the massive doors and down the steps of the residence that had graciously been made available to the former commander of the British forces in Iberia, now special envoy to the Spanish court. Waiting below were the carriages that would take Wellington and his party to the reception at the royal palace.

Some of the men who accompanied the duke tonight had been with him the last time he had entered Madrid—under far different circumstances than these. There was very little he could tell them about duty or responsibility they didn't already know. And he, more than anyone, understood that.

"He'd rather be hanged, I venture," Viscount Wetherly confided sotto voce to Sebastian as they followed their commander.

"He'd rather be charging an enemy," Sinclair responded more accurately.

"He'll find enough of those tonight. Not the sort one can take satisfaction in charging, of course. A gaggle of Spanish nobles determined to turn the clock back on the past five years. Can't be done, if you ask me."

"No one will," Sebastian assured his friend with a grin. "Politics isn't your forte, Harry. Leave the maneuvering to the Beau. At least he knows what message it is we're supposed to convey to Ferdinand and his advisors."

"That they shouldn't let the Inquisition start burning people at the stake again, I should think," Harry said. "Seems reasonable to me."

And not so far from the truth of the matter, Sebastian acknowledged ruefully, despite his comment about the viscount's lack of political understanding. Wellington had been sent by the English government to advise the Spanish court that it would be the height of folly to attempt to undo the reforms instituted in the country while its rightful king had been in exile. No one, least of all His Majesty's envoy, expected that mission to be a success.

"But will it seem reasonable to them?" Sebastian asked. "That's the question. Not that Wellington gives a damn. He'll deliver the prime minister's warning because that's what he's been asked to do. What they do in response will be up to them."

They were aware from bitter experience that Arthur Wellesley, now Duke of Wellington, had never suffered fools gladly. Riding a crest of unbelievable popularity due to his role in the defeat of Napoleon, he would have little reason to change that habitual attitude now.

"Have to confess," Harry went on as they settled into the last of the line of carriages, "I'm not nostalgic about being back in Madrid. Can't compare to the glories of Paris in the spring."

"To the glories of the dancers at the Opera, you mean."

"You're simply jealous, my dear. I can't be blamed that the loveliest preferred me," Harry chided.

It was the kind of repartee they had engaged in a thousand times through the long years of their friendship—bragging about their exploits with the fairer sex or their ability to drink or to fight, each claiming superiority. This time, however, there was a small silence after the viscount's unfortunate choice of words. And then the situation became even more awkward when Wetherly attempted to apologize for them.

"You know that ain't the truth, Sin," Harry said, his voice subdued. "No woman has *ever* preferred me to you. Not even after..."

The hesitation provided an opportunity for Sinclair to break into that nearly stuttering explanation, one which he gratefully took. "Not even after they've gotten a good look at my face?" he asked with a laugh, putting a comforting hand on his friend's shoulder.

"I didn't mean that," Harry said stiffly.

"Just because the lot of you pretend this doesn't exist," Sinclair said, touching the still-reddened scar that traversed his cheek, "doesn't mean it isn't there. Plain as the nose on Wellington's face," he said.

Sinclair never referred to the scar except mockingly, as he had done tonight and, then only in response to another's comment about it. Most people assumed it to be the result of an injury received in battle. The few friends who knew the truth of the incident said nothing to disabuse others of that notion.

"You're still the most dashing officer on the staff," Harry avowed gallantly.

"And you, sir, are its greatest liar. I wonder Wellington puts up with you."

"Keeps me around for my entertainment value."

"And me for the unquestioned beauty of my countenance," Sebastian said, grinning at him again.

"He'd be lost without us," the viscount declared, sounding relieved that his faux pas had been so gracefully handled. "Should never have won the war if we hadn't been here."

"Undoubtedly," Sebastian said, leaning back in the comfortable leather seat and closing his eyes. "Wake me when we arrive at the palace. It will be the one with all the torches."

"Arrogant English bastard," Julián Delgado said as he watched his king greet the special emissary from the Court of St. James's, "flaunting his victories and his drummed-up titles."

"Jealous, Julián?" Pilar asked.

"Of Wellesley? Hardly. I simply hate to see him lauded like some conquering hero."

"He shall make his government's request and be gone within the week. Why let his presence upset you? After all, everyone knows where the real power in Spain resides."

He turned to look at her then, perhaps in an attempt to judge if the last had been mockery. It had been, of course, but she had become extremely skilled during the past year in hiding her true feelings from her guardian. She smiled at him before she turned back to watch the English duke present the members of his small party to the king.

"I'm not sure Fernando is as convinced of that as you," Julián said, his gaze returning to the dais as well.

"I'm sure you'll take the necessary steps to see to it that he soon will be."

"As soon as possible," he agreed, not bothering to deny what she had just suggested. "The quicker he recognizes his proper place in the scheme of things, the better it will be for all of us."

"There are those who might think that smacks of treason. I should be careful where I voice that intent, if I were you."

She didn't look at him this time, knowing she was treading on very dangerous ground. Her guardian had no patience with any dissension with his opinions. Certainly not from her.

"And are you one of those, my dear?"

"On the contrary," she said. "As always, I am your most ardent admirer."

There was a prolonged silence after her lie. Through it Pilar's eyes remained focused on the ceremony taking place, as if she were unaware of the perilous undercurrents of their conversation.

"Your tongue will get you into trouble if you don't learn to control it," Julián warned, his tone softer than that in which they had been conversing. "And now, if you'll excuse me, I believe His Majesty requires my attendance."

He bowed to her formally before he turned, strolling to the front of the room. Her gibe had struck home, and Pilar's lips curved into a slight smile of satisfaction as she watched him walk away.

The rather grandiose style of his evening attire was in marked contrast to the almost severe tailoring favored by the English party. Surrounded by the sea of blazing colors that represented the court dress of the Spanish nobility, the knot of black jackets, no longer clustered around the king, again drew her eye.

The somber hue of their clothing was not the only discernible difference in the appearance of Wellington and his officers. The fine cloth of their coats stretched across shoulders broadened by years of campaigning. Knee breeches and silk stockings revealed the long, muscled thighs and shapely calves of men who had spent countless hours in the saddle.

Pilar pulled her gaze away, unwillingly reminded of another English soldier. And of the price he had paid for her foolish attempt to escape her fate. A bitter lesson, especially for someone as headstrong as she had always been.

It was one she had not forgotten, however. Nor would she, she had vowed. Never again would she embroil someone else in her troubles. It was too costly.

Grateful that Julián had been called away, providing her a few moments of freedom from the facade she maintained in his company, she began to thread her way through the close-packed throng. The doors that led to the nearby palace gardens had been left enticingly open in a fruitless attempt to permit the cooler outside air to circulate through the crowded ballroom. Her progress toward them was interrupted a few times to return greetings from those who had known her father or who were friends of her guardian.

It had been a very long time since she had been required to attend such a gathering. She knew that Julián would never have brought her tonight if he had not believed her absence might cause comment.

When she eventually reached the balcony, she was surprised to find it deserted, perhaps because the official presentations had ended such a brief time before and the dancing was to begin shortly. Julián seldom danced, so it would be some time before he would look for her.

The king's gardens lay enticingly below, free of crowds and clamor. If only she dared…

She glanced back at the ballroom, her eyes easily locating Julián's dark head. He was engaged in conversation with several others of the king's advisors. Such discussions normally occupied several hours. Surely this one would last long enough for her to escape for a few minutes that unaccustomed tumult.

Unable to resist the temptation, she hurried down the steps that led to the grounds below. It was not until she had entered the sheltering darkness under the ornamental trees, beyond the reach of the flambeaux that lined the palace walls, that she slowed, lifting her face to the breeze.

The scent of almond blossoms was heavy on the night air. If she closed her eyes she could pretend she was back on her father's estate, far from the sights and sounds and smells of the city.

Drifting out from the ballroom came the strains of the seguidilla. She smiled unconsciously, remembering the first time her dancing master had led her though its intricate patterns. Lifting the hem of her gown with her left hand, she began to parody the steps as they would be performed inside.

As she danced, she circled in and out between the slender trunks along the avenue of trees. Her outstretched fingers trailed over their bark as she moved from one to another, keeping time to the melody that floated out into the garden.

So far from the lights of the palace, she had no fear she would be seen, and only an occasional welling of anxiety that she might be missed. Surely Julián would be more concerned tonight with keeping the king in line than he would be in keeping her in line. After all—

Her fingers brushed across an unexpected texture, one that was definitely not wood or bark. Despite the brevity of the contact, she knew at once that what she had touched was flesh and bone. A living, breathing body—here, where none should be.

Her involuntary gasp broke the stillness. She stumbled backward, putting a protective distance between herself and whoever was leaning against the tree.

"I do beg your pardon," a deep voice said in English.

Her eyes found the small, glowing tip of the cigar he held. She wondered that she hadn't been aware of its pungent smell. Of course, the heady fragrance of the flowering trees and her own childish masquerade had been convenient distractions.

''Who are you?'' Pilar asked, taking another step back.

Had the man not addressed her in English, she might have been more frightened, convinced she had encountered some trespasser on the palace grounds. Given her previous interest in the Duke of Wellington's party, however, she found herself more intrigued than apprehensive.

''Merely the victim of an unfortunate vice,'' he said, his voice tinged with amused self-deprecation.

Her eyes followed the unhurried rise of the end of the cigarillo as he brought it to his lips. The tip flared briefly in the darkness as he inhaled, and then it was lowered again. This time the smoke wafted toward her, its scent as faint as the music.

Her father had smoked these same small, tightly rolled cigars, and their fragrance had lingered in his clothing. When she was a little girl, and her papa had been away too long, she would sneak into his chamber and open the door of the enormous wardrobe to breathe in the wonderful variety of smells she would always associate with him. These cigars. The oiled leather of his boots. Sandalwood and cedar. Horses. The aromas of home.

''Shall I put it out?'' the Englishman asked.

She swallowed against the force of those crowding memories and shook her head before she realized he would no more be able to see that gesture than she could see him. All she could discern was his shape, black against the lesser darkness of the night, his chest centered by the pale gleam of his cravat. And, of course, the small glowing tip of the cigarillo.

"No," she said, the word little more than a whisper.

"Is something wrong?" he asked.

Hearing the unfamiliar—and unmistakable—concern in his voice, her eyes stung with tears. She blinked, denying them.

"I wasn't expecting anyone to be here," she confessed.

"Escaping?"

The word reverberated in her consciousness. Another memory.

"For the moment," she said.

"Then we can be conspirators together."

There was a heartbeat of silence.

"You're with the English envoy."

"The Duke of Wellington. Have you met him?"

"Not yet. He seems…" She hesitated, searching for a word that would not give offense.

"Ordinary," the deep voice supplied, touched again with amusement.

Which made it even more attractive, Pilar decided. Confronted with his ease of manner, she was beginning to relax. Despite the fact that she shouldn't be here, despite the fact that he was a stranger in a dark garden, she felt no sense of foreboding in staying to talk to him.

Even if someone came looking for her, it would be easy enough to fade into the shadows. No one would ever know she had been here. With the constraints under which she was now forced to live her life, this small, harmless adventure had suddenly become unbelievably precious.

Of course, whatever interpretation she chose to put on this clandestine encounter, she had no doubt what Julián's reaction to it would be. Then she reminded herself again, almost fiercely, that he need never know. What were a few moments in a garden compared to a lifetime—

"It's all right," the Englishman went on. "Most people think him to be far less...extraordinary, somehow, than they had expected."

Wellington, she realized. He had asked her what she thought of the duke.

"I don't believe I have yet had time to form an impression," she said.

"I see," he said, the amusement in his voice still evident. "I should imagine that a lady like you has heard little about his military exploits."

"Only that they were successful," she lied.

And was rewarded by his laughter. Like his voice, it was rich and pleasing, clearly masculine, and yet, unlike her guardian's, free of mockery.

"Somewhat," he agreed after a moment.

"Did you fight under his command?"

"I was a member of his staff."

"Then I am sure you must have the greatest admiration for him."

"Of course," he agreed readily, that tantalizing hint of amusement lurking.

"And as a member of his staff, what were your duties?"

"Primarily to dance attendance."

"On the duke?"

"On whomever or whatever needed attending to.

The role of staff is to make things run as smoothly as possible. The variety of tasks we undertake to accomplish that would probably amaze you.''

''I think I should like to be amazed,'' she said promptly, realizing how much she was enjoying this.

There was no need to guard her tongue or to watch her back. She was simply a woman engaging in light flirtation with a gentleman who seemed skilled in the art.

''Carrying dispatches on the battlefield. Scouting. Procuring provisions when need be. Dancing.''

''Dancing?'' she repeated, allowing her own amusement at what seemed to be a ridiculous non sequitur.

''Oh, quite the most important requirement in a staff officer, I assure you.''

Like his laugh, like the heady sense of freedom the darkness provided, his teasing was exciting.

''The ability to dance?'' she mocked.

''*And* to be enormously charming while doing so.''

''I'm sure you excel at all of them,'' she said.

''Would you care to put that to the test?''

''Here?''

''Or inside, if you prefer.''

''Not inside,'' she said, the laughter wiped from her voice.

''Then...''

With the word, he threw the cigarillo away. Her eyes followed the glowing arc of its short flight, and when they came back, he was holding out his hand. It was close enough that she could see it, despite the darkness that obscured his face. Hesitating only long enough to draw a fortifying breath, she placed her fingers over his.

Even through the supple kid gloves she wore, she could feel its strength. A horseman's hand, she thought, remembering the muscled contours of the Englishmen's bodies, their strength more revealed than concealed by the superb cut of their clothing.

His fingers were perfectly steady, although she was aware that hers betrayed a small vibration. Anxiety or excitement? she wondered.

Then, as he moved, drawing her with him into the center of the arbor walkway, she decided it made no difference. One dance in the concealing darkness. And she was determined to make the most of it.

He turned to face her, bowing from the waist. She dropped a deep curtsy in return, and then, once more, they faced one another.

Here, away from the shadow of the trees, she could almost see his face. And her heart began to beat too quickly.

In perfect time to the measures drifting out from the ballroom, he began to lead her through the seguidilla. And she found that what he had told her was nothing but the truth. Despite the fact that the dance had never, so far as she was aware, traveled beyond her native country, his performance of the steps she had learned in childhood was faultless.

Under the spell of their perfection and the music, she began to relax again, perhaps even relishing the sense of danger in what they were doing. From that exhilaration or from the exertion of the dance, the blood in her veins began to flow more quickly, making her feel more alive than she had felt in months.

They moved together in exquisite union. His ability to anticipate the familiar rhythms of the ancient dance seemed no less than hers. She, who had been bred to feel them.

And then, as she made a turn, her eyes inadvertently found the lights of the palace. Someone was standing on the balcony, looking out into the garden. Without being able to discern anything beyond the shape and size of the figure, she knew in an instant who was there.

Like some faceless nemesis, her guardian was peering out into the shrouded darkness beneath the trees. And he was looking for her. Her fingers fell away from those of her partner, as her feet came to an abrupt stop, disrupting the pattern of the dance.

"What's wrong?" he asked.

The tone was probably no different than that of a normal conversation. To her, the question, and especially its masculine intonation, seemed magnified in the nighttime stillness. Loud enough for Julián to hear?

"I have to go," she said.

She began to turn, and his fingers closed around her wrist. Her attempt to flee was effectively halted, not only by his hold, but by her shock that he would dare detain her.

She twisted her arm, trying to wrench it free. Instead, his fingers tightened over the bone of her wrist, gripping hard enough to be painful.

"You're hurting me," she said, twisting her arm again. "Please let me go."

His hold was implacable, his determination seemingly unmoved by her plea. Heart hammering, she wondered what she could say that would make him release her before Julián found them.

As she tried to decide, her eyes again sought the figure of her guardian. He had left his position beside the balustrade and had started down the steps that led into the garden.

She wondered briefly, ridiculously, if the Englishman might be armed. But of course, no one would dare bring a weapon into the royal palace, certainly not a representative of a foreign government.

He was therefore defenseless. And Julián…

"You don't understand," she said, panic coloring her voice. "He's coming."

"Who's coming?" he asked. His tone betrayed nothing except a calm curiosity.

"My guardian. Please. He can't find me here with you."

"Of course," he said agreeably.

Rather than releasing her, he used the hand he had wrapped around her wrist to draw her into the shadows. Back under the obscuring canopy of trees they had forsaken to indulge in that dangerously exposed dance.

What had she been thinking to allow this? And the answer, when she was forced to acknowledge it, did not begin to excuse what she had done. If anything…

"You don't understand," she said again, still struggling to free her wrist.

"You don't want your guardian to find you in a dark garden with a man. Believe me, even we English can understand that concern."

"Then let me go," she demanded, her fear producing a rush of anger.

She raised her free hand, trying to pry apart his restraining fingers. It was no use. His hold, tight enough that the fingers of the hand it controlled were beginning to grow numb, didn't loosen.

"If he finds me here with you, he'll kill you," she warned. She could hear the sound of her own breathing, ragged in the darkness.

"He may certainly try," he agreed, his voice too soft.

His other hand fastened around the one she had been using to pry at his fingers. As it did, he shoved her back against the trunk of one of the trees that lined the walkway. Positioning her arms at her sides and still gripping her wrists, he held her there.

Before she could protest, his body was pressed tightly against hers, the wall of his chest painfully flattening her breasts. She had time to turn her face, so that her check lay against his shoulder rather than be crushed under it.

His heart was under her ear. Despite his calm refusal to heed her warnings, it was beating as rapidly as hers.

"Shh," he said.

In unthinking response to that command, she listened, straining to hear above the pulse of his blood.

"Pilar?"

Julián's voice. But of course, she had known it was he since she had seen that figure on the balcony.

"Shh," the Englishman warned again, the sibilance no louder than the sound of his heartbeat.

Because she had no choice, she obeyed, holding her breath so that nothing would betray their presence to the man who was hunting her. She could hear his footsteps now. Too near and far too dangerous.

Their bodies hidden from the walkway by the

trunk of the tree, the Englishman released her hands. Terrified to breathe with Julián so close, much less to move, she closed her eyes, her lips trembling in a silent prayer.

The Englishman leaned back slightly, far enough that her sense of being held captive eased. She drew a careful breath, wishing she could warn him to stillness, but Julián was too close to risk even a whisper.

Then, unexpectedly, the Englishman's palms encircled her face. He tilted it upward with pressure from his thumbs, which were beneath her chin. Startled, her eyes opened in time to watch his mouth descend toward hers.

She was too shocked to close her lips, so that his tongue had invaded before she realized his intent. His breath mingled with hers, the smoky warmth of the cigarillo pleasant.

She didn't dare protest. Not with those footsteps coming closer and closer to where their bodies, entwined like lovers, were sheltered by the tree.

That was a lesson she had learned too well. Julián did not listen to explanations. He wouldn't now. He would kill the man whose mouth was fastened over hers, his lips ravishing them expertly.

All she could hope was that the darkness would not betray them. And that what had happened before…

His mouth lifted, allowing her to draw another breath. During the past few seconds, she had forgotten how necessary that was to life. She had forgotten everything but her fear and the feel of this man's lips moving over hers.

Warm and firm and knowing. *So knowing.*

Belatedly she realized the footsteps that had terrorized her were fading. Julián was returning to the lights and the crowded ballroom, while they…

Their breathing—his as ragged as hers—was still mingled. Just as his body was still intimately pressed against hers.

As the danger that Julián would discover them lessened, she gradually became conscious of other things. Sensations she had not been aware of before. The muscles of the Englishman's chest moving against the tightening nipples of her breasts as he breathed. The strength of his erection, obvious through the silk of his knee breeches, which offered no more barrier between their bodies than the thin silk of her gown. And of long callused fingers that trembled as they touched her face.

"Why?" she whispered, finally daring that one word. "Why would you take this risk?"

"All life is risk," he said. "Nothing makes it sweeter."

"You risked death for a *kiss?*" she accused, her anger with his recklessness building again, now that the immediate danger had passed.

She raised her hands and forced his wrists apart, freeing her face. She put her palms against his chest, trying to push him away, but he refused to move.

With each passing second she had become more aware of the intimacy of their position. And for the first time, her fear of his intent was almost as great as her concern for his safety.

"Aren't your kisses worth dying for, *señorita?*" he mocked.

"You're a fool," she said, pushing more strongly against his chest.

Suddenly his hands closed over her wrists once

more, and he pulled her roughly away from the tree. Then, maintaining his hold with only his right hand, he began to drag her along behind him. Again she twisted and turned her captured arm, finally using her free hand to strike at his shoulder. He ignored the repeated blows.

"If I had a weapon, I swear I would kill you," she said.

"Steal one," he suggested. "You seem to be very good at that."

At that same moment she realized he had been dragging her *toward* the palace rather than away from it. She stopped the barrage of ineffectual blows, trying to make sense of both that destination and his words.

By the time she had realized they were too reminiscent of that terrible reality to be coincidental, he had already accomplished what he had brought her so dangerously near the palace to do. The light from the torches on the balcony above them flickered over his face, revealing the scar Julián had slashed there almost a year ago.

"We meet again, *señorita,*" he said. "And this time, I believe the advantage is mine."

Chapter Two

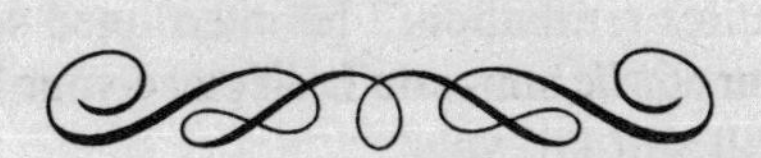

There was a definite satisfaction in watching the slow dilation of her eyes as she recognized him, Sebastian decided. It was not enough to make up for what she had done, but it was something.

"Who are you?" she whispered, her tongue moistening lips that had not seemed dry as they responded to his kiss only seconds before.

Kissing her had been a mistake. One he freely admitted. He had never been able to determine in his own mind what he would do if he found this girl. After the sensation of her mouth trembling beneath his, carrying out any of the punishments he'd devised during the past eleven months would be an impossibility.

"Sebastian Sinclair, *señorita.* I would add 'at your service,' but considering what happened the *last* time I attempted that…"

He deliberately let the sentence trail. Her eyes again traced the line of the scar, and he felt the muscles of his stomach tighten as he was forced to endure their scrutiny.

"I never meant that to happen," she said.

"His name," Sebastian demanded.

Her eyes found his, searching them.

"No," she whispered.

"Someone will tell me."

"Let them. Then, if you aren't a fool, you'll hear the name and let it disappear from your memory. What he did—"

"Requires retribution," he interrupted softly.

"If you attack him, you'll disgrace your king, and Julián will still kill you."

"Julián?"

"Colonel Julián Delgado." Despite her avowal that she wouldn't tell him, she enunciated the name deliberately, almost defiantly, as if it had weight and substance. "A man more powerful than you can possibly imagine."

"A *man,*" Sebastian mocked. "Nothing more and nothing less. He'll bleed and then he will die. Like any other man.

He fought to control the same rage he had had to conquer when he'd seen her making her way across the ballroom. He had followed her out into the darkness because, once he had found her, this confrontation was inevitable.

He had sworn he would know the name of the man who had disfigured him. Now that he did…

"He isn't a man," she said, the words low enough that for a moment he believed he must have misheard them.

The silence, broken only by the music from the palace above them, expanded as he considered what she had said. And, far more troubling, the tone in which she had said it.

"Then…what is he?" he asked, touched, in spite

of his long-held anger, by an almost superstitious dread.

A sudden noise from the balcony above their heads caused them both to turn. Three men, one carrying a torch, were descending the steps that led out into the garden. The flame streamed behind them like a banner. At the sight, the girl shrank back into the shadows of the building, drawing Sebastian with her.

''You mustn't be found here. Not with me.''

''I'm not afraid of him,'' Sebastian said.

He wasn't, despite that almost preternatural chill her characterization had created. Finding this man was something he had thought about every day since the bastard had laid open his cheek.

''You should be,'' she said. ''If nothing else, be afraid of what he will do to *me* if he finds you here.''

''Whatever tenderness I once harbored for damsels in distress was destroyed the day you allowed him to do this,'' he said, touching his cheek with the tips of his finger. He could feel the rough texture of the scar beneath them.

''*I* allowed?''

''Your intervention made it possible.''

''My intervention allowed you to escape with your life.'' She corrected his version of those events vehemently.

''Your intervention allowed *him* to escape.''

His eyes tracked the path of the torch as it was carried through the garden. Although what he had told her was true—he wasn't afraid of the man she called Julián—he also wasn't stupid enough to be caught off guard by him.

Occasionally the searchers would call her name,

but they were careful to keep their voices low so that the sound wouldn't carry to the palace. Apparently, her guardian had no desire to call attention to her disappearance.

"Whatever you choose to believe about that day..." she began.

The pause brought his eyes back to her face, long enough to realize that hers were again examining the scar.

"Whatever I believe?" he prompted caustically.

"You must never doubt that Julián would have had no compunction about killing you. To him, you are far less important than the stallion you shot."

"And what are you to him?"

"He is my guardian. And soon...soon he will become my fiancé."

For some reason, the word created a sickness in the pit of his stomach. Almost the same reaction he had felt that day by the river when he'd considered the possibility that the horseman might be her husband.

"Do you love him?"

"What a child you are," she said, her voice touched with the same bitterness he had heard then.

"Does he love you?"

She turned her head, watching the flame from the torch move in and out among the trees.

"Marriages like ours seldom have their basis in love. Nor do they in England," she added.

"So his actions that day were the result of...jealousy?" he asked. "Pride of possession?"

"Does it matter?"

"I find that it matters a great deal to me."

"He's a proud man. I had humiliated him by running away. At first, he believed you'd helped me."

"At first?"

"If he had really believed that, he would have killed you no matter what I said."

"And I have you to thank for convincing him otherwise? Are you expecting my gratitude?" he mocked.

"I'm expecting you will continue to play whatever game you are playing until he finds us here and kills you. Other than that, I assure you I have very little expectation of anything."

The bitterness was there again, more open than before. Despite the anger he had cherished toward this girl during those long months, something about her claim touched a nearly forgotten chord of chivalry.

The same emotion he'd felt the first time he had encountered her, he reminded himself. It had proven to be misplaced.

"No one can force you to marry him," he found himself saying, despite the too-clear remembrance of the last time he had attempted to intervene on her behalf. And of the price he had paid, a price he would carry to his grave, for that attempt.

She laughed, the sound abruptly cut off. She turned, again watching the flame stream through the darkness.

"You *are* a child," she said again, her voice carefully lowered. "And now, you and I will return separately to the palace, and we will act as if none of what happened tonight has occurred. If you see me or Julián again while you are in Madrid, I would advise you to pretend that you don't."

Before he could react, she slipped past him. Staying within the shadows cast by the building, she made her way to the foot of the stairs leading up to the balcony. As she stepped onto the bottom one, she turned her head, looking back to where he was standing, hidden by the shadows. One hand on the balustrade, she hesitated, her face illuminated by the flambeaux above her.

Their light glinted off the track of tears on her cheek. Then, lifting the hem of her gown, she began to climb, eventually disappearing from his sight.

''You're sure it was the same girl,'' Harry asked when they had finally achieved the privacy of the coach and could talk openly.

Sebastian had returned to the ballroom only a short time after the torchbearer and his helpers had left the garden, but he hadn't seen the girl again. His eyes had searched the perspiring mob gathered under the glow of a thousand candles, but neither of the faces he sought had been among them.

''The instant I saw her.''

''It's been nearly a year,'' the viscount reminded him hopefully.

''I'm not likely to have forgotten either of them. Besides, she didn't bother to deny it.''

He hadn't told Harry the whole. There was no reason to repeat everything that had been said—and done—during those few moments he and the girl had spent together in the garden.

Sebastian couldn't explain to his *own* satisfaction why he had kissed her. He was unwilling to try to produce an answer to his friend's inevitable questions about his motives in doing so.

''It wasn't the girl who cut your face, Sin,'' Harry reminded him. ''Actually, from what you said—''

''She knocked my pistol aside. If she hadn't—''

''If she hadn't,'' Wetherly interrupted reasonably, ''we would more than likely have found you dead with a ball in your back.''

''And you believe I prefer *this?*'' Sebastian asked savagely, touching the mark on his face.

The resulting silence lasted long enough that he knew with regret there could no longer be any pretense after tonight that he didn't care about the scar. Of course, this was Harry, who knew him well enough to understand the purpose behind that long charade.

''It was checkmate,'' Sebastian said stubbornly, trying to cling to his anger, ''until she interfered. He could have ordered them to shoot me, but I would still have taken the whoreson to hell with me.''

''Let it go, Sin,'' Harry advised gently. ''Pursuing him won't change what happened. It won't change anything at all. You must know how Wellington will feel about your carrying out some personal vendetta while we're here. Especially with the delicacy of his mission.''

''Which everyone knows is doomed to failure. I know his name, Harry. I can hunt the bastard down and—

''And do what?'' Wetherly interrupted. ''Kill him? What will that change?''

''At least it will free her,'' Sebastian said.

And it was only when he heard the words spoken aloud that he realized their implications. As did the viscount, of course.

''Bloody hell, Sin. Is that what this is about?''

Harry asked incredulously. ''You're still playing knight errant?''

''I knew then there was something wrong. She was running away because she's terrified of him. I saw it in her eyes when that bastard sent his horse down the incline. But still she stood up to him. And then tonight...it was as if she were someone completely different. All the life and fire and spirit had been sucked out of her. And she was even more terrified of him.''

''I'm not saying she isn't, Sin, but...he's her guardian. Soon to be her fiancé. They have some peculiar notions here about the sanctity of that pledge. My God, man, if they're betrothed, she's as good as married to him. Nothing you do can change that.''

''*If* they're betrothed. They aren't. Besides, she's only marrying him because he's threatening her. She as much as told me that he's holding something over her head.''

''Her family, maybe. If it's an arranged match, they would suffer if she cried off.''

''They deserve to suffer if they're forcing her to marry a man she's afraid of.''

''That's nothing to you. Let it go. There's not a thing you can do for her. Best for everyone concerned if you forget any of this ever happened.''

''Except I'm reminded every time I look into a mirror,'' Sebastian said, his voice intense.

''Did she ask you to intervene?''

She hadn't, of course. Her advice had been the same as Harry's. The same Wellington would give, if Sebastian were to lay the situation before the duke.

They were guests in a foreign country, one whose customs were very different from their own. Even in England, women were compelled to marry against their wishes. Some of them managed to make a success of their arranged matches, and the others, he supposed, eventually learned to be content with their lot. He had never before thought about the role of a woman bound in marriage to a man she not only didn't love but was frightened of.

He isn't a man.

For some reason the words and the bitterness with which they had been uttered echoed in his brain. There were so many possible connotations for them he couldn't possibly know what she had meant.

All he knew was that she wasn't in love with the man to whom she was about to be betrothed. And that he was her guardian and she was afraid of him.

"Sin?"

"She didn't ask," he admitted shortly. "She didn't ask me to do anything."

There was a small silence, unbroken except for the sound of the carriage wheels on the cobblestone street.

"Leave it," Harry urged again, his voice serious as it rarely was. "For all our sakes. This isn't the time or the place for your damned heroics. Besides, if she don't want rescuing—"

"Then I suppose I must leave her to her fate."

"Exactly," Harry said, obviously missing the sarcasm. He sounded relieved that Sebastian had been so easily persuaded to see reason. "Not really our affair, you know."

It wasn't. And it was always possible that in dwelling on what he thought he had seen in her eyes,

Sebastian was simply looking for an excuse to seek out the man who had marked his face, despite the delicacy of their mission. A reason for doing so that would carry more weight with his conscience *and* his commander than his thirst for revenge.

Besides, Harry was right about Wellington's probable reaction. Dare's, too, he supposed. Considering the distance between them, his brother's disapproval seemed less meaningful than it had while he was growing up.

Of course, despite Dare's carefully cultivated cynicism, he and Ian had been the ones who had taught him the values by which he had lived his life. Honor. Love of country. Courage in battle and in sport. And a willingness to offer his strength and his skills in defense of those who were unable to defend themselves.

You have only yourselves to blame, he mentally apprised his absent brothers. And then, in spite of the depths of his genuine, almost murderous rage, his lips curved into a small, secret smile at the thought of their probable reactions to that assertion.

''I told you,'' Pilar said, drawing her hairbrush slowly through the entire length of the strand of hair she held. As she did, she held her guardian's eyes in the mirror above the dressing table, assessing the depth of his rage.

She had dismissed her maid as soon as Julián opened the door to her chamber. She had understood very well what was about to happen. There was no need to try to delay the inevitable.

''Tell me again,'' he demanded.

''My head was aching from the heat and the

crowd and the music,'' she went on. ''I sought out an anteroom for a few minutes of peace and quiet. Someplace where the smell of a hundred perspiring bodies covered in stale scent wouldn't sicken me.''

''But you didn't think to inform me.''

''You were attending the king. I thought it best not to disturb you.''

He caught the hairbrush on its downward stroke and wrenched it from her hand. In the same movement, he put the fingers of his other hand on her shoulder, pulling her upper body around so that she was facing him.

His thumb and forefinger fastened around her chin, lifting her face to him. And then, the brush raised menacingly in his right hand, he looked down into her eyes for a long, silent moment.

She concentrated on letting nothing of what she was feeling be reflected in her eyes or in her expression. No fear. And no defiance.

She had learned that the best—indeed, the safest—way to deal with Julián, no matter his mood, was to present him with a facade of absolute calm. She made no further attempt, therefore, to convince him that what she had told him was the truth.

''Where were you?'' he asked again.

''I have told you where I was,'' she said evenly. ''And I have told you why I had taken refuge there. Do you wish to hear the explanation again?''

''What I *wish* to hear is the truth.''

He did not raise his voice, but after all these months in his control, she could no longer be lulled by the fact that he might appear to be reasonable.

He wasn't. There was nothing at all reasonable about his anger.

She eased a breath, swallowing carefully before she opened her mouth again. "The heat and the stench in the ballroom—"

He released her chin, and then, without releasing her eyes, he hurled the hairbrush at the mirror. Not heavy enough to shatter the glass, it fell onto the dressing table, overturning several of the pots and bottles arrayed there.

One of them was a perfume, the same scent she had worn to the palace tonight. As the smell permeated the heavy air, he paced away from her, his angry stride carrying him halfway across the room before he turned.

"Was your English friend there tonight?"

Her heart leapt into her throat, beating strongly enough that she prayed he wouldn't see it pulse beneath the thin silk of her *robe de chambre.*

"Was he one of those bastards with Wellington?" he demanded.

He doesn't know, she realized in relief. If he had seen the English soldier whose face he'd ruined, the tenor of this questioning would have been very different.

If Julián had known with certainty that man had been in attendance at the ball, he would not have waited until they'd reached the house. He would have dragged her from the carriage as soon as they had left the lights of the palace behind. This confrontation would have taken place in the street and not in the privacy of her bedroom.

"My...friend?" she repeated as if puzzled by the reference.

"The gallant Englishman you met by the river."

"You think...you think that a common soldier would be invited to the king's reception?"

She was pleased with the tone of her disclaimer. Disbelieving. Holding almost a note of ridicule.

"Hardly a common soldier," he said, closing the distance he had opened between them.

At his approach, her heart began to pound again. She knew it would be disastrous to let her fear gain control. Julián delighted in making people afraid. Then he delighted in using that fear to destroy them.

That was something she had sworn on her father's grave she would never let him do to her. With the thought of her father, it seemed that she could smell the acrid richness of the cigarillo the Englishman had been smoking in the garden.

The taste of it was suddenly on her tongue and her lips, along with the memory of his kiss. No one had ever kissed her like that before. No one had ever kissed her at all except Julián. And his kisses were nothing like the Englishman's.

"What is it?" Julián asked, his voice sharpening with suspicion.

He crossed the few feet that separated them and caught her chin in his fingers again, gripping hard enough that she flinched from the pain.

"What were you thinking?" he demanded.

She had let down her guard, something she could never afford to do. No mental excursions into more pleasant circumstances. Especially when he was like this.

"The scent is bringing back my headache," she lied.

"I saw something in your eyes," he said.

She shook her head, brow furrowed as if in confusion.

"I don't know what you mean."

"There was something in your face when I mentioned the Englishman."

Deliberately she widened her eyes, shaking her head again. "You're imagining things," she said.

"It should be easy enough to ascertain if you're lying."

His voice was no longer threatening. It was almost caressing, instead. And she knew from bitter experience that this was when he was most dangerous.

It *would* be easy for him to procure a list of the officers who had accompanied Wellington to Madrid. Those would be only names, however, and unless he saw the Englishman's face—

"Tonight's isn't the only entertainment planned for the English envoy," he went on, destroying that comforting hope. "There will be half a dozen activities at which Wellington and his staff will be expected to make an appearance. It's so fortunate I was wise enough to arrange it so that I should instantly know that particular officer again."

Hearing his mockery, she hated him with a renewed swell of emotion, an indulgence she had not allowed herself in a long time. The memory of the thick, reddened scar with which he had marred the visage of the man who had tried to help her was too clear. As was the pain that had been in the Englishman's eyes as he had watched her examine it.

"If I find you have lied to me about his presence in the envoy's party," Julián warned, "you know what will happen."

Despite the threat, she said nothing. She had learned that with Julián the truth often served her no better than a lie. His punishments were as capricious as his rages.

If she confessed what had happened in the garden tonight, the punishment he threatened might still be carried out in retaliation for the clandestine meeting. Just as swiftly as it would be when he discovered she was lying. And it was always possible that he would never discover that.

Anything is possible, she thought, clinging to the thinnest thread of hope. Maybe the Englishman would take to heart what she had told him. Maybe he would heed her warning and avoid the entertainments Julián had mentioned. Maybe—

"The truth," Julián demanded again.

Without a heartbeat of hesitation, her choice made for her by her previous experiences with his sense of fair play, she lied to him once more, "I have *told* you the truth."

His lips lifted into one of his rare smiles.

"Have you, my dear?" he asked softly. His thumb released her chin to trace across her mouth. "I wonder." His smile widened, his thumb moving along a line that matched the one he had carved in the English soldier's cheek.

"Shall I send for your maid?"

Her heart stopped, but she controlled her face, fighting that fear. "There is no reason for that," she said. "Please, Julián, I swear on my father's grave that I have told you the truth."

Perhaps she would go to hell for that, but it was better than sending someone else.

His eyes held hers a long moment. "Almost I wish…"

She didn't ask, because she knew what he wished for—some excuse to vent his rage at her. Now he would have to try to suppress it at least until he had proved her a liar. And when he had—

He bent, putting one hand on the top of the littered vanity and slipping the other beneath the fall of her hair. With that one, he gripped her neck strongly enough that even had she dared, she would not have been able to turn her head. His mouth fastened over hers, his tongue demanding entrance.

She didn't respond. She never did, because it made no difference to him. He preferred her impassivity. Or even, as she had learned very early in their relationship, her resistance. That was a mistake she had never made again.

As her guardian kissed her, the movement of his mouth hard, almost brutal, tears burned at the back of her eyes. Unwillingly she remembered the touch of another man's lips. Another man's kiss. Another man.

He isn't a man, she had warned the Englishman. She had known from what she had seen in his eyes that he didn't believe her. And so, even as Julián's mouth moved against hers, her mind raced, frantic to find before it was too late, some way to prevent what was about to happen to him.

Chapter Three

"My lord?" the Viscount Wetherly's batman called hesitantly.

Harry opened one bloodshot eye, briefly assessing his man's face. He was standing in the doorway to the viscount's bedroom, carefully out of range of whatever could be reached and thrown at him from the bed.

"Go away," Wetherly said, closing the eye again.

He had found nothing in those open Yorkshire features to alarm him. If Sin had gotten into serious trouble, there would surely have been some hint of it in Malford's revealing countenance.

"There's a fishmonger in the kitchen, my lord..."

The viscount's eyes opened again, very wide this time, despite the dull ache in the back of his skull. He should know better than to try to drink a Sinclair under the table, Harry acknowledged, even if that were the only way to guarantee he would know where to find him come morning.

"A fishmonger?" he repeated, imbuing his tone with every ounce of aristocratic outrage he could muster. "What the hell should I have to do with a fishmonger? Do I look like the cook, you bloody fool?''

''Indeed, no, my lord, but—''

''Go to hell and take your bleeding peddler with you,'' Wetherly ordered. ''You're interrupting my sleep.''

There were a few blessed minutes of silence, during which the viscount tried to relax the muscles that had been tightened with his unaccustomed anger. Just as it seemed he might succeed, his man spoke again.

''He is really *quite* insistent, my lord. Otherwise, I should never have dreamed of awakening you. Your instructions concerning Captain Sinclair seemed so urgent, however—''

''Sin? Good God, man, have you let Sin leave the house without arousing me?''

With the question, the viscount had tried to sit up—much too quickly. The aborted maneuver reminded him of exactly how much wine he had consumed last night. And now it seemed that through the incompetence of this idiot, that valiant effort might well have been in vain.

Clutching his head with both hands to keep it from flying off his shoulders, and moving far more prudently, Harry finally achieved an upright position, sitting on the edge of the mattress. From there he glared banefully at his servant.

''Oh, no, my lord!'' the batman hastened to assure him, apparently horrified that the viscount thought him so lax in his duty. ''Captain Sinclair hasn't stirred since we rolled him into bed. I looked in on him before I came to wake you.''

"Then why in perdition do you keep yammering on about him?"

Harry knew there must be some point to his batman's actions because, despite his accusation, the man wasn't a fool. He'd be damned, however, if he could figure out what this was about.

"Because the fishmonger's message is for *him*, my lord. At least..." The servant hesitated again, seeming determined to make him beg for every scrap of information.

"What message?" Harry asked, trying to keep his attention to the problem at hand, despite his aching head and the increasingly urgent need for the chamber pot.

He eased off the edge of the bed, staggering slightly when his stockinged feet hit the floor. The room swam sickeningly until his batman rushed forward to put a steadying hand under his arm.

Wetherly shook it off impatiently, beginning to unfasten the flap on his evening britches. At the signal Malford bent, pulling the chamber pot from beneath the bed. He arranged it at the proper position, and they both waited, their silence almost respectful, as Harry relieved himself.

"A message for the man with the scarred face," the servant said, when it seemed that objective had at last been achieved.

The viscount's hands hesitated in the act of straightening his clothing. His eyes fastened on his valet's face with the first glimmer of understanding.

"Are you telling me there's a peddler downstairs with a message for...Sin."

He had breathed the name separately, as if it had not been part of the original question. Any message intended for the man with the scarred face, Harry reasoned, would have to be for Sebastian. And a message delivered this particular morning—

"Where is he?" Harry demanded, his voice for the first time holding the authoritative tone one might expect from an officer and a gentleman.

"Still abed, my lord," Malford said, sounding puzzled.

"Not Captain Sinclair, you idiot. The fishmonger. Where's the bloody fishmonger?"

"In the kitchen, my lord. I've asked him to wait."

"Good man," Harry said, clapping him on the back and pushing him toward the door. "Now go back down and bring him up. And, Malford..."

"Yes, my lord?"

"Make sure that no one, especially not Captain Sinclair, sees him."

"Very good, my lord."

Harry sat down on the bed again, putting his head back in his hands. After a moment he spread his fingers and pushed his hair away from his eyes.

Given the mood Sin had been in after the reception last night, there was no telling how he might react to a message from the woman he'd seen there. And no telling what message she might have sent, Wetherly decided.

It would be better for all concerned if he intercepted this communication. Then, after he had the gist of it, he would be able to judge if it were one he should pass on to Sinclair. Or, and he strongly suspected this might be the case, one that should never be allowed to reach his friend.

After all, Sin wasn't thinking straight about all this. His penchant for letting his emotions embroil him in situations his intellect had a hard time extracting him from was well-known to the viscount.

Far better, Harry decided with a nod, if he handled this himself. After all, he wasn't emotionally involved with the chit. And knowing Sin, he had a good notion that more had gone on in that dark garden than his friend, as a gentleman, had revealed. If the girl were already seeking another meeting—

Far better left to me, he reiterated mentally. As a friend, his job was to make sure Sinclair's recklessness didn't get him into trouble with the Beau. Not while they were in Madrid, at any rate. Some day, when all this seeking revenge business had been forgotten, he would tell Sin what he'd done and receive his grateful thanks for keeping him out of a situation that was fraught with danger for his career.

After all, they were not only friends but fellow officers. Meeting with this woman on Sin's behalf was nothing less than his duty.

"Tell him that I'm the scarred man's representative," Wetherly said to the cook. "He may speak freely to me."

The cook began to translate, the words coming far too fast for the viscount's very limited command of Spanish to keep up with them. Again the messenger shook his head, repeating the phrase that by now even Harry understood.

"The scar-faced man ain't here, I tell you," he said, speaking slowly and loudly in English as if that might help the messenger's understanding. "I'm the best you're going to get."

The fishmonger's eyes sought the cook's, obviously waiting for a translation. Exasperated with the difficulties in making himself understood, Harry slammed both palms down on the huge wooden desk that stood in the center of his bedroom, sending a couple of pens rolling toward its edge. Wary eyes still on the viscount, the messenger managed to prevent them from falling over the edge.

"If he isn't going to give me the message," Harry said to the cook, "tell him he can hie himself back to whoever sent him and tell them he's failed."

Judging by the man's face when the translation of that was completed, Harry thought he was finally getting through. The messenger's complexion had seemed to gray and his eyes stretched wide and dark. His gaze traveled from the cook's face back to Harry's, where it rested a moment, evaluating.

The viscount was glad he had taken time to put on his boots and uniform. Far more impressive than wrinkled knee breeches and stockinged feet. He was still wearing the underclothes he had donned before the reception last night, not that anyone in the room with him was likely to notice.

When his batman had brought the peddler up from the kitchens, he had thoughtfully brought the cook with him. If he hadn't, given their combined lack of fluency in the language, this would have been a much slower process. However, the strong scent of fish clung to the man's clothing, making the condition of Harry's already queasy stomach precarious.

"What's it to be, my good man?" Harry demanded as the silence stretched.

Without waiting for a translation of that command, the messenger's focus returned to the impromptu translator, who listened diligently to the rapid stream of words that resulted. When they had stopped, however, he didn't immediately provide the viscount with a translation.

"Well?" Harry asked impatiently. "What'd he say?"

"The issue is delicate, my lord."

"Delicate?" the viscount repeated disbelievingly.

"Involving a lady," the cook leaned forward to confide.

"I knew it," Harry said. "What does she want?"

The cook's eyes flicked to the fishmonger's face before he spoke again, once more leaning forward and speaking in a near whisper. "An assignation, my lord. With the man whose face bears the scar."

"And where is this assignation to be?"

"There is a small chapel, my lord, Iglesia Santa María de la Rosa, on the western outskirts of the city. The lady will ask permission from her guardian to attend afternoon mass there. Afterward she will walk in the cemetery to visit the grave of her father. She asks that the scar-faced man join her."

"What time?"

"At the time of mass, my lord," the cook said, as if that should be clear to anyone.

"And what time would that be, you idiot?"

"Ah," the cook said. "That would be at five o'clock. The lady will wait for him in the cemetery after she has heard mass. He says it is very small and very private. No one will disturb them."

"And the lady gave him this message herself, I suppose," Harry asked.

A bold piece, he thought. She couldn't possibly be as frightened of her guardian as Sin believed her to be.

Of course, considering her antics the first time Sebastian had met her and her foray into the gardens last night, Harry wasn't surprised. Perhaps Sin couldn't see what she was up to, but he certainly could.

Given the size of the Sinclair fortune and how the current earl felt about his brothers, Sin, though a younger son, would be quite a catch. Maybe this woman had decided to throw her lot in with a rich Englishman rather than with her ill-tempered guardian.

The ramifications of that alliance for Sin would, however, be quite beyond the pale. Wellington would never put up with it, for one thing. Sebastian's career would be ruined, and Harry could only imagine his family's dismay if Sin turned up in England with a Spanish adventuress in tow. He knew what his own father would have to say to that.

"She communicated it to him through her maid, he says." The cook finished the laborious process of translating Wetherly's question and the messenger's answer. "This man knows the woman personally, however. There is no doubt the communication is genuine."

"And the lady's name?" Harry asked.

"Doña Maria del Pilar Mendoza y Aranjúez," came the eventual reply.

"Then he may tell Doña Aranjúez," Harry avowed, not perfectly sure of the style of Spanish titles, but soldiering on despite that minor setback, "that the appointment she seeks will be kept."

He reached into the pocket of his jacket and divided the coins he found there between the two men. He had very little idea what he had given them, but since their expressions revealed nothing but pleasure, he assumed he'd done well by them. Probably too bloody well, he decided, watching them hurriedly pocket their payment.

He'd get it back, one way or another. Sin might have better luck with the ladies, but Harry usually held the upper hand at cards. And if he couldn't retrieve his investment that way, one day he might tell Sin exactly what it had cost him to mount his rescue from this Spanish temptress's snares. Not, of course, until they were safely home in England.

When Sebastian opened his eyes, he could tell by the slant of the sun coming into his room that the day was well advanced. It was probable that everyone else had also slept late after last night's reception. Everyone except Wellington, of course, who would have been up at his usual hour, working on his internal reports.

The duke, however, hadn't been party to the private drinking session that had followed the official entertainment. Only he and Harry had broached those additional bottles, and they would pay the price for it this morning, he acknowledged, easing his head back down on the pillow.

He closed his eyes, remembering the events that had precipitated that schoolboy bout of overindulgence. Of all the places he might have imagined finding the girl he had met on that riverbank, the royal palace had been the last.

Despite the fact she had spoken impeccable English, assuring that she was a member of a class much higher than the clothing she'd worn that day had indicated, he had not had the slightest premonition that he would see her at any of the entertainments they would attend in Madrid.

The sight of her crossing the ballroom last night had struck him with the force of a blow. More shocking because it was so unexpected.

He still didn't know her full name. Only that of her guardian. And to think of her under the absolute power of that arrogant bastard…

Harry was right, he told himself, destroying the unwanted image. She was Delgado's ward. There was nothing he could do to change that, even if she wanted him to. And she had made it very clear that she didn't.

He wouldn't see her again in the time they would be here. After her escapade in disappearing from the ballroom last night, her guardian would probably see to it that she was duly chastised.

The word impacted in his gut, stirring a nausea that had as much to do with the image it produced as did his overindulgence in Harry's wine. And yet he knew that allowing himself to worry about what might have happened to her last night after she had disappeared was simply another form of self-indulgence. One he couldn't afford.

Harry was right about that, too. No matter his quarrel with Delgado, he was here as a representative of the crown. Any attempt to seek a personal vengeance, an act which might have repercussions on the success of this mission and even on future relations between the two countries, would be little more than treason. As much as he needed the satisfaction of driving his sword through the heart of the man who had marked his face, that sweet retaliation would have to wait.

Thanks to the girl, at least he knew the bastard's name. There would come a time, more appropriate than this, for the revenge he had sworn by the river that day. All he could do now was to exercise the patience Ian had tried so hard to instill.

At the thought of his brother, invalided out of the army two years ago and enduring his long convalescence without complaint, Sebastian opened his eyes. Despite everything, he was still a soldier. He had duties to perform. None of which involved lying abed all day licking old wounds.

In time, he vowed silently. *In time, you bastard.*

''Gone where?'' Sebastian demanded of Harry's batman almost three hours after he'd awakened.

He had taken time to have them send up a bath. Despite the dregs of a headache, he was feeling almost human again and sober enough to realize that a great deal of what Harry had argued last night made sense. Which was surprising, he admitted, considering the viscount's usual inability to say anything more serious than 'Good morning.'

He had come to Wetherly's rooms to thank him and had found him gone. Although it was curious Harry hadn't informed him of his plans to be away this afternoon, if it hadn't been for his servant's almost furtive behavior, Sebastian might have let it go.

After all, both he and Harry were supposed to attend a small private dinner in the duke's honor hosted by one of the very nobles whose influence Wellington was trying to overcome. He could have given his thanks to Harry then, of course, if Malford's secretiveness hadn't set off alarms.

"I believe he had an errand, sir," the man managed finally.

"What kind of errand?" Sebastian persisted.

And was rewarded with a guilty silence.

"What kind of errand?" he asked again, that warning finger of unease brushing along his spine.

"Something for the duke, I think."

Accustomed to judging men and their words, it was obvious to Sin that the batman was lying. What wasn't obvious was why.

"Are you telling me His Grace sent Lord Wetherly on an errand *here?*"

Harry had less Spanish than any other member of the staff. Despite the years they had spent in Iberia, the viscount spoke none of its languages well enough to communicate on his own. Even his French, which he had learned at his governess's knee, was atrocious.

His lack of proficiency in languages had been the subject of a long-standing raillery among the officers. The duke, who knew everything, would almost certainly be aware of it.

"Perhaps it was a private meeting," the batman said, and then, as Sebastian watched, his smoothly shaven cheeks reddened. "Errand," he corrected, but of course, that had come too late.

"A meeting with whom?"

"I am sure it was not my place to inquire, Captain Sinclair."

"And Lord Wetherly didn't volunteer the information."

"Alas, no, he did not. I'm sorry that I can't be of more help—"

The last word became a yelp as Sebastian grabbed

the man by the front of his jacket and lifted him until he dangled, toes barely touching the floor. "The truth, if you please, Malford."

"I beg you, Captain Sinclair—"

"The truth," Sebastian said, shaking him.

The flush spread upward, suffusing the man's entire face. His top lip was beaded with sweat.

"There was a...message," Malford stammered.

"We seem to be making progress," Sebastian said, shaking him again. "A message from whom?"

The man's eyes held on his, and then he swallowed. "A fishmonger brought it to the kitchens this afternoon."

"From whom?" Sebastian repeated.

"I'm sure if Lord Wetherly had wished this meeting to be made public—"

"Hardly public. I'm his best friend. And you know as well as I do that if your master *didn't* tell me about this meeting, it's because he's hiding something from me. As, I suspect, are you."

In the back of Sebastian's mind the thought was beginning to form that Harry's mysterious disappearance might have something to do with what had happened at the palace reception last night. And if it did...

"I assure you, Captain Sinclair—"

Sebastian shook him again. The lie was cut off as the man's teeth snapped together with the violence of that motion.

"Enough. We are in a foreign country. We are here at the sufferance of its monarch. And your master doesn't speak the language. If you don't tell me where he has gone this instant, I shall go to the duke and ask him to get to the bottom of your deception.

That is something I doubt any of us, especially you, should wish to happen. Now, where the hell is Lord Wetherly?"

There was a prolonged silence as the servant again considered Sebastian's eyes. Apparently what he saw there wasn't entirely convincing, because his lips flattened, just as if he had reached a conscious decision to keep them closed.

Furious, Sebastian threw the batman backward. He landed against the side of the high bed, but Sebastian hadn't even watched after he'd released him. He had turned on his heel and headed to the door of the bedchamber instead.

"It was from a woman," the batman said when he realized that intent.

Sebastian stopped in the act of reaching for the knob. And then he slowly turned, looking over his shoulder. The man was still lying where he had fallen.

"A woman?" Sinclair repeated softly.

As far as he was aware, Harry hadn't met any women since they had been here. Unlike their time in Paris, they had been busy enough with their official duties that there had been no opportunity for that particular kind of entertainment.

"A lady," Malford amended.

"A *lady?*" Sebastian mocked. Spanish ladies didn't make private assignations with soldiers, of course, especially foreign ones. "And this lady's name?"

"I only heard it once. And my Spanish—"

"As much as you remember," Sebastian demanded.

"María del Pilar..."

The tone of the information he'd just imparted had been almost sullen, but Sebastian was hardly aware of that, considering its import. *Pilar.* And the timing—

"She sent *Harry* a message?"

Again the batman seemed reluctant, and finally losing patience with the delay caused by having to drag each bit of information out of him, Sebastian started back across the room. This time, whatever the man read in his face seemed to have the desired effect.

"Not to Lord Wetherly. The message was for you. The viscount intercepted it. He's gone to meet her."

"Where?"

One word, and its intonation left no doubt that his patience with evasion was at an end.

"At a chapel called Santa María de la Rosa. She's waiting in the cemetery."

"How long has he been gone?"

"An hour. Maybe less."

Harry, Sebastian thought, trepidation crowding his throat. *Oh, Harry. You poor stupid bastard.*

By the time Sebastian had secured both a horse and directions, the trickle of anxiety with which he had left Harry's bedroom had become a raging torrent. As he guided his mount through the last of the narrow, winding streets of the city and then dug in his heels as he had finally reached the open countryside, he reminded himself that the viscount had never in his life managed to follow directions. *Or* to arrive at any destination on time. Please God, he prayed, today would be no exception.

The secluded chapel, when he found it, appeared to sleep in the heat of the late afternoon. The only sound as he approached, slowing his horse to a cautious canter, was the low hum of the cicadas.

The cemetery beside the church stretched along a hillside, shaded by numerous stands of trees. From what he could see as he dismounted, almost before the gelding had come to a full stop, it was deserted. All the same, glancing back toward the chapel, he drew his sword from its scabbard, the slide of metal loud in the somnolent stillness.

It was *too* quiet here, almost like the breathless hush before battle. That eerie waiting they all were forced to endure until the drums began their tattoo.

The hair on the back of his neck had begun to lift, a soldier's premonition. And despite the fact that the place seemed deserted—or perhaps because of it—he knew he had been right to fear for his friend.

He's not a man. The echo of that phrase added to his sense of foreboding as he opened the gate of the low iron fence that surrounded the shadowed graveyard and stepped inside. He didn't bother to close it behind him, but stood listening to the strange quality of the silence instead.

Even the hum of the insects had ceased and now the only sound was the pulse of his own blood, rushing too quickly through his veins. Yet somehow he knew he wasn't alone. Every instinct warned him.

Moving noiselessly, he began to search the cemetery. Senses alert, he threaded his way between aged headstones, their letters eroded with rain and sun and wind and the long, slow passage of the years. Death was all around him, the sense of it so strong it was almost a physical presence.

Gradually he was forced to accept that there was no one else here. Not Harry. Not the girl he had kissed last night. Only the sleeping dead.

He had begun to turn, intending to go back to the gate when an anomaly in the monotoned pattern of dry earth, gnarled olive trees and weathered stone caught his eye. Something lay on the ground among the most distant of the graves, those which dotted the rise of the gentle slope.

They were in the deepest shade, and yet whatever he saw was far darker than the hues that surrounded it. It seemed a spill of pure black against the silent shadows.

His sword at the ready, he crossed the distance carefully. If the message that had brought him here was a trap, as he suspected, then this would be the most dangerous moment. An enemy might be waiting just beyond that rise. Actually, any number of men could be concealed there by having them lie flat against the ground on the other side.

As he approached it, the patch of darkness he had noticed resolved itself into a piece of cloth, which he eventually drew close enough to recognize as a cloak. Of rich black velvet, it was of the type a gentlewoman in England might have worn to an evening entertainment.

His heart rate accelerated when he made that identification, but it quickly became obvious that no body lay concealed under the garment. It was as if it had been dropped or perhaps pulled from the wearer's shoulders.

Pulled away as she fled? he wondered, his eyes searching the area that surrounded it for any sign of a struggle.

He resisted the urge to touch the cloak, finally stepping across it instead. Then, keeping low, he climbed to the top of the slope, which proved steeper than it had appeared from below.

As he approached the summit, he crouched close to the ground, listening for any sound from beyond the rise. Some movement. The same slide of metal against metal the unsheathing of his own sword had created. The cocking of a pistol.

There was nothing. Nothing except that same cold sickness of premonition he had felt from the first.

Something was wrong. Something—

Without giving himself a chance to succumb to that almost superstitious presentiment, he pushed up off the ground, charging over the top of the rise as if he were attacking a barricade.

As long as he lived, he would never forget the sight that awaited him there. In less than a heartbeat, he was kneeling beside his friend. The man who had come to keep a treacherous assignation that had been meant for him. And who had met, instead, the fate intended for Sebastian.

The front of Wetherly's uniform was literally soaked with blood. It was obvious where the ball had entered his chest, too near the heart for him to have ever had a chance. Hands trembling, Sebastian touched the bloodless cheek, turning Harry's face toward him.

As he did, the hazel eyes opened. They were sightless, already glazed with the unmistakable sheen of death Sebastian had seen too many times in the past three years to mistake for anything else.

''Mother?'' Harry whispered.

''It's Sin, you great goose,'' Sebastian said, fighting tears as he found the cold, white fingers and enclosed them in his own, trying desperately to warm them. "Why did you come, Harry? What the hell did you think you were doing?"

There was a silence as Wetherly seemed to try to focus on his face, and then his eyes closed again as if he were too tired to make the effort. Sebastian bowed his head, the moisture he had fought running unchecked down his cheeks.

"Couldn't let you have *all* the pretty ones," the breathless whisper came. "Reputation to consider, you know."

The last had been a gasp. The handsome face contorted hard before it cleared, seeming at peace again. And because he understood he could do nothing for Harry, Sebastian now wanted that.

Still, he had to know. If he were going to do anything about this, he had to know.

"What happened, Harry? What happened to the girl?"

The eyes opened again, and this time they seemed to find Sebastian's face. A trick of the shadows perhaps, caused by the hot wind moving through the twisted branches of the trees above their heads.

Then, as quickly as it had appeared, awareness faded. The eyes didn't close, but the faint flicker of animation that had been within them was suddenly gone, snuffed out like night's last candle.

Sebastian Sinclair lifted the hand he held and brought it to his lips, pressing a kiss against the cold knuckles. And then he raised his own eyes, blinded by the hot scald of tears.

"Oh, God, Harry," he whispered. "Don't go. Not you, too. Not now."

It was supposed to be over. The long years when they buried a friend at twilight and pushed the memory of the loss out of their heads by dawn, so they could go out and kill again, never knowing which comrade would fall that day. Never knowing if the next shell would shatter their own limbs or those of the man who ate and slept and fought beside them.

He and Harry had survived it all. Now, when it was supposed to be over, Harry was dead.

And it was his fault. His thirst for revenge had brought his best friend here in an attempt to protect Sebastian from his own impulsiveness.

He lowered his head, looking down into the face of a man he had loved as dearly as his brothers, and the sentimental words he would never have spoken aloud to any of them whispered through his mind.

We happy few. This band of brothers.

He put the palm of his hand over the staring eyes, closing them gently. ''Rest in peace, Harry,'' he whispered, his voice breaking over the name.

He didn't bother with vows or promises. There were no words for what was in his heart. Wetherly, of all people, would understand that he would make this right. As right as his world could ever be again without Harry in it.

Chapter Four

Wellington's eyes never left Sebastian's face throughout the painful recital. It had even seemed there was within them the occasional gleam of sympathy. Or perhaps that was something else, he thought. A hint of moisture that had appeared in response to his own.

When it was done, when Sebastian had laid everything that had happened before him, the duke rose. He walked away from the enormous desk where he had been working, its surface cluttered with the usual reports and dispatches, and stood with his back to Sebastian, looking out the window.

"There's nothing you can do, you know," Wellington said after a moment.

There was no logical reason for the swell of disappointment that was evoked by hearing the words. He had known before he came that it was ridiculous to hope the duke might suggest some course of action that would allow him to avenge Harry's death. And in these circumstances, of course, his commander's advice was nothing less than an order.

Wellington turned, his lips slightly pursed as he

considered Sebastian's face. "First of all, you have no proof of what you suspect. Even if the fishmonger could be forced to verify the source of the message he gave, there would be no point in compelling him to do so. The man you believe guilty of Harry's death is too powerful for such testimony to carry weight with the Spanish Court."

"You're saying that even though he murdered Harry, he's untouchable," Sebastian said bluntly.

"Untouchable by you. Taking into account our current mission and his past service to the crown. Colonel Delgado led what was perhaps the most effective of the juntas that helped to restore Ferdinand to the throne. The king is unlikely to reward him by having him arrested."

Little more than private armies, the juntas had been organized by individual commanders and operated independently of any allied command. They had fought the French using tactics which, although undeniably effective, differed strikingly from the more traditional methods employed by the British army. Rather than engaging the enemy in pitched battles, the juntas harried the French forces with series of quick strikes and quicker retreats, fighting a multitude of "little wars." Or, as they were called in Spanish, *guerrillas.*

If Delgado had been one of their more successful leaders, Sebastian acknowledged, then Wellington was right. Ferdinand's gratitude would preclude any action being taken against him, no matter what proof might be presented of his role in the viscount's murder.

And as of now, of course, he had no such proof.

He had nothing but his own absolute surety that Delgado had been responsible for Harry's death.

"The only thing you can do," his commander went on, "the thing you *must* do, is to put this as well as what happened a year ago, from your mind. Considering the king's negative response to the prime minister's suggestions, we shall be in Madrid only a few more days at any rate. I think you have no choice but to let this go."

"Are you saying I should let Wetherly's murder go unpunished, your grace?" Sebastian asked with a soft bitterness.

Locking his hands behind his back in a characteristic pose, Wellington walked back across the room. Surprisingly, he didn't stop at his desk. He approached Sebastian's chair and put his hand on the younger man's shoulder.

"You've lost comrades before, Sin. We all have. This is no different. Simply another sort of battle. A diplomatic one, if you will."

"*I* was the one who was supposed to die this afternoon, your grace. Not Harry. That ambush was directed at me."

"Then consider that Wetherly, as your friend, gave his life for yours. Honor that sacrifice."

"By letting the man who killed him get away with it?"

"By remembering who we are and why we are here," Wellington said simply.

He had told them the same thing before the reception. And Harry had even echoed it after the incident in the gardens. Then, perhaps, it had made sense. Now, however...

"I have a letter for you, by the way," the duke

said, his tone as different as the change of subject. ''It was included with the latest dispatches. I was about to send for you when they told me you were waiting outside to see me.''

Sebastian raised his gaze to his commander's face. The piercing eyes seemed full of kindness, their normally stern expression exuding warmth.

Sympathy for Harry? Or was it possible…

''Ian?'' he asked, fear tightening his throat. He couldn't bear another loss of this magnitude.

''If the news were bad, I'm sure the earl would have asked that I give it to you personally. Since he hasn't, we must presume Major Sinclair continues to recuperate from his wounds.''

Wellington, notoriously unable to dissemble, appeared to be telling the truth, and Sebastian remembered to breathe.

''Maybe this will be good news on that front at least,'' the duke continued with his quick smile.

Giving Sebastian's shoulder a light squeeze, he strode over to his desk and began sifting through the papers there. After a moment he held up the one he had sought among that confusion and walked back to hand it over.

Dare, with his customary decisiveness, had pressed his signet firmly into the wax, the impression it left both crisp and clean. Seeing the family crest brought a wave of nostalgia, which produced another embarrassing pricking at the back of Sebastian's eyes.

He lowered them to hide the emotion, breaking the seal on his letter and spreading open the single sheet. As he scanned his brother's scrawl, he realized with relief that Wellington had been right.

"Ian has married," he said, trying to determine Dare's opinion of the match by reading between the lines of the sparse information the earl had given him.

"Please add my congratulations to your own when you write," the duke said. "I shall be glad to make a place for your reply within the next diplomatic pouch. And with it, you may include the welcome news that we will be home before next month is out."

Home.

After three years of hard fighting, the idea of returning to the almost idyllic life he had led as the youngest son of a well-to-do and indulgent family seemed nearly fantastical. Sebastian looked up from his letter to find those blue eyes still fastened on his face.

"Don't do anything that might jeopardize a reunion with your brothers, Sebastian," Wellington warned. "Not now. Not so near the end."

Not now. Those were the same words he had breathed to Harry. And with the remembrance of them came the knowledge that in spite of what his commander had said, his friend's death was not something he could "let go." No matter what avenging it might cost him.

"I shall write to the viscount's father," the duke went on, thankfully unaware of that realization, "although given the unusual circumstances surrounding his death, I shouldn't imagine he will be fully satisfied by my recital of these events."

"I'm sure you will say all that is proper, your grace," Sebastian managed, refolding Dare's letter.

"Perhaps when you return to England, you could

visit them. I think Harry's parents would find comfort in knowing that you were with him at the end.''

''I shall, your grace,'' Sebastian said, understanding from both the words and the finality of their tone that this interview was at an end. And after all, Wellington had told him only what he had expected to hear.

''Sebastian.'' The duke's voice stopped him as he reached the door.

''Your grace?''

''I shouldn't say anything to the others about what you believe happened this afternoon. Harry was well liked. Some of them might not be so wise in their reaction as you have been.''

Sebastian didn't turn, hiding the caustic smile the duke's compliment produced.

''Of course, your grace,'' he said before he opened the door and stepped out into the hall. And, for the first time in three years, out of Wellington's iron control.

''The question is a simple one. I wish to know who sent the message that was intercepted by Viscount Wetherly.''

The process necessary to arrange this interrogation had been tedious in the extreme. He had questioned Harry's batman first, and, his eyes touched with the same nearly paralyzing grief Sebastian felt, this time Malford had been cooperative.

The cook, when approached, had been reluctant to reveal the name of the peddler. Having acquired the man's identity through a combination of intimidation and bribery, Sebastian had finally tracked him down this morning to find that the messenger was terrified to talk to him.

"I told his lordship yesterday," the man began, his eyes shifting nervously from Sebastian to Malford.

"Tell *me.*"

"It was the lady, my lord."

"I'm not a lord," Sebastian corrected. "And I need the lady's name."

The man swallowed nervously, the reaction strong enough to be visible. "Doña María del Pilar Mendoza y Aranjúez. Just as I told the other one."

"And you spoke to Señorita Mendoza yourself?"

"To her maid, my lord. She gave me a message to be delivered to the scar-faced man—" He stopped, his eyes quickly examining Sebastian's features, apparently attempting to judge if the words had offended him.

"Go on," Sebastian urged.

"And then I came here." Again his gaze shifted to the batman's face as if hoping for affirmation.

"Where did you meet her?" Sebastian asked.

"My lord?"

"The maid. Did she come to you?"

His round face lightened in comprehension. "No, no, my lord. I call there as I call here, bringing fish for the kitchen."

"And Doña Pilar's maid gave you the message while you were there?"

"Yes, my lord."

"And you know the woman? You're sure it was Doña Pilar's maid."

"I have known her for many years, even before she went to work for the lady."

''Can you take me there?''

The fishmonger shook his head, his brow furrowing in confusion. ''My lord?''

''Can you take me to where Doña Pilar lives.''

''But of course, my lord,'' the man said, his face clearing as he finally understood what he was being asked to do. ''Anyone in Madrid could direct you to the house of Colonel Delgado.''

The hardest part of the past two days, Sebastian acknowledged as he watched the front of Delgado's house, had been those moments when he had found himself thinking he wanted to tell Harry something or to seek his advice, ramshackled as that might be. Then, with a welling of renewed grief, almost as powerful as that he had felt as he'd knelt beside his dying friend, he would realize that he would never again be able to do either of those things.

Harry was gone, and there was only one thing Sebastian could do for him now. And despite what Wellington had advised, it was not to gratefully accept his sacrifice.

The time for the English envoy's departure from Madrid was, however, growing ever closer. If he were going to succeed in his quest without being forced to become a deserter—something which would bring dishonor not only on his own head, but also to his family—he would have to devise a way to confront Delgado within the next few days. Something he had thus far found impossible to do.

He leaned back against the wall behind him and closed his eyes. Between maintaining some semblance of attendance to his duties, slight though they were now that it was obvious their mission had failed, and trying to discover a way to get past the formidable defenses with which Delgado had surrounded himself, he couldn't remember the last time he had gotten more than two consecutive hours of sleep. Certainly not since the night…

His mind flinched from the memory of Wetherly's expression, solemn as an owl's, as he had attempted to pour the last of that final bottle of wine they had shared into Sebastian's cup. The viscount had missed the rim widely, which had struck him as enormously amusing. The sound of Harry's laughter, the last time Sebastian would ever hear it, echoed still in his heart.

A noise at the front of the colonel's house drew his attention. Eager for something else to think about, he opened his eyes, watching as a large black coach, pulled by a perfectly matched team of four was driven up to the front entrance. As soon as it arrived, a boy carrying a torch emerged from the shadowed portico of the house.

Following in its light, a man swept purposefully down the low steps, his cloak, as black as midnight, swirling dramatically behind him. In spite of his exhaustion, a thrill of excitement ran like a restorative through Sebastian's veins.

Almost without his conscious volition, his hand fastened around the butt of the pistol he had concealed under his own cloak. Although he knew a shot fired from here would not be within the narrow range of the weapon, he still had to fight not to level the gun at the Spaniard's black heart and shoot him down like the mongrel cur he was.

He had never planned an assassination. He wanted to give Delgado what the Spaniard hadn't given poor Harry. He wanted to beat him in a fair fight. And before he killed him, he wanted to make sure the bastard understood exactly why he was dying.

Sebastian stepped forward, intending to stop Delgado before he could enter the coach. Almost immediately, the courtyard began to fill with horsemen, no doubt the same ones who had been with the colonel that day by the river, obviously part of the junta Wellington had described.

If he revealed himself now, Sebastian realized, he would never be allowed to get close enough to their leader to challenge him. And if he failed in this attempt, Delgado would escape punishment for what he had done. Working to control his disappointment, he retreated into the shadows, pressing close to the wall from where he had been watching.

When the men were assembled, Delgado put his foot onto the first of the carriage steps. Before he climbed in, he turned once more to face the house. It became apparent to Sebastian only then that someone was standing at the top of the steps, almost hidden by the shadows from the overhang.

"Watch her," Delgado ordered, raising his voice to be heard over the noise of the milling horses. "Your own life depends upon it."

The reply, if there was one, was too soft for Sebastian to hear. Turning, the Spaniard raised his hand, giving the signal for departure. As he entered the carriage, half of the troop cantered across the courtyard and out of the gates that guarded the house. The carriage followed, with the remainder of the horsemen bringing up the rear.

Watch her. Your own life depends upon it. Obviously, the order referred to Delgado's ward.

Would he issue such a threat, Sebastian wondered, if he were going to be away for only a few hours? There was no way to know. Not for sure.

He did know, however, that the time in which he had to accomplish his goal was running out. During the past two days, he had felt the passage of each separate minute as if he were watching the fall of sand in an hourglass. The slow, inevitable drop of each grain had tightened the tension. If he couldn't manage to catch Delgado alone before Wellington's party left Madrid…

Then, almost as if an answer to prayer, an idea sprang into his head. It went against every precept of honor he had ever been taught, but desperate times called for desperate measures. And having seen Delgado's jealousy, he knew without any doubt there *was* a way to lure the man away from his fortress and his cadre of devoted followers.

Delgado was both arrogant and possessive enough to make it work, Sebastian thought. He would take the bait. Just as poor Harry had done.

The plan was so perfect, Sebastian wondered why he hadn't considered it before. Of course, he had had no idea that Delgado would leave tonight, taking his "garrison" with him. And if Sebastian didn't find some way to take advantage of the unexpected opportunity he had just been given, he deserved to fail.

The boy with the torch turned and began to remount the steps. The figure that had been in the shadows at the top of them had disappeared, apparently moving back into the interior.

And the girl called Pilar? Sebastian wondered. Had she kissed her fiancé farewell before he left? Had she bid that bastard Godspeed on his journey?

He had spent hours during the past two days wondering about her role in Harry's death. Perhaps she hadn't understood Delgado's intent when he had sent her to that cemetery. Or perhaps she had been an unwilling accomplice, forced to play her part under duress. After all, it had been clear that night in the garden that she feared her guardian.

Her *guardian.* Soon to be her fiancé.

For some reason the knowledge that the girl was living with Delgado had eaten at Sebastian like acid since he'd discovered it. He had supposed Spanish society to be at least as strict in its conventions as his own. Apparently he had been wrong.

It made no difference to him that, according to the fishmonger who had directed him here, the arrangement was sanctioned by the presence of a female relative within the household. The situation was still unsavory, especially since the girl had openly admitted they were soon to be betrothed.

Under duress? If so, just as he had told Harry, when he killed the bastard, he would, at the same time, free the girl.

When the courtyard was again completely deserted, he eased along in the shadows of the garden wall from where he'd been watching. He had spent part of the last forty-eight hours finding out as much as he could about the arrangement of the dwelling in case, as a last resort, he had to break into it in order to bring about the confrontation he sought.

Since it was too dangerous to ask questions of anyone who might have that information, he had been forced to rely upon his own observations. He had learned which rooms belonged to Pilar because he had caught a glimpse of her last night.

The floor-to-ceiling window she had been standing in led onto a small patio surrounded by a low wall. The cloud of midnight hair that had been artfully arranged in curls atop her head on the night of the ball had again been allowed to drift loosely around her shoulders. He had even been able to discern the color of the dressing gown she wore, a deep crimson, made richer by the glow of the candlelight from the room behind her.

Moving silently through the darkness, he had now arrived outside that same patio. Tonight the shutters on the window were closed. In the light that filtered through the wooden slats, Sebastian could see that a guard had been posted outside it.

Luckily he didn't seem to be taking his duties seriously. His musket had been propped against the same wall he was leaning against as he smoked. The scent of his cigar wafted into the darkness.

For a second Sebastian hesitated. *Don't do anything that might jeopardize a reunion with your brothers,* Wellington had advised. In his mind's eye, he could see their faces as clearly as he had seen Harry's, and the temptation to turn away from the dangerous course he had chosen before it was too late was incredibly strong.

If he did, there might never be another opportunity. With that acknowledgment, Sebastian Sinclair vaulted lightly over the wall that separated him from Delgado's sentry and ultimately from the woman that guard was supposed to protect.

* * *

Despite the fact that she was even more closely watched when Julián was away, Pilar still felt an undeniable sense of escape, a subtle relaxation of the ever-present tension, when her guardian left her alone. As he had tonight.

He hadn't told her the import of the message that had called him away. He seldom shared that kind of information. All she knew was that it had been unexpected. And apparently urgent.

She was sitting now before her dressing table, her unseeing eyes focused on its mirror. She held her hairbrush rather than employing it, as she thought about Julián's behavior during the past few days.

Something had happened. Something he hadn't told her about. She knew because, up until tonight, his mood had been unusually buoyant.

It was possible, of course, that whatever had caused the almost visible aura of accomplishment that had surrounded him had to do with the political situation. Once or twice, however, she had lifted her eyes to find him contemplating her with an expression that had looked very much like satisfaction.

Then, becoming aware of her gaze, he had smiled at her. A slow, triumphant smile that seemed to denote victory.

Whatever he thought he had achieved, therefore, had something to do with her. And the only thing she could imagine that would give him cause to think he had had some triumph over her would concern the English soldier.

Sebastian Sinclair. Although she had tried since the reception to put his name out of her mind, she found it reverberating in her memory at the oddest moments.

That had happened once when she had heard a strain of music floating in through the windows of her bedroom. She had opened the shutters in order to listen to the distant, haunting melody, as faint as that which had drifted into the palace gardens the night of the reception.

The other incident had occurred at dinner last night. As she absently watched Julián's long, white fingers toy with his wineglass, she had realized she was unconsciously contrasting them to the sunburned ones that had fastened around her wrist. It seemed she could feel their callused warmth even now.

There was a slight noise outside her window. Her eyes lifted, looking into the mirror at the reflection of the shutters her maid had closed before she had left.

She listened, trying to determine the origin of the sound she'd heard. Not the regular footsteps of the guard who would be stationed there tonight. This had sounded like a scuffle. Almost as if blows were being exchanged. And then…

At the sudden silence, she laid down her brush and turned toward the window. As she watched, the shutters opened inward, revealing the figure of a man. He was standing on the patio outside, his shape outlined against the deep purple of the evening sky.

The identification made viscerally rather than visually, she knew at once who it was. An overwhelming sense of terror, more powerful than that which she'd felt as he held her prisoner in the garden, blossomed in her chest.

She rose instinctively, but she could think of nothing to say. There was no warning she could give him that she hadn't already made. No other reason she could think of to convince him that being here was nothing less than suicide.

"You have five minutes to get dressed," Sebastian Sinclair said. "I've never known any woman who could accomplish that, but I warn you that if you don't, I shall take you in your rail."

"Take me?" she repeated, latching onto the salient part of that. "Take me where?"

"With me," he said simply.

"No," she whispered. "I told you—"

"The choice isn't yours, my lady. I have need of you. And therefore, you *will* come."

Her feelings about this man were so tangled there was some part of her that exulted in the fact that he was here. He had come for her.

That heady sense of pleasure was short-lived. Whatever his purpose, if she were foolish enough to go with him, there could be only one outcome. She had always known that.

"Need me for what?"

"To lure your *guardian* to his death." There was a slight emphasis on the word "guardian," the tone mocking.

"Julián? You're insane."

"Four minutes," he said, striding across the room to throw open her wardrobe.

She turned to watch, too stunned to protest as he began to paw through the garments stored there, selecting one or two items from among them. He brought those over to where she was standing, tossing them down carelessly onto the stool of her dressing table.

"Of course, if you prefer to go as you are..." His smile reminded her of Julián's—cold and sardonic.

"Why are you doing this?" she demanded. "Don't you understand that he'll kill you?"

"That particular threat grows old, my lady. You should find a new one. Did you enjoy your excursion to mass?"

Perhaps he *had* suddenly gone mad. Something about him had changed.

What Julián had done to his face might explain what had become of the gallant cavalier who had attempted to save her that day by the river. She could imagine no reason, however, for the alteration that seemed to have occurred between the kiss they had shared in the garden three nights ago and what was now in his eyes.

"I haven't been to mass," she said. There was too much she could never confess, so she refused to go and make a mockery.

"Only to the cemetery, I suppose. And you lost your cloak. A pity. You might have worn *it* tonight instead of having the bother of getting dressed."

She shook her head, feeling more and more as if she had stumbled into a nightmare from which she couldn't awaken. The Englishman was in her bedchamber, and he was demanding she go with him so that he might kill Julián. The danger that he might be discovered increased minute by minute, yet he continued to bandy nonsense about lost cloaks and graveyards.

"I don't understand," she said. "What cloak?"

He picked up one of the garments he'd laid on the stool and tossed it toward her. It was the jacket of her riding habit, she realized, as she automatically caught it, clutching it protectively to her breasts.

"Are you waiting for me to avert my eyes?" he asked.

"I am waiting for you to tell me why you are here."

"I have told you. I'm here to take you with me."

She tried to think what she could possibly say to him that she hadn't already said. Of course, one didn't reason with a madman.

"I'm not going," she said instead. "I can't."

She expected argument. Another accusation. Something. Instead his eyes simply considered her face, his mouth still arranged in that mocking half smile.

"You profess to fear your guardian," he said. "Yet, when given the opportunity to escape him, you refuse to accept it."

"Because I know we'll never be allowed to leave the grounds," she said. "He has guards everywhere."

"Most of whom have just ridden out with him. As for the rest, with their master gone, I should imagine they are even less diligent than the one outside your windows was."

She hadn't been sure he was aware Julián wasn't here. And of course, he couldn't understand the implications of her guardian's absence. Contrary to what he was suggesting, security around her would be increased rather than lessened.

"Even if we did get past the guards—"

The soft knock on her door cut into those words of protest as sharply as a knife. Her eyes, widened in shock and fear, met his. Removing a pistol from beneath his cloak, the Englishman reached out to grasp her wrist as he had in the garden, pulling her toward the window.

Dropping the jacket he'd thrown at her, she pushed ineffectively at the fingers gripping her arm like an iron band. It was the only form of protest she dared with someone standing outside her door.

Inexorably the Englishman's strength overcame hers as he dragged her toward the open shutters. Desperate, she struck at his face with her free hand until he averted it, protecting himself from the blows by hunching his shoulder to provide her less of a target.

As she struggled, she worried that the sound of those slaps might alert whoever was outside. Then, finally, she realized she was losing the silent battle. They were almost at the window and in only a few seconds—

He straightened, no longer forced to avoid her flailing hand. Without releasing her wrist, he looked over his shoulder, surveying the patio beyond the window before he turned, meeting her eyes.

Seeing what was in them, she realized that he wouldn't be denied. If he had to, he would carry her out of the house, and the only protest she could possibly make—

She raised her free hand, clenching it into a fist. With her closed hand, she struck him as hard as she could in the nose. At the same time, she gave one last desperate jerk of her captured wrist, panic lending her strength.

Her hand came free, but it happened so unexpectedly that she stumbled backward even as he grabbed for her again. As she staggered, off balance, her foot became entangled in the folds of the riding jacket she had dropped.

Arms flailing in a vain attempt to right herself, she knew she was falling, and yet there was nothing she could do to stop it. Almost as soon as the realization formed, the back of her head struck the footboard of the high bed.

There was a fraction of a second during which the impact registered before blackness closed around her like fog. The Englishman's shocked face, his hand still outstretched toward her, was the last thing she remembered.

Chapter Five

Awkwardly shifting the burden he held in his arms, Sebastian raised his right fist, hammering it against the heavy wooden door. With Ferdinand's soldiers guarding the front entrances of the house that had been provided for the English envoy's stay in Madrid, this was a last resort.

He turned, his eyes searching the darkness behind him. Despite the knock on the door of Pilar's bedroom, no alarm had been sounded as he'd carried her out of Delgado's house. And so far he had seen no sign of pursuit. That had seemed a stroke of incredible luck, since he'd had no destination in mind when he'd started this.

When he'd made that spur-of-the-moment decision to use the girl to lure Delgado to come to him, he had never considered that he might have to take her by force. He had thought she would welcome the chance to escape her guardian's control.

He still believed he would eventually have been able to convince her if they hadn't been interrupted. At least that's what he had told himself, fighting the guilt he felt over this abduction, a guilt that increased with each passing minute. Especially when he looked down to consider the pale face of the girl who still slept in his arms.

After she'd hit her head, he had rushed to her side, realizing immediately she was deeply unconscious. The knock on the door had sounded again, accompanied this time by a woman's voice calling Doña Pilar's name.

Without much thought about the consequences, he had bent, picking the girl up and settling her across his shoulder. It was the same method he had used innumerable times to carry a wounded comrade.

Once outside, he had somehow managed to hold on to her and mount the gelding he'd hidden behind a neighboring house. Then, as he had guided the horse through the dark, twisting streets of Madrid, he had held the girl before him, her body frighteningly still and limp.

During the course of the journey, she had drifted briefly into consciousness. She had turned her head to look up. Her eyes had appeared almost dazed, and after only a moment they had closed again.

Despite the time that had passed since then, she had not regained consciousness. Apparently the impact to her head had been more severe than he'd realized at the time, and anxiety roiled in his gut.

"Who is it?"

Although the voice was muffled by the thickness of the wooden door between them, Sebastian recognized it with a prayer of thanksgiving. At last, something had gone right.

"Sinclair," he said. Then, realizing his name might not be sufficient identification for the speaker, he added something that he knew would be. ''The man with the scarred face. I need your help.''

There were no more questions, but it seemed an eternity before he heard the sound of the bar being removed from the inside of the door. When it opened, the figure of the fat cook who had served as translator between Harry and the fishmonger was revealed.

Sebastian already knew the man was amenable to bribes. And tonight he was ready to offer him anything for his help.

Due to the lateness of the hour, the cook had already donned his nightclothes, including a long, almost comical night cap. In one hand, he held a candle, which he raised to verify Sebastian's identity.

Without giving him time to speak, Sebastian put his shoulder against the door, pushing it open widely enough to allow him to carry the girl inside. To his credit, the cook didn't try to block his entrance. Instead, he shut the door quickly after them, and, setting down his candle, lifted the bar and placed it back in its place.

''I need a bed and some mulled wine,'' Sebastian said. ''You'll be well paid for your trouble.''

Despite the fact that he was at this man's mercy, he did what he knew Dare or Wellington would have done in the circumstances. He assumed command. If you did that convincingly enough, his eldest brother had always said, people usually responded exactly as you wished them to.

''Is she dead?'' the cook asked, holding the candle so that its light fell on the girl's face.

Her eyes were still closed, fine blue veins visible under the fragile skin of the lids. She lay so still that for a heartbeat Sebastian feared she might be. Then he felt, as he had since he'd lifted her from the floor of her bedroom, the rise and fall of her breasts, moving tantalizingly against his chest as she breathed.

"If she were, I should need neither of the things I've asked you to provide. Since she isn't—"

He inclined his head, raising one brow in the same autocratic manner the earl used so effectively, and pinned the cook with a look that demanded action. Surprisingly, it worked as well for him as it always had for Dare.

"This way," the cook said, turning to lead him through the dark kitchens, his solitary candle lighting the passage.

Drawing a breath in relief, Sebastian shifted the girl in his arms so that his hold was more secure. He glanced back at the outside door, verifying that it was again impregnable, at least for the time being. Then he, too, turned, following the wavering light of that single candle.

"Drink this. It will help your head."

Pilar opened her eyes to find the English soldier, in full uniform now, stooping beside her. He slipped his arm beneath her shoulders to raise her upper body as he placed the rim of a cup against her lips.

She had a vague recollection, almost like something from a dream, that he had done this before. It had been night then, the only light in the room a candle. And every time she had opened her eyes, she remembered now, he had been beside her.

Once he had put his hand against her forehead, as if feeling for fever. As she had looked up at him then, he had laid his palm against her cheek, the motion almost a caress.

His fingers had been cool on her heated skin, seeming to soothe the throbbing in her skull. She'd had to resist the urge to turn her face into them, rubbing against them like a cat.

"Drink it," he said again, his tone this time more commanding.

Obedient as a child, she opened her mouth, taking a tentative swallow of whatever the cup contained. Some kind of infusion, she decided. The taste was slightly bitter. Medicinal. Despite that, just as his hand against her cheek had been last night, its coolness was welcome against the incredible dryness of her mouth.

When he began to remove the cup, her lips followed, clinging to the rim. Only now did she realize how thirsty she was. And there was still a dull ache at the back of her head, although that was not so bad as when she had awakened before.

"More?" he asked.

At her nod, he tilted the cup, and she drank from it greedily. When she signaled that she'd finished, he eased her down on the pillows once more. Then he turned to set the cup on a table beside the bed, where the candle had been last night.

Daylight revealed their surroundings. The room was small, with only one window, thinly curtained against the morning sun. The light that filtered through revealed furnishings that were both primitive and sparse.

"Where are we?" she asked, her eyes returning to his face.

The angle of that diffused sunlight seemed to emphasize the cruel line of the scar. It didn't detract from his looks, she decided. Without it, they might even have been too refined. Too much the proper English gentleman.

The mark added a certain dangerous appeal to the classically handsome features. She knew, of course, that her assessment of its effect would not be the same as his. Even if the man were totally lacking in vanity, the manner of the scar's acquisition would guarantee it would be despised.

"Someplace where you'll be safe," he said. "At least for the time being."

Safe? Safe from...? Julián.

At the realization that her guardian would surely be looking for her, she put her hands against the mattress, pushing up too quickly. Then she lowered her head, closing her eyes as she fought the resulting flood of vertigo.

Sebastian's arm came around her, offering support. For the moment, she was forced to accept it, leaning weakly against his chest, too disoriented to do anything else.

As soon as the worst had passed, she straightened, pushing away from that impersonal embrace. He released her immediately.

"Why did you do this?" she whispered, searching his face. "Why did you bring me here?"

"I told you," he said.

Despite their color, his eyes seemed dark and very cold. But then, his purpose in taking her was both. He *had* told her last night exactly what it was.

I need you, he had said. *To lure your guardian to his death.*

"When I've killed him," he went on, "I promise to convey you to your family."

"I *have* no family," she said bitterly. "Julián has already seen to that."

His eyes narrowed. She could almost read his horror in them. "Are you saying that your guardian—"

"I tried to tell you," she interrupted, feeling her anger build again because he hadn't listened. Now, when it seemed he was willing to, it was far too late. "You refuse to believe what he's capable of."

There was a small silence, and then he broke it, his tone completely different. As biting as hers.

"Believe me, I *know* what he's capable of. The day after the king's reception, your guardian set a trap. It was intended for me, but one of my friends stumbled into it instead."

The day *after* the reception. Which meant that whatever Julián had done was the result of her foolish escapade in the garden.

"I should never have left the ballroom," she whispered. "If there is one thing I've learned—"

She stopped because it was painfully obvious she had *not* learned, despite Julián's repeated attempts to teach her, the uselessness of rebellion. Instead, she had dared to slip away from the reception, enjoying what she had convinced herself would be a brief, harmless interlude.

She should have known that nothing like that moment of freedom could ever be harmless where she was concerned. After all, Julián had done everything in his power to teach her.

After her father's death, he had tightened his control over every aspect of her life. Eventually her pride had rebelled against his restrictions.

That had led to her attempted escape. The one during which she had met this man and discovered that, even if she were willing to die rather than surrender to Julián's control, she was incapable of sacrificing anyone else to that goal.

When she had thought her disobedience would cost the English soldier his life, she had begged Julián for it. Since her guardian had enjoyed seeing her reduced to the role of supplicant, Sebastian Sinclair had not died that day.

Now, again because of her foolishness, another man had. That was the triumph Julián had been taking such delight in the past two days, she realized. Someone had paid the ultimate price for her disappearance from an overcrowded ballroom. And this time she had not been given a chance to beg Julián to spare that life.

''What did he do?'' she asked, not because she wanted to know, but because each piece of treachery painted a clearer portrait, if she needed one, of her guardian's soullessness.

''Your maid delivered your message through a peddler who calls here as well as at Delgado's.''

''*My* message?'' she repeated. She had sent no messages. But of course, Anna would do anything Julián told her to do. Any of the servants who worked for him would. ''I promise you that I never—''

''It was meant for me,'' he continued, without allowing her to complete the denial, ''but to protect me, my friend intercepted it. He went to meet you in my stead.''

''In...a cemetery,'' she guessed, finally making

sense of the accusation he'd thrown at her last night. "I knew nothing about that, I swear to you."

"*Someone* was there when he arrived. Someone wearing a woman's cloak."

Anna? The maid had asked for permission to go to confession the day after the reception. Pilar had never thought of refusing.

"Given this," Sebastian said, long fingers lifting to touch the scar Julián had slashed across his face, "it must have become obvious at some point that Harry *wasn't* his intended victim. Your guardian killed him all the same."

Another death that might be laid at her door. Just as Sebastian Sinclair's would eventually be.

"No life but Julián's has value to him," she said. "If he wants something, he is absolutely ruthless in the acquisition of it. God help anyone who gets in his way."

"Is that what happened to your family? They got in his way?"

It was, of course, but she hadn't realized that until much later. And unless Julián chose one day to taunt her with the knowledge, she would never know if her father had understood why he had to die.

"My mother died when I was born. Despite a great deal of pressure from his family, my father never remarried."

None of them could understand that refusal, but none of them had witnessed, as she had, his profound and lifelong grief. She believed he was still grieving the loss of her mother on the day he'd died.

That was the only thing that had given her any peace when Julián had told her about her father's death—the idea that they would at last be reunited.

It was that thought alone that had kept her sane when she had finally realized what Julián had done and why he had done it.

"My father had dedicated himself to ridding Spain of the French domination. That's how he became involved with Julián. Given their positions, their paths would never have crossed, except for the war."

"Their positions?"

"My father was a grandee. The Conde del Castillo. Bonaparte abolished the designation, but he couldn't abolish the years of power and influence behind it. Julián was a minor hidalgo. Only in the cause of independence would they have ever become friends.

"They did, because my father admired him both as a soldier and a patriot. He didn't suspect the kind of man Julián was or he would never have brought him to our home. When Julián saw me, he decided that I would make the perfect wife for him. My father...didn't agree."

Although she had known nothing about Delgado, other than his friendship with her father and his avowed dedication to their mutual cause, there had been something about him that had made her view the possibility of such a union with near loathing. Without even consulting her, however, her father had refused the offer, having no intention of seeing her wed to a common soldier. Neither of them had understood then that Julián could not endure to be refused. Not anything.

"My father's dedication to his king and his country were based on his family's long loyalty and service to the crown. Julián, on the other hand..."

Even now it was difficult for her to articulate what he had done. If the Englishman were to have any chance at all in this insane quest, however, he had to know everything.

"Julián is an opportunist. Had he believed Napoleon could hope to maintain control of Iberia, I have no doubt he would have backed the other side. It's possible he did that in the early years of the war. Then he came to the realization that the French would eventually be driven out. And, far more important for him, to the realization that those who helped to bring about their defeat would be suitably rewarded."

"As he has been," Sebastian said.

She lifted her eyes, shutting out those painful images from the past. For the first time she noticed the signs of exhaustion in his face. The skin under his eyes was dark with fatigue. Of course, since he had kept watch over her all night...

The memory of that vigil touched her. It had been a long time since anyone had been truly concerned about her well-being. Those who were expected to care for her now did so, not out of love or even loyalty, but out of fear.

"He has the king's favor," she said, "but he has not yet been rewarded to the extent he expects to be. That's why my father had to die."

Julián had made it seem as if her father's death had nothing to do with his proposal. Even then, even before she had come to understand the kind of man he was, she had known in her heart that he was somehow responsible.

"Delgado killed him?"

"In the midst of a war it's easy to rid yourself of

someone who stands in the way of what you want.'' She took a breath, remembering her shock the day she had listened to Julián's explanation of her father's death and his supposed dying wish for her future. ''Julián claimed that before he died, my father appointed him my guardian. He produced a document to that effect, although...''

The words faded. She had been convinced that the wavering signature had been forged or—and the thought of this was far more horrifying—that it had been obtained by force.

Since her father was dead and conveniently unable to dispute the claim, however, the document had been accepted as authentic. Julián had gotten his way. He always did.

''My father's death gave Julián the opportunity he needed. He took over the army my father had raised, and he used it to great effect in the waning days of the war. Then, as soon as the king was restored to the throne, he began his petitions. He's been promised his answer in a matter of weeks. Considering the king's gratitude, what that answer will be is a foregone conclusion.''

''Petitioning the king for what?''

The Englishman couldn't possibly have followed that part of her explanation, she realized. Not without knowing something of the men who were involved, as well as the laws governing inheritances.

''For permission to marry his ward, of course. And in doing so, to inherit the lands and titles that belonged to her father, Antonio Rafael Lázaro Mendoza de Covadonga, Conde del Castillo. You didn't imagine Julián wanted to marry me for love, did you?''

She had told him that in the garden. She had believed then she would never see this man again, so she hadn't tried to explain the complicated motivations that drove Delgado.

"Don't worry, Captain Sinclair. Wealth is a much greater enticement to Julián than love. He'll do what you want. He'll come after me because, if he doesn't, he stands to lose a great deal. Or perhaps I should say, he'll come after you. And when he finds you, he'll do exactly what I convinced him *not* to do that day by the river. He'll kill you as slowly and as painfully as he possibly can."

"I think he can be trusted," Sebastian said. "I've paid him enough to assure his silence, but..."

"You want me to keep an eye on things," Malford said. "See to it that he doesn't leave the house."

"And especially that he doesn't send a message to anyone outside it."

Last night it had seemed he had no choice in trusting the cook. He had felt then that bringing Pilar here was a reasonable solution. In the light of day, however, he had realized there were a great number of things that could go wrong.

The cook's reluctance to give him the fishmonger's name might well speak to his ability to keep his mouth shut, but an offer of money had loosened his tongue quickly enough. And he imagined Delgado had much more with which to bargain than he had.

"I'll look sharp," Harry's batman promised. "Don't you worry on that score, Captain Sinclair.

You concentrate on finding the bastard that killed Lord Wetherly."

"Good man," Sebastian said, gripping his shoulder.

Malford was the ideal conspirator, virtually without duties now that his master was dead, and with his own grudge against Harry's murderer. It had taken Sebastian only a few minutes of mental debate to decide to let the batman in on what was going on. He would certainly be more trustworthy than the accomplice who had been thrust upon him last night.

"Oh," Malford said, turning back after he had gone part of the way down the passage that led to the kitchens. "I almost forgot. His Grace is looking for you. Sent word near half an hour ago."

Sebastian's response to that information was the same as when one of the masters at school had sent for him, magnified perhaps a hundredfold. A cold dread settled in the pit of his stomach like a stone.

He thought of asking Malford if he had any idea what the summons was about. Only the knowledge that, even if Wellington had somehow learned what was going on, he would have to face the accounting prevented him.

"Thank you," he said instead.

He watched until the batman had disappeared, and then, running his finger around the collar of his uniform, which seemed to have tightened against his throat, he turned and headed upstairs. If the duke had been waiting for half an hour, any further delay could only exacerbate his always uncertain temper.

Even if Wellington had no idea what Sebastian had done, he was probably in for an unpleasant few minutes. If the duke *had* somehow gotten word that one of his officers had kidnapped the ward of the Spanish king's favorite...

Then being late was going to be the least of his problems, Sebastian acknowledged. The very least.

"Captain Sinclair," Wellington said, looking up from the papers spread across the surface of his desk.

Sebastian was experienced enough with the moods of his commander to know that the tone didn't connote displeasure, and the knot that had settled in his stomach began to dissolve. Whatever this was about, it wasn't the disaster he'd been anticipating.

"Your grace?"

"I received some news this morning that I thought you would be interested in. It concerns the subject we discussed privately the last time we met," the duke said somewhat cryptically.

"Lord Wetherly's death," Sebastian said, refusing to avoid a direct reference to the topic.

"In a way. I've inquired, of course, but it seems there were no witnesses to what took place in the church yard of Santa María de la Rosa that afternoon."

It would be the rare murder that was carried out in front of witnesses, of course, but Sebastian refrained from pointing out the obvious.

"No, my news concerns the Spanish gentleman we spoke of," the duke continued.

"Julián Delgado."

"Who is to be, it seems, His Majesty's ambassador to the court of his royal cousin, Louis of France. He was given the appointment yesterday afternoon. Short notice, especially if he is expected to reach Paris before the agreements that are to be the products of the current negotiations are signed. Or perhaps that isn't the intent. Perhaps Ferdinand simply feels it necessary to have a representative there at this critical juncture."

"Forgive me, your grace," Sebastian said, almost interrupting the spate of speculation. "Are you saying Delgado is going to Paris?"

"*Has* gone, according to my informants."

Wellington had always had remarkably well-informed "correspondents," as he had called his secret sources during the war. Apparently, some of those were still in operation, and given the accuracy of their past communiques, Sebastian had little cause to doubt what the duke had been told.

"I must confess, knowing how you felt about Wetherly and what you believe about Delgado's role in his death, I was relieved to hear of his departure," Wellington said.

The implications of this appointment were only now beginning to penetrate. The primary one was, of course, that Delgado was no longer within his reach because he was no longer in Madrid. It was even possible, Sebastian realized, that he had watched Julián's departure for France last night.

His servants had been placed under the threat of death to keep his ward secured until he returned. Perhaps they hadn't been particularly eager to track Delgado down in order to inform him that she was missing.

"By the way," the duke added, "the colonel's been given a title commensurate with his new duties. Apparently he had been petitioning for it for some time. Ferdinand decided that his representative should carry with him all the pomp and circumstances of the Spanish court—the pre-Bonaparte court, of course.''

''And Delgado is now Conde del Castillo,'' Sebastian said.

It seemed the bastard had succeeded in what Pilar believed he had set out at the beginning to accomplish.

''It appears your sources are as good as mine, Captain Sinclair. How surprising.''

Wellington was no fool. Sebastian could only hope that in the press of his own duties, his commander wouldn't have time to wonder too long about how he, a lowly staff officer, had obtained information about the inner workings of the Spanish court.

''And with the count in Paris,'' the duke went on, ''you must do exactly as I advised you before. Whatever your suspicions, he is certainly beyond the reach of them now. I should suppose his ward is traveling with him. I understand they are to be married soon. Perhaps they will honeymoon in Paris, something no one but the French have been able to do since the Peace of Amiens.''

This time Sebastian was wise enough to hold his tongue. Whatever Delgado would be doing in Paris, it would not involve his ward, the girl he had hidden in the kitchens of this very house.

''As for the rest of us, we shall be leaving soon for Bordeaux to meet the transport ships there. I promised you should be home before the end of June, and so you shall. I'm very glad you did nothing to jeopardize what should be a joyous reunion with your family. I suspect Dare should never have forgiven me if I'd allowed you to come to harm after the dangers of war were past. As it is, you may be home in time to interrupt Major Sinclair's honeymoon, which, I assume, is *not* taking place in Paris.''

Wellington was almost jovial. He had probably been worried that Sebastian would do exactly what he *had* done. Now, of course, he believed the danger of the youngest Sinclair precipitating an international incident had passed. And his relief was obvious, both as His Majesty's envoy and as the Earl of Dare's friend.

''I think you may safely make that assumption, your grace.''

Wellington smiled. ''I confess, Sin, the idea of your attempting to avenge Harry's death gave me more than a few sleepless hours. Given your previous...shall we say impetuousness, I applaud your control in this situation. I can only imagine what a temptation it must have been to act upon your suspicions. The fact that you chose not to demonstrates a maturity and attention to duty I commend. I know your brothers would be very proud if they knew.''

''Thank you, your grace,'' Sebastian answered, because there was literally nothing else he could say.

Delgado was gone, and in a few days he himself would be leaving for England. And the only thing left to be settled...

For a moment the image of the girl's face, as she had lain in his arms last night, filled his head. He had taken her by force. And in doing so, he had promised her that he would kill her guardian and free her from the bastard's control.

It seemed that accomplishing the first was now an impossibility. And as for the second, he could think of only one way he could possibly guarantee that now.

Chapter Six

"And there's none braver, my lady," Malford said. "Lord Wetherly always said he'd rather have Captain Sinclair—Sin, as he called him—by his side in a hard fight than anyone else in the whole army. A very fine officer, as well as a gentleman from an old and distinguished family. A younger son and untitled, you understand, but much favored by his brothers. Or so I've been told."

In the circle in which Pilar had grown up, it would have been considered highly improper to entertain servants' gossip and almost unforgivable to solicit it. In these circumstances, however, it had seemed this might be the only way to obtain information about the man who had abducted her. And Lord Wetherly's valet had proven a veritable font of that.

Now she had a much clearer understanding of the relationship that had existed between Malford's late master and Sebastian Sinclair. She had also been provided with more details about Julián's deception, which had led to the viscount's death. Hearing them, she understood why the captain had been suspicious of her role. She also knew why he was so bent on revenge.

As she had listened to Malford's praise, she found she was considering the tantalizing possibility that Sebastian might actually succeed in his goal. Given both his courage and ability, believing that he might be the one who could best Julián was a temptation.

"And his oldest brother is an earl, I believe you said?"

"The Earl of Dare, my lady. Friend of the Duke of Wellington as well as a member of the Regent's inner circle, if you take my meaning."

They turned almost guiltily as a soft knock sounded at the door. It opened before either of them had time to respond. Sebastian stepped into the room, closing the door quickly behind him.

His eyes had sought Pilar first, and he seemed surprised she was sitting on the edge of the bed rather than lying upon it as he'd left her. Or perhaps it was her appearance that shocked him. Since he had abducted her in her nightgown, however, just as he had threatened, she had been left little choice in her attire.

She had managed to fashion a shawl from the thin coverlet she'd found at the foot of the bed. Draped about her shoulders and held together over the front of her rail, the makeshift garment was more modest than her ball gown had been. Sebastian's eyes had made a quick downward survey of its arrangement before they fastened on her face.

"Your headache seems improved."

She couldn't decide if there had been a note of censure in the comment. Even if there were, her answer would be the same.

"Yes, it is, thank you," she said almost formally.

His eyes held on hers for a moment before he turned to the batman. The tilt of his head toward the door was almost imperceptible, but Malford responded eagerly, springing up from the windowsill where he'd propped his hip.

"If you'll excuse me, my lady," he said, as he started across the room, "I'm sure I've taken up enough of your day with my chatter."

She inclined her head, smiling an unnecessary dismissal. After all, it was very apparent from whom he was taking his orders.

As soon as he had slipped out the door, closing it behind him as furtively as Sinclair had opened it, Pilar looked back at the man who had kidnapped her. He was watching her with what could only be called speculation. Seeing it, she raised her brows questioningly.

"What is it?" she asked.

When he didn't answer immediately, anxiety began to tighten her chest, making it difficult to breathe.

"It seems your guardian is no longer in Madrid."

His tone had been without inflection, but as she absorbed the news, she realized what a bitter disappointment this must have been for him. It was not until several seconds later that she even thought to wonder what it would portend for her.

"Then…where is he?"

Normally she would think that the farther away Julián was, the better. In this situation…

"King Ferdinand has sent him to Paris."

"To *Paris?*"

"As his representative. There are talks going on

there between the ambassadors of the crowned heads of Europe concerning what to do with France's conquered territories, now that Napoleon has abdicated."

"And the king sent *Julián* to represent Spain?"

Despite Ferdinand's gratitude over her guardian's efforts in his cause, it was bizarre that a man without any official standing at the royal court should have been given such a responsibility.

"It seems your guardian's petition has been granted," Sebastian said softly.

Still coming to terms with the shock that Julián was no longer in Spain, it took longer than it should have for that more emotionally significant piece of information to register. When it did, she felt a flood of renewed grief and bitterness on her father's behalf.

"The king has given him my father's titles."

"Apparently he felt that would be in keeping with Delgado's appointment."

"And the rest?" she asked.

A small crease formed between the midnight brows. "I would assume the lands are attached to the title, although I have to confess, I was told nothing of what was entailed in the appointment."

"I had reference to the other." She wondered if he had forgotten what she had told him or if it were simply unimportant to him.

"The other?"

She took a breath before she asked, attempting to slow her heart. "I was merely curious as to whether His Majesty has also granted permission for Julián to marry the daughter of the man he murdered."

Had the king given her away as casually as he

had disposed of the lands and titles that had once belonged to a man who had raised an army to help restore him to the throne?

"As I've been reminded rather frequently of late, one must have proof in order to accuse the king's favorite. I doubt you could prove that accusation any more than I am likely to be able to prove he murdered my friend."

"So he has escaped again," she said.

"For the time being. Will they send word to France that you're missing?"

She thought about the panic that would have ensued within the household when it was discovered she was gone. She could almost picture her maid's frantic search of her room and her resulting wails of terror. Poor Anna.

"The servants would be too afraid to tell him, I think. I don't know which of his men went with Julián to Paris, but...I suppose it's possible that whoever he left in charge here *might* be foolish enough to send him word."

"Foolish because confessing they had failed would be dangerous?"

She laughed, the sound without humor. Failure was always dangerous. Everyone who worked for Julián knew that.

They would be terrified to tell him and equally terrified that he might somehow find out that they hadn't. She herself had been in that same position on several occasions. And she had always opted to keep silent in the hope that whatever she was hiding wouldn't come out.

This man couldn't possibly understand the dread Julián's staff would be feeling this morning when they discovered she was gone. Despite her firsthand knowledge, she still found it difficult to grasp the scope of her guardian's cruelty, both to those who worked for him and to his soldiers, who followed him from fear rather than any sense of loyalty.

"Whoever was in charge will pay with his life for my disappearance—*if* he is foolish enough to wait there until Julián returns. Unless I can be found or return on my own."

She couldn't be sure who would be held responsible. And no matter who it was, the servants or one of Julián's men, if they didn't run away, they would be made to suffer for something that was not their fault.

"You *want* to go back to him?" Sebastian asked, his tone incredulous. "Believing that he was responsible for your father's death?"

"Giving him an excuse to add another death to that toll won't bring my father back. Or your friend. Believe me, the guilt I already bear for inciting Julián's rages is quite sufficient already."

"The guilt *you* bear? You aren't responsible for what he does."

"You don't understand. Every time I disobey him—"

"What I understand," he broke in, "is that your guardian set out to create the perfect wife, someone who is properly cowed and submissive. Apparently he's succeeded. And considering what you once were, that's the real tragedy of your life."

What you once were... He meant that day by the river.

The accusation that she was no longer the girl who had been brave enough to threaten him with his own sword cut her to the heart. That day, however, had been a turning point in her relationship with her guardian.

She, who had been taught courage and honor from the cradle, had been forced since the incident by the river to balance the demands of the two in ways no one should have to. Whatever else Julián was, he was a man who understood human nature. When she had begged for Sebastian Sinclair's life, her guardian had been given the key to understanding hers.

From then on, any disobedience to his will resulted in swift and brutal punishments, but those were never inflicted on her. That she would have borne. In some perverse way, she would even have welcomed them as a form of penance for having been unknowingly responsible for her father's death. Instead of punishing her, however, Julián made others suffer in her stead.

"If I am late one minute in returning from a ride," she said, trying to make this arrogant English soldier with his talk of submission understand what her life had been, "then the groom who accompanies me is beaten. If I displease Julián in my dress or my demeanor, especially when we are in public, my maid is beaten when we return home. Often I'm not even aware that I've given offense until I'm forced to witness his retaliation against some innocent victim. And so I freely confess that I try never to displease him."

It wasn't fair that this man would take that hard-learned lesson and use it as a scourge against her. She understood what was at stake if she defied Julián. He didn't.

"It doesn't matter what you think of me," she

went on. "You may believe me cowed and submissive. Or even a coward if you choose. I do what I do to keep others from being hurt in my stead. Like the anger you felt for the friend who died in your place, I can't bear the thought of someone else paying the price for my supposed transgressions. Not even, God help me, if that person is you."

She had once compared his smile to Julián's. This time, his eyes locked on hers, it was very slow in coming. When it did, there was no mockery in it. No coldness. And seeing it, inexplicably her heart lifted.

"No matter what you fear," he said, "for me or for others, I swear to you that if you will do what I ask of you, he'll never use that threat to control you again. You have my word, as an officer and a gentleman, as well as my word as a Sinclair. And I promise you, I can make no pledge more binding than that."

There was a steadfast assurance in the quiet words. Despite what she knew of her guardian, she found herself believing Sebastian. Perhaps because she wanted to so much. And so, almost mesmerized by the promise of what he had offered, she nodded.

"We'll embark from Bordeaux. There's always confusion in any operation of that size, but especially in this one, where a large number of dependents are to be transported as well as the troops."

"And I would go on board as one of those dependents?" she asked.

The idea of leaving Spain and traveling to a foreign country with a man who was virtually a stranger was almost more frightening than the thought of returning to Julián's house to deal with the consequences of her disappearance. Almost. If she had not read the absolute sincerity, as well as the certainty, in those blue eyes, she might not have been willing to listen to even this much of his plan.

"The safest way will be for you to travel disguised as Malford's..." He hesitated, his lips compressing briefly before he opened them to say the words. "As his wife."

"His *wife?*"

"Not in reality, of course. No documentation will be required. The army is very lenient in accepting the word of a soldier that a woman is...attached to him."

"He would claim we were married?"

"You need have no fear that Malford would in any way take advantage of the situation. It would merely be a ploy to get you safely on board."

She wondered why he didn't suggest that she travel as *his* wife. Of course, as an officer and a gentleman, a phrase she seemed to be hearing with a deal of frequency lately, it might be difficult for him to later disavow knowledge of such a dependent. Especially if he were forced to make that claim in front of his fellow officers. For a common soldier, like Lord Wetherly's batman, there would be no questions asked about what had become of his "wife" once they disembarked in England.

"As soon as we arrive, I'll convey you to my brother. Even if you don't trust me to keep you safe, I assure you that you may put your faith in Dare's abilities and, more important, in his connections. The Conde del Castillo will find it difficult to question protection sanctioned by the Prince Regent."

It seemed that he had considered every aspect of his plan. She couldn't find fault with anything he had said. He had a powerful family, with powerful friends, who would undoubtedly be able to offer her the sanctuary he had promised. So the only question was…

"Why are you doing this? Are you hoping Julián will follow me to England so you may kill him there?"

There was a small silence before he asked, "Do you believe he will?"

She couldn't read any emotion, neither hope nor anticipation, in the question, so she answered it with the truth.

"He has what he wanted all along. And he's managed to achieve it without having to marry me. I think if you still want to kill Julián, you'll have to come back to the Continent and hunt him down."

"And kill him like the cur he is," Sebastian finished softly.

She let the silence build for a moment before she broke it. "But it's foxes you hunt in England, isn't it," she asked, holding his eyes. "Believe me, Captain Sinclair, you'll find that to be a far more fitting analogy for Julián Delgado."

When the soft knock sounded again on the door of the room where she was hidden, it was after dusk. For a moment she didn't respond, expecting it to open immediately as it had this morning.

Malford, she decided, when it didn't. Or perhaps the kind, fat man who brought her meals. In any case, not Sebastian, and despite the feelings she had cautioned herself against all day, there was a swell of disappointment.

She crossed the room, and then, just as she reached the door, her steps slowed. What if this were *not* one of the three trusted people who knew about her presence? What if this were another of the servants, the scullery boy or a maid come to clean the room? Or, the thought far more frightening than the others, what if Julián were standing on the other side?

And then she ridiculed her own fear. Her guardian would hardly wait to be given permission to enter. He would break down the door and drag her out by her hair.

As she hesitated, the knock sounded again, slightly louder this time. And she recognized the voice that spoke her name immediately after it.

She opened the door and looked up into Sebastian Sinclair's eyes. Illuminated by the candle he held, they seemed almost luminous in the dimness of the stone passageway. As blue as the sapphires in her mother's parure.

For a moment she couldn't seem to think of anything else. Not to step back and let him in. Not even to draw the next breath.

His eyes looked down into hers with an intensity she could feel. And although they were both standing in the open doorway, he seemed oblivious to the danger that someone might see her.

Then he moved, breaking the spell that held them motionless. She stepped back, allowing him room to enter. She closed the door behind him, being careful to make as little noise as possible.

"I've brought you some clothing," he said.

He held the bundle he was carrying in his left hand out to her like a gift. When she had taken it, he crossed the room and set the candle down on the table beside the bed.

As she watched him, she was again conscious of the fit of his uniform, tailored to cover those broad shoulders without a wrinkle. The smooth line of his pantaloons, which disappeared into the top of high boots, emphasized the same play of muscle she had been aware of that night at the reception. The night that had begun this.

Except, of course, it hadn't. Her relationship with this man had begun months before, when she had stolen his sword and put the point of it against his throat. For an instant, the memory as intense as his eyes had been in the hallway, she pictured those wet drawers clinging like a second skin to his lean frame.

"This is not your spare uniform, I take it?"

He turned, his eyes slightly widened. Then the stern line of his lips relaxed. Again the image of the laughing gallant who had showed neither fear nor anger over her attempt to rob him was in her head. His eyes had simply held on hers that day, just as they had a moment ago at the door. Just as they were now.

"I think you will be less conspicuous in *those,*" he said.

She lowered her gaze to the bundle, beginning to unfold the garments that made it up.

"I don't believe I ever asked what you intended to do with my uniform after you'd stolen it."

She glanced up and found that his lips had arranged themselves into a smile. Not quite as open as the one she had seen that day by the river. Of course, in the time since she had encountered him again, he had had little enough to smile about.

"I was going to disguise myself as an English soldier."

"A soldier in a very badly fitting uniform," he suggested.

"Not everyone is blessed with your tailor, Captain Sinclair."

"I shall take that as a compliment."

"Somehow I was sure that you would."

Hiding her own smile, she again lowered her eyes to examine the items he'd brought. They were much the same as the garments she had stolen from Anna that day. Perhaps not so fine. Or so clean, she acknowledged with a tiny wrinkle of her nose.

"I owe you an apology," he said.

Her eyes came up to find he was watching her, the amusement gone. His features were as set as when she had told him the story of her father. As stern as when he had talked about his friend's death.

"An apology, Captain Sinclair? Whatever for?"

Actually, there were any number of things in his treatment of her that a gentleman might wish to apologize for. Stealing a kiss in a dark garden. Holding her wrists. Causing her to fall and strike her head. Abducting her.

"I believe...I believe I was mistaken about the disappearance of the girl I met by the river that day."

"Mistaken?"

"I think she still exists. Her spirit may have been subdued, but given what has happened to her, that might be expected. I didn't understand all the reasons for why she did the things she did. I humbly beg her pardon for accusing her of being a coward.''

Perhaps her emotions were still too exposed, too near the surface. Whatever the reason, her eyes unexpectedly began to fill with tears. She controlled them through sheer will, refusing to allow them to fall.

''I believe you once made a claim to being both charming and entertaining, Captain Sinclair. The prime duties of a staff officer, I think you said.''

''English arrogance.''

''Indeed? And I was about to compliment you on having told nothing less than the truth that night.''

''I'm sorry then that I suggested it was arrogance. I don't suppose you would be willing to acquit me of—''

''Of being charming,'' she interrupted quickly, smiling at him. ''But of course. If that's what you wish.''

''What I wish—''

For some reason, he broke the sentence abruptly. She waited through the pause, wondering because the phrase had such intriguing possibilities. *What I wish...*

''Captain Sinclair?'' she prompted finally.

''I wish you would call me Sebastian,'' he said, the alignment of his mouth changing again, almost a tilt. ''It seems we are on far too intimate terms for the formality of titles.''

Intimate. The word had so many connotations, she wasn't sure which he meant. They had shared a kiss. He had carried her while she was wearing only her nightgown. Watched over her as she slept. All of which might be considered intimate. Far too intimate by some.

"If you wish," she said.

He hadn't asked permission to address her by name. Although her father had seen to it that she was educated in its literature and language, she was not perfectly certain of the niceties of social protocol in England. Perhaps it would be improper for him to call her Pilar.

And then, as she thought that, she realized the absurdity of worrying about proper forms of address from a man with whom she was conversing while wearing only her rail. A man who had once kissed her while holding her so tightly that her breasts had been crushed against his chest. A man who had seen to her physical needs throughout a long night during which she had been helpless. Completely in his power.

"My name is Pilar," she said.

"Doña Pilar," he repeated softly.

It was her title, just as his brother would be called Lord Dare, but…

"Pilar," she corrected, her voice as low as his. "Our acquaintance, although brief, is, as you say, of a certain intimacy."

His lips lifted again, but this time the movement was quickly controlled.

"Are you laughing at me, Sebastian?"

"Forgive me. It seems a long time since I've found anything even remotely amusing."

"And you find *me* amusing?"

Again there was a brief hesitation before he responded. "I find you both charming *and* entertaining, my lady," he said. "You would indeed have made a very fine staff officer. *If* you had only had my tailor, of course."

He was flirting with her, she realized with a touch of shock. Just as he had during the first few minutes they had spent together in the garden that night, before she had known who he was or why he was there.

That had been a deliberate deception. But this? This was probably as natural to him as breathing.

Charming *and* entertaining. And as she had then, she was again responding. This time without any sense of impending doom.

Perhaps that was because she knew her fiancé was no longer in the country. Perhaps it was because she was safely hidden in the house of the English envoy. Or perhaps it was because she was with a man who had sworn to protect her. And who, for some inexplicable reason, she believed might really be able to.

"Ready?" Sebastian asked.

She nodded, although her face seemed unnaturally pale in the candlelight.

The envoy's party was to leave Madrid at dawn. Therefore, they had to get Pilar out of the house tonight so she could be hidden among the women and children who would be accompanying the English soldiers as they departed.

Some of the garrison force, which had been left behind when the main British army had crossed the frontier last winter, were to serve as an escort for the duke. Together they would make their way to Bordeaux to join the rest of the troops awaiting the transports.

If it hadn't been for those units and the camp

followers who had attached themselves to them, Sebastian wasn't sure how he would have smuggled the ward of the Conde del Castillo out of the Spanish capital. As it was, Pilar must blend in among those other women, just as she would have to on board ship.

This was the part of the plan that worried him the most, although he couldn't see any way around it. Having her out of his sight for any length of time, even if she were in disguise and hidden among the camp followers, seemed dangerous.

"Malford will stay as close to you as he can. So will I, of course. There may be some occasion, however—"

"I know," she interrupted.

They had been over this a dozen times. He had tried to think of anything that might go wrong, until he was anticipating problems that would, in all likelihood, never happen.

He nodded to Malford, who lifted the bar and then opened the kitchen door. The alley behind the house was dark and seemed deserted. Moving as silently as ghosts, the three of them slipped out of the house, leaving the door ajar behind them.

Sebastian would have to return before dawn. His absence during the morning's departure would be too conspicuous.

He could only hope no one would notice that Harry's batman was missing. Or notice when he rejoined them later tomorrow, as soon as the duke's party met with the units that would accompany them into France.

Sebastian led the way down the narrow, twisting passage, keeping to the shadows of the building.

Their footsteps seemed to echo too loudly. When they reached the end of the alley, he realized that his hand had been resting on the hilt of his sword throughout the journey.

Considering the stillness around them, he began to believe he wouldn't be called upon to use it. He had no premonition of danger. No cold finger touched the back of his neck. He felt none of those intangible warnings that had served him so well in the past.

From this point, they had only a few streets to traverse before they reached the stables. Malford would ride Harry's horse, and Sebastian would ride double, carrying the girl.

Earlier this afternoon the batman had gone out to visit the encampment, which lay only a mile or so outside the city. Aided by the money Sebastian had provided, he had had no trouble in arranging a seat for Pilar in one of the numerous carts and wagons carrying the baggage.

Everything had gone according to plan. And there was no reason to believe that it wouldn't the rest of the way.

Taking a quick look up and down the street, he ran lightly across it and into the concealing shadows of the adjacent alley. He was aware by the sound of their footsteps that Pilar and Malford had followed him.

When she reached the other side, the girl stopped behind him, her quickened breathing audible in the darkness. He waited until he heard the sounds of the batman's arrival a second or two later.

He had already lifted his foot to take the next step when he heard the distinctive snick of a blade being withdrawn from its scabbard. It was a sound like no other, unmistakable to someone who had heard it as many times as he.

He turned, eyes straining against the darkness. He could see nothing, but just as their own footsteps had probably betrayed them, he could now hear those of whoever pursued them.

With a sweep of his arm he shoved the girl behind him, and in almost the same motion, drew his own sword. He heard Malford do the same.

Then, standing breathless in the midnight blackness that surrounded them, they listened to the rapid approach of their assailants. Despite the fact that he knew Delgado was in Paris, Sebastian couldn't deny the chill at the thought that his enemy might be out there, screened by the night.

The girl between them, he and Malford faced in opposite directions, swords drawn. Both of them had been in this kind of situation before, protecting a wounded comrade in the middle of a battlefield. At least in this case, there was a wall at their backs. One less direction to watch for the enemy's approach.

And when they finally came, pouring in from either end of the alley, uncaring of the noise they made, there were far more of them than Sebastian had anticipated. At least five or six, he guessed, forcing himself to stand his ground, despite the flood of adrenaline that demanded he advance to meet their charge.

Their only chance against such one-sided odds was to hold this position as long as they could, using the wall to their advantage. And of course, to dispatch each attacker as quickly as possible.

And perhaps to pray, he added as, eyes adjusting to the darkness, he saw the first of them materialize before him, his blade raised to strike. Sebastian parried the blow, disengaging as quickly as he could to thrust his sword at the nearly invisible target. Surprisingly, the man gasped, his forward momentum checked as he ran into that blind jab.

Behind him he could hear steel striking steel as Malford fought. He had no idea whether or not the man had any skill. If not, he thought, parrying and feinting almost mechanically now, he would find out soon enough.

It seemed to go on forever. They had been lucky at first in that he had quickly dispatched one of his attackers, and Malford had somehow had success against another. The odds were too great for that luck to continue. Sebastian didn't have time to glance to his right to confirm whether Malford was also being forced to fend off the combined attack of two opponents. It was all he could do to successfully ward off the blows aimed at him.

And he was beginning to tire. His arm was incredibly heavy, each movement of the sword an effort. If it hadn't been for his awareness of the girl behind him and the equally heavy breathing of his adversaries, he might well have succumbed to that exhaustion. They were tiring as rapidly as he was, he told himself. If he could only hold on…

He heard an outcry, an English profanity, and knew it must therefore have come from the batman. Malford staggered backward, bumping into his arm and disrupting the now mindless rhythm of parry and thrust he and his opponents had established.

Pushing Malford with his shoulder, Sebastian

tried to help the batman regain his balance. On some level, he acknowledged that if Malford went down, they were done for. There was no way he could fight off the ones who were left and protect the girl by himself.

Knowing that didn't prevent the next stroke of his sword, while he was still half supporting the weight of the man at his side. There wasn't breath enough to ask if he were all right. Nor a second to glance at him. There was nothing left in his world now but the girl at his back and the flash and fire of the two blades, which came at him almost simultaneously, striking sparks from his in the darkness.

And then, terrifyingly, he realized he could no longer feel Pilar behind him. He had been aware that the batman must be attempting to right himself because he was no longer leaning against Sebastian. Perhaps Pilar had moved from her protected position in a misguided attempt to help Malford.

That hopeful image lasted until he heard a sword clatter onto the cobblestones and realized, despairing, that it did not belong to either of his opponents. He renewed his attack against them, will and not strength driving the motion of his arm, which was so fatigued he could no longer feel it.

He was fighting, as he had done often enough before, in a mindless haze of exhaustion. At the same time he was attempting to move to his right. To locate and defend his comrades.

Then, almost like a miracle, he heard a shout that seemed to come from the alley they had just left. The same one that ran behind the house currently occupied by the duke. Apparently the noise of the fight had aroused his household.

Charging his opponents with the last of his strength, Sebastian drove them far enough back that he could risk a glance to the side. The cook was running across the street toward them, brandishing above his head what looked for all the world like an ax.

At the same time, out of the corner of his eye, Sebastian caught a flash of white. He identified it only after his gaze had returned to his own adversaries. Pilar's blouse. Which meant…

She was wielding the sword the batman had dropped. She was trying to wage a fight against the same swordsman who had brought Malford down.

Knowing there wasn't a second to lose, he tried a trick Dare had taught him. He retreated as much as he could with the wall at his back, exposing himself recklessly as if he were at the end of his stamina.

Emboldened, the more skilled of the two opponents immediately closed in for the kill. As the man extended his sword, aiming for his heart, Sebastian moved with a speed that belied his weariness, ducking and going in under it.

It was a dangerous tactic. And this time it came dangerously close to getting him killed. The blade pricked his shoulder, but his own thrust was straight and deep.

He even heard the rush of blood and air as he pulled his sword free, turning his attention to the remaining man. By that time the cook had reached them, breathing as loud as if he had been fighting with them the whole time.

The weapon he had brought impacted against the head of the swordsman Pilar had been fighting, the sound like a hammer striking a ripe melon. Although Sebastian didn't have time to draw breath in relief, a weight lifted from his heart, and with it, new vigor flowed through his veins.

Without distraction now, his total concentration devoted to his opponent for the first time in the fight, he was able to get in under his guard with the next series of feints. The man cried out, the noise distressingly loud in the sleeping neighborhood. Then he stumbled backward, falling against the wall on the opposite side of the alley before sliding down it.

Panting, held upright by his sword, which he had allowed to lower until its tip rested on the stones of the street, Sebastian realized it was finally over. He closed his mouth, attempting to control his breathing as he turned. Both Pilar and the cook were bending over Malford, but at least the batman was sitting up, leaning back against the wall.

"How bad is it?" he asked, gasping the words.

In spite of his genuine concern for Harry's man, he was equally concerned for the impact of Malford's injury on the plan they had made to get Pilar out of Madrid.

"Turned my ankle on one of the uneven stones, Captain Sinclair. Dropped the sword before I could catch my balance, and the bastard rushed me. Begging your pardon, my lady," Malford said, looking up at Pilar, who was still stooping beside him.

Sebastian glanced at the cook, trying to gauge his reaction. He might wish Malford hadn't referred to Pilar by that title, but it was hard to fault the man for not thinking right now about the possible danger in doing so. And after all, the cook *had* come charging to their rescue, hardly the actions of a man who was planning to betray them.

"I know this one," Pilar said, looking at one of the bodies.

"Julián's man?" he asked, although he supposed that was obvious.

"Yes, but *not* one of my father's."

He wondered if that were significant. Or if it was simply that those who still maintained any loyalty to the real conde had chosen not to try to find his daughter and drag her back.

"Maybe the others have all left," he said.

"I hope," she said softly.

He was too far away to read her expression, but even in the darkness he could tell that her head had lifted, and that her face was turned toward him.

"How did they find us?" she asked after a moment.

"Some of them may have been in on the attack on Harry. They would have known enough from that to track me here. They've probably been watching the house, waiting for something like tonight's expedition."

He had always been aware of the possibility that the house was being watched. That's why he had been so furtive about leaving. That and the fact that he didn't want to risk waking anyone in the duke's party and having to answer awkward questions from his commander.

"What now?" she asked.

"That depends on Malford."

"Nothing to worry about here," the batman said, using the support of the cook's arm to lift himself to his feet. "Bound to be tender, I suppose," he continued, hopping gingerly on one foot. "If it's swollen tomorrow that will give me an excuse to ride in the carts."

Which would keep him nearer to Pilar, Sebastian realized. Given tonight's attack, that would be reassuring.

"Then we shall hope for massive swelling and discoloration," Sebastian said. "At least severe enough to keep you off your feet until we reach Bordeaux."

The cook held out his hand to Pilar. Taking it without hesitation, she also got to her feet. When she had, she leaned forward, pressing a kiss against his rounded cheek.

"Gracias," she said, *"Muchas gracias."*

The man shook his head, and then ducked it in embarrassment. Pilar twisted a ring off her finger and, taking his hand, she opened the thick fingers and laid it in his palm.

"It was my father's," she said, still speaking in Spanish.

"I can't take your father's ring, my lady."

She folded his fingers around the band of gold. "I want you to have it. *He* would want you to have it for saving his daughter's life. If you hadn't come when you did.."

Recognizing the bitter truth of that, Sebastian sheathed his sword, closing the distance between them. He draped Malford's arm around his shoulder.

"We need to go," he reminded her.

"Vaya con Dios," the cook said, the words seeming almost a blessing. And God, of course, would know how much they needed one.

Chapter Seven

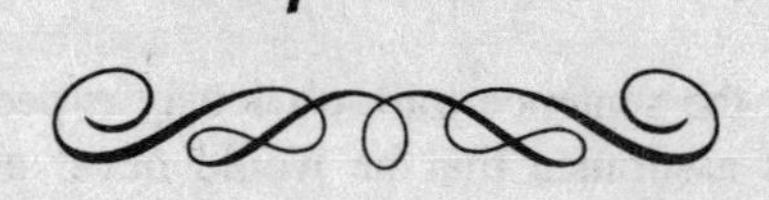

A week later
Bordeaux, France

"To *Paris,* your grace?"

"Briefly. And then on to England. It will mean only a slight delay in the reunion with your brothers, Captain Sinclair. We'll still be back to London before the month is out, I assure you."

Sebastian couldn't begin to explain what he had felt on hearing that destination. This should be the very thing he had wished for. Only a few days ago, it would have been.

After all, Julián Delgado was in Paris, and Wellington had just presented him with the perfect opportunity to do what he had sworn over Harry's body he would do.

Now, however, he had made another vow. A promise that must surely, on his honor, be given equal weight.

It was possible, of course, that it was not his honor that balked at the thought of abandoning his plan to get Pilar out of the reach of the newly created conde. Perhaps it was something else, something new and fragile that had slowly grown in the days since he had abducted her.

"I haven't forgotten that Delgado is there," the duke said, when Sebastian didn't respond. "If you feel that you'll be unable to contain your animosity..."

He let the sentence trail, obviously expecting Sebastian's assurance that he would never allow his personal feelings to impinge on doing his duty. The only problem with making that assurance was that he wasn't certain he would be able to carry through with it.

He couldn't take Pilar to Paris. Not only would it be impossible to hide her as he had among the larger force with which they had traveled from Madrid, it would put her much too close to her guardian. As reliable as Malford was, Sebastian couldn't entrust her entirely to the care of Wetherly's batman, not in port and certainly not aboard a crowded troop ship.

Malford would do his best to look after her, but as an enlisted man, he wouldn't have the standing to protect her from the more despicable elements of the British army, the ones Wellington had once referred to as "the scum of the earth."

Despite the caliber of the men he had personally served with, after the past three years Sebastian was well aware that there were a number of another kind within the ranks. Men who would, at the first opportunity, seek to take advantage of any unprotected woman. Especially one so exquisitely tempting as Pilar.

Which was hardly the kind of thinking he should

be engaging in, he acknowledged. Not about a woman to whom he had sworn to provide protection.

Protection was the crux of the problem. He had promised to protect her, and that meant from both her guardian and from the entire British army if necessary.

Forgive me, Harry, he prayed silently.

''Actually, your grace..'' he began.

He was reluctant to destroy whatever goodwill the duke might still feel for him after his near dereliction of duty during the past few days. He knew Wellington had put that down to grief over Wetherly's death, but if he refused to go to Paris...

There really was no other option, he decided. At least not that he could see.

''On reflection, I think it might be better if I were *not* in the same city with Delgado. My conviction that he murdered Lord Wetherly hasn't lessened, I assure you. If anything, it has strengthened with the passage of time.''

''Indeed?'' Wellington said, seeming surprised by the comment. His lips pursed as they always did when he was thinking, and his eyes focused keenly on Sebastian's face. ''I confess that I'm surprised, Captain Sinclair. Are you requesting to be relieved of your duties?''

''Only this one, your grace. I believe you may be satisfied that I have never shirked my more difficult obligations. This, however...I would be very grateful if you could find some way—''

''If you don't wish to come with me to Paris, you need say no more,'' the duke said sharply.

It was obvious both from his tone and his closed expression that he was displeased. His gaze had already fallen to the ever-present papers on his desk. And the additional request Sebastian was about to make would not, he believed, restore him to his commander's good graces.

"If I may, your grace—"

The blue eyes came up, quite cold. "There's something else, Captain Sinclair?"

"Harry's batman. I wonder if I might have permission to keep him here with me in Bordeaux. I would assume that with his master gone..."

"Thinking of taking him into service, are you?"

As plausible a lie as any, Sebastian supposed. "With your permission."

"A far more honorable obligation than *some* you seem to feel."

As Wellington's reproofs went, this one was mild. He hated, however, to end his career in his commander's disfavor.

"I'm very sorry, your grace," he said.

The piercing eyes lifted again, seeming to search his face. "You've been a fine officer on the whole, Sin. A bit rash and impetuous at times, at least in comparison to the steadiness of *Major* Sinclair."

"Few men could live up to that standard, your grace. I beg you won't compare me to Ian. Dare, on the other hand—"

Wellington laughed, the distinctive sound that was almost a bray. His eyes had become less cold.

"Perhaps I'm wrong in being disappointed in your decision," he said. "To err on the side of caution is, in your case, probably a wise thing. I'm sure that we shall manage to function in Paris without your support. God speed you on your journey, Captain Sinclair. And please don't forget to offer my congratulations to your brother on his recent nuptials when you see him again in London.''

''Apparently none of the women are being allowed to board the ships.'' As he talked, Malford's eyes darted back and forth from Sebastian's face to Pilar, who was sitting in the back of a small wagon with a group of other women.

Given her vibrant beauty, she blended in with them as well as one could expect, Sebastian supposed. However, looking at the rough mob surrounding them, he could understand the batman's diligence in keeping an eye on her.

When they'd arrived in the French port, they had found nothing short of chaos. Far too many people were crowded into every available inch of space around the docks, some of them having been here for weeks.

The Peninsular army was being disbanded. These hardened veterans were to be dispatched to England, Ireland or a variety of other postings. Some were destined to immediately join the British forces fighting in America.

Now they were awaiting orders to board the transports that had been sent to collect them. And noisily waiting with them were the Spanish and Portuguese women who had followed this army during the course of the long war.

''What do you mean they aren't being allowed to board?'' Sebastian demanded, raising his voice in order to be heard above the din.

''Quartermaster general's orders,'' Malford said, shouting back. ''Some of the troopers have documentation showing they've made a lawful union with their women. Even those are being turned away."

"This can't be Wellington's idea," Sebastian said. "These women don't speak French. If they're left here without any means of support..."

He didn't bother to finish the sentence. Malford knew as well as he what would become of them.

Through the long years the English had fought in Iberia, the camp followers had washed their clothes, cooked their meals and cared for their sick and wounded. Although some had undoubtedly been passed from soldier to soldier, for the most part that had only been after their original protector had been killed in battle. With so few females to such a large number of males, it took no more than a few hours before a woman so deprived had moved her possessions into another soldier's tent. To treat them now as nothing more than prostitutes seemed nearly criminal.

There was nothing Sebastian could do to change the quartermaster general's orders. Not even if, as he suspected, they had not been sanctioned by the commander in chief. His concerns were more immediate. And more personal.

"I did exactly what you said, Captain Sinclair. I told them the lady was my wife, but they refused to let me take her on board. They didn't even listen," Malford said, his eyes troubled.

"Perhaps they'll listen to me," Sebastian said. "Who did you talk to?"

Malford pointed to the man seated at the end of one of the long tables where the lists of those boarding each transport were being compiled. Several soldiers could be seen arguing with him, their women wailing behind them. Although Sebastian was too far away to hear what was being said, the obstinate set of the man's jaw and the way in which he answered each inquiry with a shake of his head spoke to the veracity of Malford's claim.

"Not even if they have their marriage lines, you say?" Sebastian asked, who had been wondering about the possibility of finding someone capable of forging such a document.

"No matter what kind of papers they can produce. Unless, of course, you're an officer."

"They're letting the *officers* take women on board?"

"With proof they've taken the woman to wife."

"What kind of proof are they accepting?"

"I don't know about the documents that are being presented, but I can tell you that they aren't looking at any of them too closely. Even the quartermaster general don't want to take a chance on insulting an officer's wife by accusing her of being a camp follower."

With proof they've taken the woman to wife. The solution to the problem seemed obvious. And, Sebastian realized, just as obviously impossible.

Pilar was not only the daughter of a Spanish grandee, she was undoubtedly a Catholic. He had promised he would convey her to England and that once there he would put her into the capable hands of his brother and under the protection of the Sinclair family and the crown. How could he now demand that she marry him in order to accomplish that?

Besides, in this madness, how could he hope to arrange any kind of ceremony she would agree to?

To arrange any kind of ceremony at all, he amended, looking around him.

With the recent abdication of Napoleon, he wasn't even sure which laws governed France right now. Of course, that might mean that no one else associated with the British army could be perfectly certain of them either.

He had a vague recollection that religion had been abolished during the Revolution, but he wasn't clear about what had happened to the churches under Bonaparte. And with the recent Bourbon restoration…

Surely there were still priests in the country. The question was whether any one of them would agree to join in matrimony a Catholic girl to a heretic Englishman, albeit one in fairly good standing with his own church.

Of course, admitting that might very well put a swift end to any attempt to get them wed. And without Wellington's help or advice—

"This woman says that none of the dependents are being let on board those ships."

He turned and found Pilar standing at his elbow. She was holding the arm of a woman who was dressed in clothing almost identical to that with which he had provided her.

Despite the similarity of their costumes, the difference in the women themselves was striking. Pilar's bearing seemed to shout she was an aristocrat playing at masquerade. He could only pray she did not stand out from this crowd as much as he was imagining she did.

The woman with her was older and heavier, her face tight with anxiety. In her arms she carried a baby of perhaps three months, closely swaddled despite the heat. Her dark eyes looked hopefully into Sebastian's, as if she believed he might be able to help them, perhaps because of the uniform he wore.

"I'm afraid she may be right," he admitted.

The girl's eyes widened, but instead of remonstrating about the news he had given her, she turned to the older woman beside her and repeated it. There was a few seconds of animated conversation, before Pilar turned back and spoke to him again.

"She asks me what they are to do. Surely the English don't intend to leave all these women behind in Bordeaux. They'll starve."

"Or worse," Malford said darkly. Seeing Pilar's expression, he added, "Begging your pardon, my lady."

"Become whores? Is that what you mean? Is that what your great Lord Wellington intends for these women to do? To support themselves and their children by selling their bodies on the streets."

"I don't believe the duke can be aware of what's happening," Sebastian said stiffly.

"Then he should be *made* aware. These women have borne the children of *his* soldiers. Those men can't mean to leave their families behind."

"They won't have no choice, my lady," Malford explained, his voice subdued by the reality of what was about to happen. "They'll board those ships when they're told or they'll be deserters."

"Leaving their wives and children behind to starve," Pilar said, her disgust with the British army clear.

She was right, of course. Whoever had made this

decision, it was indefensible. And unless Sebastian could figure out something within the next hour...

"We need a priest," he said.

"A priest," Malford and Pilar repeated simultaneously.

"She's already married," Pilar said, drawing the woman closer. "Show him your paper," she instructed in Spanish.

Obediently the mother of the baby drew a neatly folded sheet of paper from inside her blouse. She handed it to Pilar, her eyes still focused hopefully on Sebastian.

"See. Magdalena Sistallo and John Ridgely," Pilar read the names as she held the document out to him. "Joined in matrimony on the fourth of March, 1814."

"I didn't mean a priest for *her,*" he said, without taking the proffered paper.

After a second or two, her eyes lifted from it to fasten on his face. "Then...for whom *do* you need a priest?"

"They're allowing the officers to bring their wives on board *if* they can provide documentation of the marriage."

He hadn't as yet confirmed what Malford had told him with anyone in authority, but he might as well gauge her reaction in case it turned out to be true.

"Officers' wives are being allowed to go?"

"As long as they have documentation."

"Are you suggesting...?" Her voice faltered, but her gaze remained locked on his face.

"It seems we have no alternative," he said truthfully.

Some infinitesimal change occurred in the depths

of her eyes before they were veiled by the fall of her lashes. And when they lifted once more, whatever he had seen within them had disappeared.

"I see," Pilar said.

"I'm not certain about the laws governing marriage in France at the moment, but surely, if we can find a priest who will agree to marry us—"

"Are you Catholic, Captain Sinclair?"

He noticed that she was no longer calling him Sebastian. "I am a member of the Church of England. In this situation, however—"

"Because if you aren't," Pilar continued as if he hadn't spoken, "then no priest is going to consent to celebrate a nuptial mass between us."

Sebastian could only assume she was right. After all, her knowledge of a priest's likely response to that request was certainly more accurate than his.

There was a prolonged silence as he tried to think of some other way to accomplish what he was realizing more with each passing minute must be accomplished. He was aware that the eyes of the woman with the baby, as well as the eyes of the girl he had promised to see safely to England, had not left his face.

"If I may be so bold..." Malford said, drawing everyone's attention.

"If you have a solution, man, then for God's sake offer it," Sebastian said. He hadn't intended that demand to sound so harsh, but the batman didn't seem put off by his tone.

"Somehow, I doubt our good John Ridgely is Catholic either," he said.

John Ridgely. The name of the man on the paper

Pilar had tried to show him. John Ridgely, who was apparently married to—

"Ask her," he commanded Pilar as soon as he understood what Malford was suggesting.

Pilar's eyes held on his a moment longer before she turned to obey. The resulting exchange was rapid, and except for the occasional idiomatic word, he was able to follow it.

"She says they were married in camp by...a heretic?" Pilar repeated uncertainly, when she had turned back to him.

It took Sebastian only a moment to arrive at the correct translation. "Not a heretic. A dissenter. Some kind of lay preacher perhaps."

"There are a few of those with the army," Malford offered. "Come over to save our immortal souls by preaching hellfire and brimstone at us, all the while protecting us from the dread influence of the Papists."

The batman was right. Some of the officers had objected to Wellington about the presence of the evangelists among the enlisted men. In the end no one had been willing to deny the possibility that they might provide spiritual comfort or some moral guidance to the troops, who had much need of both.

"The question is will any of them have come to Bordeaux?"

"It's where the army is, isn't it. The problem as I see it, Captain Sinclair, is going to be locating one of them in this mob."

Not to mention the problem of getting him to agree to perform the marriage. Sebastian had no idea what such a ceremony would involve, but he had seen a few drumhead marriages in camp. He wasn't sure how binding that simple exchange of vows would be for two people, neither of whom shared the religion under which those vows were given.

"What is a dissenter?" Pilar asked.

Sebastian glanced at Malford, seeking help with the explanation. None was forthcoming. The batman shrugged his shoulders, leaving it to him to try to explain.

"Someone who objects—"

Sebastian broke off the sentence when he realized that knowledge of exactly which elements within the Church of England the dissenters objected to would not be helpful in convincing Pilar to let one of their preachers conduct the ceremony. *If* he could manage to convince one of them to agree to do so.

"Someone who objects to certain elements contained within the practices of the Church of England," he finished carefully.

"They object to the *church.* That is allowed in your country?"

"To some extent." Far more than it had been during the previous centuries, he conceded.

"And you believe that such a man would—"

"Marry us?" he said, finally putting into words the gist of what they had been talking around. "I have no idea, but unless we can locate a priest who doesn't have a problem with the fact that I'm not Catholic and you are, I think we're going to be forced to find out."

After Sebastian had verified Malford's information about the wives of officers being allowed to board, it had proven remarkably easy to locate an evangelist. All they had had to do was wander through the crowd until they found someone preaching loudly enough to be heard over the noise. The man had attracted a small group of troopers, most of whom appeared to be listening out of boredom rather than from any religious fervor.

Of course, their boredom was understandable. These men no longer had a mission or a purpose. They had found themselves confined for several days in a city where most of them didn't speak the language. And based on his firsthand knowledge of the British soldier, Sebastian speculated that they had probably drunk up or gambled away whatever pay had remained in their pockets. The evangelist's harangue was for them simply a form of free entertainment.

And not a very comforting one, Sebastian decided as he listened. The man seemed to be chronicling the gory punishments that would follow in the next world for every vice that had ever found favor with the British soldier.

Most of which he himself had been guilty of at one time or another, he admitted. He couldn't quite imagine the gentle, elderly vicar Dare maintained ever mentioning any of them in a sermon to his flock, however.

"You intend to ask *him* to marry us?" Pilar asked loudly enough to cause a few heads to turn.

"If he will," Sebastian responded, lowering his voice in the hope that she would do the same.

"Why would he refuse? We are respectable people." It was obvious by her tone that she didn't believe the evangelist was.

"Considering the narrowness of his theology, I doubt many here would qualify as respectable. Besides, there is the additional problem of our own religions."

"This won't be a mass," she said. "He's not a priest."

"He's a minister. The marriage will, of necessity, not...be a mass," he finished awkwardly.

"And therefore not a real marriage."

Not to her, he realized. And Sebastian had already acknowledged he had no idea about the legal ramification of such a match. However...

"It may possibly be considered real by the courts."

"The French courts or the English ones? What could either possibly have to do with this?"

"*If* the question arose," he hedged.

"If Julián contested the marriage, do you mean?"

That hadn't been what he meant, but it was a consideration. "Your guardian or anyone else," he said. "I know that to you any vows we exchange before this man would be meaningless. I'm simply telling you that to others they may not be."

"And to you? What would such vows mean to you?"

What *would* they mean? he wondered, trying to be both logical and objective. Would he consider himself bound by such a union? "Til death do us part" bound?

If, for example, Pilar chose to deny that the vows were binding once they reached England, would he still consider himself married. Then he realized that was not really the question.

If she chose to deny those vows, would he be able to let her go? Would he be able to watch her hold her head at that proud tilt as she placed her hand on that of some simpering London fop and danced away from him? Even worse, would he let Delgado arrive, with all the pomp of the Spanish court behind him, and reclaim his fiancée?

As he hesitated, her eyes held his. When the answer to her question had been delayed too long, she turned her face away, the angle of her chin rising even as he watched.

"They would mean," he said, putting his hands on her upper arms and forcing her to face him, "that I have no other way to get you out of France and away from your guardian. When we get to England, we can sort through the legal ramifications of what we're being forced to do here."

For a moment, she said nothing. "Then perhaps it would be better if you conveyed me to Paris, Captain Sinclair."

"To...Delgado?"

"At least I understand his motives."

"His motives in what?" he said, feeling a surge of resentment that, after all he had tried to do, she was comparing him unfavorably to that bastard. "His motives in killing your father," he reminded her brutally.

Her mouth tightened. "In desiring to marry me," she said.

"Apparently he had the same motives for both. I'm trying to keep you safe, from him *and* from what you see around you. If you truly prefer either of those choices, then I assure you I won't insist on this marriage."

Her eyes left his face to consider the rough-hewn, battle-weary veterans around her. Unwashed, wearing threadbare uniforms that had seen them through years of service, they were also unkempt, untutored and uncultured.

When her gaze finally returned to his face, his voice was lower and more intense. "Or perhaps you would like me to find you another British officer to marry so that *he* might then convey you safely to England. My brother would, I assure you, still honor my promise of protection."

"Your comments are insulting, Captain Sinclair."

"My comments are simply the reiteration of your choices, Doña Pilar. Which of them you make is up to you."

He had once called her a coward. That was not the word he wanted to use now, but he couldn't see that telling her how pigheaded she was being was apt to win her agreement.

The breath she finally took was deep enough to lift her breasts, making him too aware of the low neckline of the blouse she wore. Something he *didn't* want to think about.

Not now. Not while he was trying to convince her to enter into a very necessary marriage of convenience. A marriage that might not be either a marriage or convenient, but one that was, in these circumstances, certainly necessary.

"That man isn't a priest," she said again.

"Perhaps not," he conceded, "but if he agrees to marry us, will you let him? Will you exchange vows with me, and trust that as soon as I get you to England and to safety, I shall endeavor to do whatever is within my power to make this right?"

Exactly what that might be, he admitted, he had no idea.

* * *

"A Papist?" the Reverend Dargood Reynolds said.

His mud-colored eyes considered the flawless skin and midnight hair of the daughter of the late Conde del Castillo as if they were somehow offensive.

"My betrothed is Catholic," Sebastian confirmed, since there was little point in denying the obvious.

"And now she wishes to join the covenant of true believers?"

If it would get this man's signature on a document proclaiming he and Pilar were husband and wife, Sebastian thought, then he would agree that she did. Agree that they both did. At this point, he would have agreed to anything short of eternal perdition. And he doubted, given their predicament, that lie would come close to qualifying him for that punishment.

"She wishes to marry me," he said. "And I wish to marry her."

"To save her immortal soul?"

To save her body from a brutal and despicable madman.

"Yes."

As the lie came out of his mouth, it seemed he caught a whiff of sulfur lingering in the air from the sermon they had just heard.

"Does she believe in the Lord Jesus as her savior?"

"Of course," Pilar said disdainfully.

Sebastian had cautioned her to silence, but he could tell by her tone that she was rapidly approaching the point where she would turn and walk away, even if it meant accepting another of those choices he had threatened her with.

"Will you wed us?" he asked Reynolds, pressing the decision.

"You seem to be in a great hurry."

"In case you hadn't noticed, those transports are loading," Sebastian said in exasperation, pointing at the waiting ships. "According to the quartermaster, I need documentation that this marriage has taken place in order to take this woman aboard them. If you don't wish to help me save her immortal soul, then perhaps you'll be good enough to direct me to another of your brethren who won't be so stingy with his authority to offer that salvation."

"My authority comes from God, sir, and you have no right to question it."

"I'm not questioning it. I'm asking you to use it to wed me to this Papist, so that as her lawful husband I may teach her the errors of her ways."

His fingers tightened around Pilar's shoulder so hard that he felt her flinch. It was as forceful a reminder to keep her mouth shut as he could manage under the circumstances.

Incredibly, it seemed to work. As he and Reynolds watched, her chin came up. Her dark eyes flashed him a look that spoke volumes. Her mouth, however, remained closed in a line that could be called nothing short of obstinate.

"You're sure, my son, that you're up to the job?" the Reverend Dargood Reynolds asked.

Sebastian could have sworn he'd heard a note of sympathy in the question.

"I'm sure that if I don't undertake to try, no one else in her country or in this one ever shall. She'll be lost forever. Do you really wish to have that on your conscience?"

He could feel the small shoulder stiffen indignantly beneath his fingers, but he didn't ease his hold. Instead, his fingers tightened warningly again.

"And you promise to instruct her in the true path?"

Vague enough to win his agreement, Sebastian decided. And apparently vague enough to win Pilar's too, for remarkably she continued to hold her tongue.

"To the very best of my ability," Sebastian said, and again felt the depth of the breath the woman beside him took as the preacher nodded his agreement.

"It seems very...small," Pilar said, looking doubtfully around the cabin they'd been assigned.

"At least we'll have some privacy," Sebastian responded.

Having seen the other parts of the ship as they made their way here, she knew that it was incredibly crowded below decks. Sebastian had told her that many of the soldiers would simply spread a makeshift pallet topside tonight, sleeping under the stars. Providing, of course, that they had calm weather for the crossing.

"Are you a good sailor?" he asked.

She turned at the question, but found it difficult to meet his eyes. She'd had difficulty doing so since they had gone through the exchange of vows back on the dock.

As much as she might try to convince herself that there was nothing binding about a marriage ceremony that was not a mass performed by someone who was not a priest, the pledges they had repeated seemed to argue otherwise. Despite the fiery sermon they had listened to, the Reverend Reynolds had spoken the simple words with a dignity she'd found unexpectedly moving. And Sebastian's deep voice, when he had made those vows, had seemed incredibly solemn.

"I don't know," she confessed. "I've never been on a boat."

"Ship," he corrected, smiling at her, more out of relief that they were aboard, she believed, than from pleasure in her company. "Then we must hope for a smooth crossing."

That was a hope, however, which was not destined to come to fruition. They sailed with the evening tide and before they were out of the harbor, the motion of the ship, along with the smells that permeated the area below deck—tar and fish and the scent of too many unwashed bodies pressed too closely into the space—had given Pilar the answer to his question.

"I think..." she whispered, having controlled her growing nausea as long as she thought possible. "I think that perhaps I am *not* a good sailor."

In the darkness, she heard Sebastian rise to light the lantern that hung from a hook in the middle of the cabin. He knelt beside the narrow bunk on which she was lying, looking down into her face, just as he had when he'd taken her to the house in Madrid.

The lantern moved with the motion of the ship, alternately lighting and then casting his face into shadow. Fighting her sickness, she managed to hold her eyes open long enough to discover that he was neither angry nor disgusted with her weakness. Actually, she thought, he seemed to be slightly amused.

"Some fresh air, I think," he said, putting his hand under her arm to urge her up.

She didn't want to move, afraid that she might embarrass herself if she did, but the thought of breathing something other than the stale, malodorous assortment of scents below deck was enticing. Enough so that she let him help her off the bunk and lead her to the door.

Once there, Sebastian removed his cloak from the hook to wrap it around her. Then, just as he had while he'd talked to the man who had married them, he kept his arm around her shoulders. He guided her unerringly through the darkness, down the passageway and past the sleeping troopers, none of whom stirred.

As they climbed the narrow stairs that led up to the deck, like a miracle, the first inhalation of brine-scented breeze dispelled her queasiness. She lifted her face into a fine mist, either the remnants of a storm or of the spray produced as the ship cut through the water.

"Better?" he asked.

She nodded, her eyes shifting upward to watch the full-bellied sails snap taut in the wind. Above them, the clouds had parted to reveal a few stars dotting a midnight sky.

"Not the sea, then," he said.

She lowered her eyes, to find his on the water of the channel, which churned whitely along the hull. "*Not* the sea?"

"You weren't seasick," he said, turning to look at her. "Humanity sick, perhaps. All those bodies packed too tightly together."

The imagery the phrase produced wasn't that of

the sleeping men below. It was of a dark garden instead, and of the muscled wall of his chest pressed against her breasts. For a moment, it seemed she could again feel him breathing, his body moving in unison with her own.

The motion of the ship, she told herself resolutely. Still, in the back of her mind she couldn't disavow the knowledge that this man was now her husband. Perhaps the church might not recognize their union, but one made just the same. Whether or not it could legally be dissolved when they reached England…

"Tell me about your family," she said, realizing only now how much she was dreading what was to come.

"My mother and father are both dead," Sebastian said, his voice distant. Nostalgic, perhaps. "They died within a year of each other. My father first, and then… As strange as it may sound, I think my mother chose to follow him as quickly as she could arrange it."

"Not…suicide."

He laughed, and the chill she had felt at his choice of words dissipated. "Not suicide. Grief perhaps. Loneliness. They were the whole world to one another."

The whole world to one another. Just as her own mother and father had been. Just as she had always imagined…

"What of her children?" she asked. She could not bear to dwell on what she had always imagined about this moment. Her wedding night. "Didn't she think of them?"

"We were grown men by that time. At least we thought we were," he said, his voice still touched with amusement. "At least I *thought* I was. Since they're older, I'm sure that was true for my brothers as well."

His eyes were focused once more on the sea. She studied his profile, willing to wait for the rest. And when it came, the amusement had been supplanted again by the nostalgia she had heard before.

"Dare inherited the title, and I can think of no one more suited to it. Aristocratic to the core," he said. "He can freeze you with a look. Incredible presence."

"And a friend of the Regent," she said, repeating what Malford had told her.

"A trusted member of Prinny's inner circle. There's a difference, you know."

"I'm not sure—"

"It doesn't matter. When you meet him, you may form your own opinion. I would prefer that. And then there's Ian. My second brother."

Perhaps because she couldn't see his face, his voice seemed more revealing than it ever had before. There was within it now a warmth, a subtle relaxation of the tone in which he had discussed the earl.

"I've learned only recently that he wed," he added.

"And the earl?" she asked. "Is he also married?"

"For almost a year now. I haven't met her, but Ian tells me that she is...remarkable," he said.

Remarkable. There had been a definite note of admiration in that. She wondered exactly what he had been told about a woman he had never met to cause it to be there.

"Brave, beautiful and erudite," he said, answering the question she hadn't asked.

All things he obviously felt a woman should be. And Pilar wasn't sure she herself possessed any of those attributes.

Despite her gift for languages, she could not claim to be erudite, a trait that would hardly be valued in a woman of her culture in any case. He had already deemed her a coward. And considering that only once in their acquaintance had he seen her dressed in anything remotely resembling the attire of a gentlewoman...

"That's the extent of my family. Two brothers, as different as daylight and dark. And two sisters-in-law, neither of whom I have yet met."

"What will they think of our...situation?" she asked.

She had finally settled on that word because she could not bring herself to claim this was a marriage. Something he had entered into, by his own admission, only because there was no other way to get her out of France.

"I'm sure they'll feel as I did. That there was no other alternative."

He had never misled her about his motives. And unlike Julián's, they were totally unselfish. Still...

The hiss and snap of the sail drew her eyes. As she watched, it swelled with the wind, carrying them nearer to England and away from everything she had ever known. Suddenly the clarity of the white cloth and the scattered stars above it blurred until she was forced to blink to clear her vision. Unwanted, his words echoed over and over again in her head.

I'm sure they'll feel as I did. That there was no other alternative.

Chapter Eight

London

"I regret to inform you, sir, that the earl is presently at dinner. If I may be so bold as to inquire who's calling, I shall have word sent to him immediately when he's finished."

"My name is Sebastian. Please inform Lord Dare that we've not yet dined. If between them, he and Ian haven't yet managed to devour every scrap of food the kitchen sent up..."

He raised one inquiring brow at the butler, again consciously imitating his eldest brother's mannerism. By that time, comprehension, swiftly followed by consternation, had begun to dawn over the face of what Sebastian believed, knowing Dare, would be the perfect majordomo.

"Sebastian?" the man repeated. "Then you must be—"

"Captain the Honorable Sebastian Sinclair. Late of His Majesty's forces engaged in fighting the

French. Surely someone in London has thought to mention that the war is over."

"Of course, Captain Sinclair. Forgive me, *please,*" the butler said, a deep flush spreading into his closely shaven jowls. "No one told me to expect you tonight, sir."

"Perhaps because no one knew we'd be arriving. Actually, we didn't know," Sebastian said. And then he realized that any explanation as to why they had arrived, without prior warning, at the door of the earl's town house should properly be made to his brother rather than his brother's butler. "Would you be so kind as to tell them we *have* arrived, please..." He hesitated, searching his memory for the name. "I'm sorry. I'm afraid I don't know your name."

"Watson, sir."

"Then would you tell the earl, Watson, that we're here."

"Of course, Captain Sinclair."

The butler bowed formally, and when he straightened, his eyes touched on Pilar before they even more briefly considered Malford, who was standing behind the two of them. Those examinations weren't prolonged enough to solicit a correction, but still, the shock of what he had seen was apparent in the man's eyes.

And after all, Sebastian acknowledged, choosing to ignore the breach, why wouldn't he be shocked?

All of them had, of necessity, been wearing the same clothing for several days. Sebastian hadn't managed a shave since they'd left Bordeaux, and with her hair spilling around her shoulders and her complexion darkened by the sun, Pilar resembled nothing so much as a Gypsy girl. Their appearances were certainly less villainous than that of Harry's batman, who had not had the luxury of a private cabin during the crossing.

The butler said nothing of what he was obviously thinking. He simply turned on his heel and disappeared down the wide hallway, moving as rapidly as the dignity of his office would permit.

"For the servant of an earl," Pilar said, "he seems very poorly trained."

"I suppose your father's servants would have handled the arrival of unexpected guests in the middle of dinner better than that."

"My father's servants would never have dared to gawk at *anyone* who came to his door, no matter how they were dressed. But then, they *were* well trained."

"My apologies for the ineptitude of my brother's servants. I suppose you believe I should have chastised the man, but we *are* rather rough looking, you will admit. I confess I'm far too glad to be home to quibble over something that minor."

Pilar had managed the rigors of the journey from Madrid to Bordeaux and the even more trying channel crossing, where they had been forced to share a cabin, without voicing one single complaint. He could only suppose her criticism of Dare's majordomo had its roots in an exhaustion which, given her femininity, must surely exceed his own. And his was staggering.

When he glanced down at her face, about to attempt an apology for his brusqueness, he realized she had gone very pale. Her fingers lifted to the neckline of the blouse she wore, tugging it upward to cover the beginning curve of her breasts, which was exposed by its low cut. It was then Sebastian saw that her hands were trembling.

Exhaustion or…anxiety? Of course anyone would be anxious, given what probably lay ahead.

A door opened somewhere down the hall, the sound traveling clearly along that vast expanse of marble. He looked up, feeling his throat close with emotion as he saw his brothers coming toward him.

With his characteristic arrogance, Dare led the way, his long stride eating the distance between them. Limping slightly, Ian followed closely behind him.

"You might have given us some warning, you know," the earl said. "I could probably have managed to delay dinner for perhaps half an hour. Any longer, I'm afraid, and my cook would return to his former position at Carlton House."

"Hello, Val," Sebastian said softly, his blue eyes locking with an identical pair. "It would never do to anger your cook. I shouldn't expect you to. Not for me."

"No, you shouldn't," his brother said, putting out his right hand to grasp his. At the same time he gripped Sebastian's shoulder with his left. "You've had a very long journey, however. Exceptions might have been made," Dare said, smiling at him.

"But I shouldn't dream of asking for them. Not so long as you've something left that's eatable."

"Given the circumstances, I believe we might even persuade the kitchen to prepare another meal," Ian said, stepping around the earl to get to his younger brother. "The fatted calf, perhaps. Was that what you were hoping for by staging this unannounced arrival, you rascal?"

"Good English beef," Sebastian said, laughing. "There were times, I confess..." For some reason, his throat closed completely this time, preventing him from finishing.

In the steady hazel eyes of the middle Sinclair brother was a perfect understanding. Of course, Ian understood everything. He might not approve, but he had always understood.

"I know," Ian said now, pulling him into an embrace that was strong enough to give hope that his terrible injuries were at last almost healed.

And then, just at the proper moment, before Sebastian's emotions might succumb to the heartfelt honesty of that gesture, Ian put his hands on his shoulders, holding him away as if to evaluate him.

"It becomes you," Ian said. "Gives your face a rather charmingly cutthroat aspect. You always were far too beautiful to be a proper Sinclair."

The scar, Sebastian realized. Neither of them had seen it, and the way in which he had acquired it was hardly a story he would have included in any of his rare letters home. And thinking of that now—

He began to step back, and Ian's hands released immediately. Sebastian half turned, intending to include Pilar in the homecoming by introducing her to his brothers.

Her face was paler now than it had been before, making the contrast between the ivory skin and that midnight hair and her eyes more striking. She was standing with her hands clasped together at her waist. Although her expression was perfectly composed, it was somehow obvious to him that she truly was afraid of what was to come.

Surprisingly, now that he had once again been welcomed into the camaraderie that he had shared with his brothers since childhood, he no longer minded the revelation he would have to make. This was his family, and no matter the circumstances of his marriage, he knew they would eventually accept it. Just as they would accept Pilar.

It might be better, however, not to demand that they do so immediately. Not with her watching for their reaction. Surely the necessary explanation could be made after they'd both had a chance to eat and to rest.

"This is Pilar," he said. "The reasons are complicated, but I have promised on my honor as a Sinclair that she'll not only be welcomed here, but also protected."

Two sets of eyes, one sapphire and the other hazel, fastened on the girl's face before they returned questioningly to his.

"Protected?" Dare repeated carefully.

"The reasons for that are not something I wish to go into now, if you don't mind," Sebastian said. "Perhaps after we've eaten."

It was as near a warning off as he could give without revealing that he was hiding something. Without waiting for their response, although he had no real doubt as to what that would be, he turned back to take Harry's batman by the elbow, bringing him forward.

"And this is Malford. My...valet," he said. That was no more the whole truth, of course, than his introduction of Pilar had been. "If Watson would see to his comfort, I would be grateful. We've all traveled a very long way."

"Certainly," Dare said, that dark brow still raised.

The earl's eyes, focused intently on Sebastian's face, said a great deal more, but at least he wasn't asking the awkward questions he would ask eventually. Although Sebastian had had time to prepare to answer them, he still wasn't perfectly sure what he would say when his brothers demanded an explanation for what he'd done.

They had always considered him reckless and impulsive. He imagined this episode was unlikely to change that perception.

"I think that perhaps introductions are in order."

The suggestion, which had been made in a strong but unmistakably feminine voice, brought every Sinclair's gaze to the same doorway from which Dare and Ian had emerged moments before. Two women stood together there.

The one who had spoken was tall and, despite the cunning placement of an embroidered silk shawl, the ends of which had been crossed over her waistline, she was very obviously pregnant. Her hair was so light as to appear gilt in the glow of the overhead chandelier. It was arranged in curls on top of her head, which was held as regally as a queen's on a long, graceful neck. Her eyes were almost the same crystalline blue as those of two of the three Sinclair brothers.

The other woman, in contrast, seemed little more than a girl. She was both smaller and less imposing than the blonde. Her eyes, a warm brown, were focused not on the men, but on the girl standing at Sebastian's side. And she was smiling.

"We are in the process of making our introductions," the earl said.

"I meant introductions of *us,* my dear," his countess responded. "Unless, of course, you consider us in some way unpresentable."

"I believe I'm the one he considers unpresentable," Sebastian said, walking toward them. "He's right, of course. You must be Dare's Elizabeth. Forgive me for appearing before you in all my dirt, as well as for disrupting your dinner table."

By that time he had reached the pair. He wasn't sure what the proper procedure for greeting sisters-in-law might be, never having met one before. His indecision lasted only a second or two—long enough, however, to discern a gleam of amusement in Elizabeth's eyes.

When she put out her hand, he took it into his. The contrast between his grimy, sunburned fingers and the white patrician ones she'd offered was as glaringly obvious as her pregnancy. Undeterred by the incongruity, he brought her fingers to his lips, pressing a kiss on the backs of them just as if he were bathed, clean shaven, and properly attired in evening clothes like his brothers. When he looked up, still bent over her hand, Elizabeth was smiling at him.

"Welcome home, Sebastian Sinclair," she said softly. "Now, finally, the circle is complete."

Again that peculiar tightness thickened his throat, so that he couldn't even attempt a response. He turned instead to smile at the smaller of the two women, who was waiting patiently by the countess's side.

"And I'm Anne," she said.

"Ian's Anne."

A subtle change occurred within her eyes. It didn't destroy the friendliness Sebastian had found there, but there had been some flicker of emotion, an unexpected darkness perhaps, in the aura of welcoming acceptance that had seemed to surround her.

"Ian's Anne," she repeated, as if the words meant something beyond the simple acknowledgment of her identity that he had intended. "Welcome home, *dear* Sebastian," she said, extending her hand and then pressing her other atop his when he took it. "We are all so very pleased to have you here at last."

Her voice was as attractive as her eyes, he decided. Although Anne would never have the commanding presence Dare's Elizabeth exuded effortlessly, she possessed something that was equally compelling. A warmth which immediately put one at ease.

"And your friends?" she said now, freeing her hand from his. "I believe Elizabeth and I missed your introduction of them."

She crossed to where his brothers stood, watching Sebastian's meeting with their wives. At Anne's reminder, they all looked toward Pilar and poor Harry's batman, still waiting by the door, almost forgotten in the unabashed joy of this homecoming.

"I'm Anne Sinclair," his new sister-in-law said to Pilar. And then, the gesture seeming both uncontrived and sincere, she put her arm gently around the girl's shoulders. "You must be exhausted after your journey. Please forgive our rudeness. Or at least accept our apologies for it. We're so delighted that Sebastian has come home safely, you see."

At the moment when Ian's wife touched her, Pilar's back had visibly stiffened, so much so that Sebastian was afraid she intended to step away from that embrace or perhaps even to say something cutting about its familiarity. Instead, after a moment she seemed to force herself to relax.

"Thank you," she said, her smile as unconsciously regal as that of the countess.

Why shouldn't it be? Sebastian thought. She is, after all, the daughter of a count.

"You've had a very long journey," Anne said. "After you've eaten, you shall have a hot bath and a clean nightgown and be tucked up in one of Elizabeth's comfortable beds. I've always thought that there's nothing like a bath and clean clothing to make you feel much more the thing—no matter what chaos is going on around you. And men never think about those things, of course."

Pilar's eyes found Sebastian's briefly before she turned her gaze back to the smiling face of Ian's wife. "I'm really not very hungry, but a bath... I think I should like that above all things."

"Then you shall have it at once. *And* one of Elizabeth's nightgowns. Hers are all much finer than mine," Anne confided.

Her arm still around Pilar's shoulders, she began to lead the girl toward the staircase, chatting easily the entire time. She was still talking as they climbed the stairs to disappear onto the landing.

Unconsciously, Sebastian's gaze had followed their progress. And it was only when he turned that he realized everyone, including Malford, was looking at him.

They were expecting some explanation for Pilar's presence. Dare's brow was lifted, a sure sign that he was waiting. He would simply have to continue to wait, Sebastian decided. At least until they were in private.

"You were going to ask Watson to provide for my man," he reminded.

"Of course," the earl said.

"And I believe someone mentioned food."

"I shall send to the kitchen for something hot," Elizabeth said, turning to put her intent into motion.

"Forgive me," Sebastian said. "I find I'm far more concerned with the immediacy of the food than with its temperature. Besides, I doubt I've eaten a hot meal within the past year."

"Of course," Elizabeth said after a minute's hesitation, her eyes meeting her husband's. Apparently some silent communication had passed between them, for she said, "I'll see if there is anything Anne needs. I believe she mentioned borrowing one of my nightgowns."

"The dining room," the earl said, gesturing toward the open door at the end of the hall.

Somehow, what should have been an invitation had become a summons. Sebastian had known the time of reckoning would come, and he supposed now was as good a time as any to get this out of the way. As if, he thought meeting his brother's eyes, he was going to have any other choice.

"So...I took her," Sebastian said, deciding there was no point in trying to make that kidnapping seem anything other than what it had been.

"You *abducted* her?" Ian clarified, his tone disbelieving. "You abducted that girl from her guardian's home?"

"I didn't have any other choice."

"I would think it should be obvious even to you—" Dare began.

"You weren't there. And don't try to make me believe you would have done any differently. The man had murdered her father to gain control of her and her fortune. He did this—" his finger touched the scar that was a constant reminder of Delgado's cruelty "—because I interfered with him when she tried to run away. Then, despite knowing he had the wrong man, he killed Viscount Wetherly in a trap that had been set for me. I was hardly able to leave the girl in his hands after that. Especially knowing what I knew about how he was controlling her."

There was a prolonged silence. Undaunted, Sebastian took advantage of it to spear another slice of rare roast beef from the pile on his plate. He had eaten his fill, but the habit of continuing to eat when there was such an abundance would be hard to break.

"I hid her in the house where the duke's party was staying and then smuggled her out of Madrid among the camp followers," he said when the earl's disapproving quietness had stretched beyond even his tolerance for such tactics.

He had been the victim of them too many times in the past to be truly cowed. Besides, after years spent fighting the French, he was no longer the boy who wilted at the first sign of Dare's displeasure.

He was truly satisfied in his own mind that he had done the only thing possible in the situation. If his brother disapproved, then Dare would simply have to learn to deal with the reality that Sebastian was making his own decisions now.

"Then the king gave Delgado her father's titles and sent him to Paris as his ambassador. When Wellington decided to visit the French capital before he returned to London, I knew I couldn't take Pilar there and risk Delgado seeing her. That's why I'm home before the duke. And why I arrived unannounced."

"What titles?" Ian asked.

"The only one I'm sure of is the Conde del Castillo. I'm not certain of any of the lesser ones her father held. And by the way, Val, she seems to feel that your butler is not so well trained as her father's servants were. I thought you might want to know."

He managed to take another bite while Ian's eyes met Dare's. This time it was the brows of his second brother that had inched upward.

"Are you telling me," Ian asked, when he turned back to face him, "that you have kidnapped the daughter of a Spanish grandee and dragged her unescorted across Spain and France in order to bring her here."

Surprisingly, Sebastian found that he was beginning to enjoy himself. It wasn't often that he could truly shock his brothers.

"She wasn't unescorted. Malford was with her during any time when, because of my duties, I couldn't be. Not at night, of course. She slept with the camp followers then."

Another silence.

"You *do* realize you'll have to marry the girl," Ian said, the pronouncement awful in its solemnity. As it had obviously been intended to be.

"Actually..." Sebastian let the word trail, looking from one face to the other. "You see, once all those women—the camp followers—got to Bordeaux, the army refused to let them on the transports. Those were the quartermaster general's idiotic orders, but I couldn't think of any way to get around them. We had planned to pretend that she was Malford's wife, but once we found out that they were allowing only the officers' wives on board—"

"You married her," Dare breathed, sounding relieved.

"*If* you can consider it a marriage. I'm not sure Pilar does."

"Why wouldn't she?" Dare asked.

"Because she's Catholic for one thing. No French priest was going to agree to marry us, so we were married by a dissenter. Some kind of lay preacher attached to one of the Protestant sects. I don't believe either of us thought to ask which. The vows are probably not binding because I'm not sure any of it was legal."

"But surely—" That was Ian, who was certain to argue that any marriage, if it had been conducted by a minister, might be considered binding.

"With the chaos in France, you see," Sebastian continued, "no one seemed perfectly certain which set of laws are in force right now."

The silence after that lasted an inordinate amount of time, but Sebastian was determined he would not be the one who broke it. Let his brothers see if they could have come up with a better solution than what he had done.

It wouldn't really be a fair comparison, he thought, even if they did. They had the luxury of time and no one was trying to kill them. If they believed they might have found one, however, he was perfectly willing to listen to it.

"Then you must be married again here and as quickly as we can arrange it," the earl said finally.

"Special license," Ian suggested.

"Hmm..." Dare said, still looking at Sebastian. And seeing what was in his face, his tone quickly changed. "What's the matter now?"

"I'm not sure she'll agree. She didn't want to marry me before, but of course she was afraid, as I was, that if we didn't get onto the transports, Julián's men might find us again."

"Again?" Ian repeated.

"We were attacked the night we left Madrid. While we were sneaking Pilar out of the house to take her to the encampment and hide her among the women. If it hadn't been for the cook coming to our rescue with an ax, I don't know how we would have escaped. I must tell you, however, that Pilar was holding her own with the swordsman who had put Malford out of commission. I think that attack and the possibility that it might be repeated if we didn't get out of the country were the only reasons she agreed to marry me."

"Good God," Ian said.

"Exactly," Sebastian complimented, smiling at him.

"You seem to think this is all some sort of joke," Dare accused, anger infusing his voice for the first time. "Some juvenile prank, undertaken, perhaps, to prove how daring you are."

With that accusation, the amusement Sebastian had felt evaporated, to be replaced by an unexpected anger of his own.

"The bastard I took her away from tied me down and did this with my sword, simply because I had tried to help her," he said, gesturing again toward his face. "At that time, he had already murdered her father. Then he murdered my best friend, a man I owed my life to on more occasions than I can recount. He beats Pilar's servants when she displeases him. He has stolen everything of value she has ever possessed, including her family and her name. I don't know what else he may have done to her."

Pilar had been living in Julián Delgado's home for almost a year. Although she had never hinted at anything sexually inappropriate in her guardian's behavior, now that Sebastian understood the depths of depravity of which the man was capable, he had begun to wonder what other horrors had been inflicted on her.

He hadn't realized that particular fear lay so near the surface until he had put it into words. As soon as he had, he wished he might take them back.

Neither of his brothers, however, said anything in response to that litany of abuses. Finally, both of them seemed to be listening to, and more important, *hearing,* what he was saying about her situation.

"I took her away from him," he said again. "I smuggled her out of Spain, despite the efforts of his people, who were looking for us. I tricked her into a marriage she didn't want in order to get her out of France. And I promised her the protection of the

Sinclairs. Believe me, Val, I don't consider any of what has happened to be a prank."

"Our first consideration must be what is best for the girl," Ian said, his voice without any trace of censure.

"I have done nothing less than that from the beginning—at least, as soon as I fully understood her situation. I don't need you and Val second-guessing my actions now. Believe me, they were well considered."

That was only partially true, he admitted. After the abduction, however, her well-being *had* been his primary concern. There had been something about the act of carrying a helpless woman in his arms that had made him more aware of the proper role of a gentleman than he had ever been before in his life.

"What does *she* want to do now?" Dare asked.

That was a question Sebastian couldn't possibly answer. They hadn't discussed what she wanted. All along, they had only had time to discuss what had to be done.

"I don't know. At least, not beyond wanting *not* to go back to her guardian."

"Is he likely to try to force her to?"

"Perhaps. *If* he knew where she was. I don't believe he does. Pilar seems to think that since he has gotten what he was after—her father's lands and titles—he will be willing to let her go."

"What do *you* believe?" Ian asked, perhaps recognizing from his tone that it wasn't an opinion he shared.

Sebastian thought about what he really expected Delgado to do now. And although he had far less knowledge of the man than Pilar...

"I'm not sure he'll give up so easily. She was his possession. He didn't strike me as a man who will surrender anything that belongs to him without a fight."

Her bedroom door opened soundlessly, and Anne Sinclair peered through the opening. When she realized Pilar was still awake, she smiled at her.

"May I come in?" she asked.

Reluctant to appear more rude than she already had, Pilar hesitated only a second before she agreed. "Of course."

"I thought you might like some warm milk. It will help you sleep," Anne suggested, carrying a glass on a saucer as she came across the room. She stopped beside the high bed, looking down on her.

In a matter of minutes after she had led Pilar upstairs, the earl's servants had provided a steaming bath, which they had set before the fire in this beautifully appointed chamber. She had also been provided with a maid—a smiling, freckle-faced girl, who had rhapsodized over Pilar's now-clean hair as she had combed the tangles out. And, just as had been promised, she had been lent a nightgown to sleep in, one that was as fine as anything her father had ever bought for her before the war.

There had been nothing in anyone's treatment that could be considered the slightest bit insulting or patronizing. She had truly been cared for like a cherished guest. There had been questions in their eyes, perhaps, but they hadn't yet asked any of them. And she had been profoundly grateful not to have to deal with those tonight.

"I don't believe I shall have any trouble sleeping,'' she said truthfully, but she smiled to soften the denial.

''Just as soon as you are given the opportunity,'' Anne suggested with an answering smile, as she set the milk on the table beside the bed.

''I didn't mean to imply—''

''Then you should. I have no business bothering you. I just wanted to tell you that if you need anything during the night—anything at all—not to hesitate to send for me. Or for Elizabeth, if you prefer.''

Pilar knew very well that she wouldn't send for either of them. But, she acknowledged, if she ever had to call on one of them for a favor, she also knew without any doubt which of them it would be.

''Elizabeth is really very kind,'' Anne said, exactly as if she had read her mind. ''And don't be put off by the earl's manner. I've discovered in the short time I've been a member of this family that it's all bluff, at least as far as his brothers are concerned.''

''You haven't been married long?'' Pilar asked.

For some reason she was surprised by that information. Anne seemed perfectly at ease in the presence of her imposing sister-in-law, even teasing about the loan of her nightgown.

''Not so long that it isn't still...'' Anne hesitated, and then, her eyes smiling again, she finished softly, ''Magical.''

''Magical?'' Pilar repeated questioningly, not sure that was the word that had been used. It seemed strange in that context.

And then she realized that her mother and father's marriage must have had that quality. She had never thought of the love they shared as magical, but she understood the concept, based on the devotion they had obviously felt for one another. She had always dreamed that one day—

Anne laughed, interrupting that memory. She reached down to take Pilar's hand, which was lying outside the covers. She held it in her palm, her other hand almost absently stroking the back of it.

The gesture was again too familiar, just as when she had put her arm around Pilar's shoulders downstairs. For some reason, now as then, Pilar wasn't offended. Ian's wife seemed to radiate an innate kindness, so that one was quite unable to take offense at her familiarity.

"A strange word, I suppose. And I would believe that marriage is magical only between Ian and me, except I know that it is for Dare and Elizabeth as well. Perhaps it's only Sinclair marriages that are magical," she said, smiling at Pilar. "Except that's too narrow, too, of course. It's not *only* the Sinclairs who make such marriages. I'm sure any marriage based on true love shares that quality. Ours simply happen to be the only marriages with which I have an intimate acquaintance."

An intimate acquaintance. *Intimate.* It was the same word Sebastian had used to describe *their* relationship. Too intimate for titles, he had said. Yet during the time that had passed between then and now…

If the Sinclairs had a tendency to marriages that might indeed be characterized as magical, then something had gone very wrong in this one. She and Sebastian were married, and there was nothing of love or intimacy involved.

He treated her almost exactly as Malford did. And

almost, she acknowledged bitterly, exactly as he treated Malford.

"What is it?" Anne asked softly. Her smile had faded, possibly because of whatever was reflected in Pilar's face. "Have I said something to upset you?"

"Of course not," Pilar lied.

"Well, I shan't keep you from your rest," Anne said. "I just wanted to make sure that you have everything you need. And to wish you pleasant dreams."

She smiled again, laying Pilar's hand back down on the coverlet. Then she crossed the room, closing the door behind her.

As soon as she was alone, Pilar took a deep breath, thinking how much her life had changed. And thinking, despite her intention not to—at least not tonight—about what lay ahead.

She was at last free from Julián's hated domination. She was in England, under the protection of a family that had powerful connections. And she was married, not to her despised guardian, but to a man…

To a man who had been forced into that marriage by their circumstances. *There was no other alternative.* His words had been unequivocal; the opinion they expressed undeniably accurate.

Sebastian had never misled her about why he was doing what he had done. He had married her to rescue her. To protect her. To get her away from Julián.

He had married her, but at no time had he ever indicated that he desired to be her husband. If Anne really thought that all Sinclair marriages were magical, then it would probably be painful for her to learn exactly how far from that ideal this one fell.

Not nearly so painful, Pilar acknowledged, as that realization had been for her.

Chapter Nine

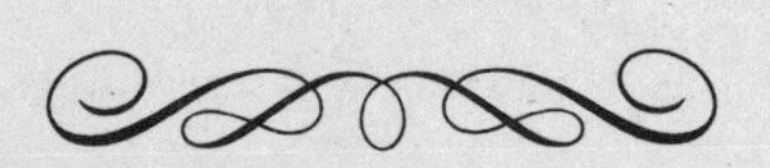

"Quite the loveliest emigré London has seen in a very long time," Anne Sinclair said admiringly.

She was sitting in the center of her bed, her skirts rucked carelessly around her, as she watched the abigail put the finishing touches on Pilar's toilette.

"Refugee, I should think," Pilar corrected absently, adjusting the sleeve of the morning gown she had been given.

The shade of green was not one she would have chosen. However, with the current darkness of her complexion, it was unexpectedly becoming. Very becoming, she amended, unable to prevent turning a small pirouette before the cheval glass to admire the dress from every angle.

"Of course," Anne agreed, unembarrassed over the mistake. "You could hardly be an emigré, could you, since you aren't French."

"I believe that will do, thank you," Pilar said, smiling a dismissal at the hovering maid.

When she had turned back to consider the image in the glass, she thought that it—and she—would do very well, indeed. Even wearing a hastily altered gown that had been created for someone whose coloring and figure were very different. It was almost miraculous what a bath, a good night's sleep and a fashionable dress could accomplish.

When the maid had gone, Pilar turned away from her own reflection to face the girl on the bed. She had never met anyone less pretentious or kinder than Anne Sinclair.

"Thank you," she said sincerely, gesturing toward the dozens of other dresses, which were spread, it seemed, over every available inch of space in the room. Not all of the ones Anne had tried to give her could be adjusted to fit, but there were at least four or five that had proven to be quite suitable.

More than suitable, she acknowledged, resisting the urge to glance back at her reflection.

"You're very welcome. In truth, this isn't nearly the sacrifice you seem to think. I have far more than I can possibly wear, and by next year I fear they will be sadly out of date for London. This was to be my Season, you see. You can't imagine the sums Ian spent."

"Ian spent?"

"He was my guardian before he was my husband. Oh, dear," Anne said, her eyes still smiling, "I've managed to shock you quite thoroughly."

"Please believe me when I tell you that I am *not* so easily shocked," Pilar said truthfully. After all, this was no different than her own situation. "It's just that I had thought..." She paused, unwilling to judge a relationship or a society about which she knew nothing.

"No, it *isn't* the 'accepted thing' in England for a guardian to marry his ward. And especially not accepted when his ward is also heiress to a considerable fortune."

"And you were."

"I'm afraid so," Anne said. "Ian was as reluctant as any man of honor could be, but..." For a second or two, the smile seemed forced, and that strange hint of melancholy was again in her eyes.

"But you overcame his scruples," Pilar suggested, watching her face.

The brown eyes came back from wherever they had been, and the smile expanded, becoming almost mischievous. "How can you be so certain it wasn't the other way 'round?" she teased.

"Because there's something about your husband..."

Unconsciously, Pilar shook her head, unable to put into words the feeling that of all the Sinclairs, Ian was the one who lived his life most strictly by the rules. Or, she amended, by the dictates of honor.

Sebastian was governed by his emotions, of course. Everything he had done since she had known him had been based on how he felt about a particular situation. Everything except their marriage.

She wasn't sure yet what the guiding principal of the earl's life might be, but like the youngest Sinclair, there was a bit too much devil-may-care in those eyes to believe the world's opinion mattered. His opinion of himself was quite high enough to make up for any lack of respect society might offer.

"You're right again, of course," Anne said, her voice no longer teasing. "Someday, when I know you better, I shall tell you why, despite those quite formidable barriers to our relationship, Ian was persuaded to ask me to marry him."

When I know you better... Despite her doubts that she would be here long enough to earn Anne's friendship to that extent, Pilar said, "And why *you* accepted, perhaps?"

"But you've met him," Anne responded, smiling again. "I'm sure you can see for yourself why I accepted."

Since Anne had described her marriage as "magical," she probably couldn't imagine anyone who would *not* fall head over heels in love with Ian Sinclair. And Pilar found that she was almost jealous.

"Do you think it's possible that if two people marry, but it's not for love..." She hesitated, regretting, despite Anne's kindness, having begun the question.

"If they didn't marry for love," Anne said after a moment, "then why did they marry?"

"Perhaps because one of them felt there was no option other than marriage in the situation they had found themselves in."

How ridiculous that sounded. And how melodramatic.

"It seems to me that there are always options," Anne said, "no matter the situation. We tend to choose those that make the most sense to us. So that if love *is* involved—"

A knock on the door interrupted whatever she had intended to say. Although Anne could not possibly understand what it felt like to have the man you'd fallen in love with offer to marry you out of expediency, Pilar had found herself listening avidly to what had sounded like a promising beginning. She would be extremely disappointed not to hear the end of it.

"Come in," Anne called, without troubling to scramble off the bed.

The door opened to reveal Watson, Dare's dignified majordomo. He nodded to Ian's wife before he turned to address Pilar.

"The earl asks if you would join him in his study, madam."

"Now?"

"I believe he's waiting for you there. However, if you wish me to take a message to him..."

"Never mind," Pilar said, giving in. The earl's questions were inevitable. Buoyed by a new dress and a night's rest, she felt now was as good a time as any to try to answer them. Besides, there were a few things she wanted to ask Dare as well.

"If you would follow me," Watson suggested.

"Of course," she said.

She glanced at Anne, grimacing. She was careful, however, that the face she'd made was hidden from the butler.

"Remember what I told you," Anne advised.

About the earl, Pilar realized. *It's all bluff.*

Anne meant his arrogance, she supposed. Or the aura of unspoken authority that surrounded him. Since she wasn't his family, however, no matter what Anne had meant to reassure her about, it wouldn't apply to his treatment of her.

"You sent for me," Pilar said.

"I hope I should never be so gauche as to 'send' for a guest," the Earl of Dare protested.

He had risen when she'd entered the room, and he was standing now as if he expected her to walk across and present her hand. She didn't. If pressed, she could not have explained why she had chosen not to.

"I merely asked if you would agree to see me," her host continued, willing to overlook her reluctance. "If my messenger implied anything other than that, I apologize for his ineptitude."

"Your messenger delivered your summons impeccably, Lord Dare," Pilar said.

Dare's lips moved slightly at the corners, almost a tilt. Other than that, he ignored the gibe, gesturing her to the chair opposite his instead of pursuing her interpretation of his request.

It was early enough that she had not yet seen Sebastian. She had no idea, therefore, what he had told his oldest brother about what had occurred in Spain. Or, more important, in France.

If he had told him anything at all, she suspected it was the latter events about which the earl was concerned. If Sebastian had mentioned their marriage, there was no doubt that Dare, as head of the Sinclair family, intended to determine with whom its youngest member had gotten himself entangled.

"Would you care for coffee?" he asked as soon as she had settled herself in the chair.

There was no tray in sight, so she supposed he intended to ring for one to be brought if she said that she did. And since that might have the effect of unnecessarily prolonging this interview…

"Thank you, but no. I had tea in my room."

She didn't add that it had been accompanied by what had seemed, even for a household of this size and obvious wealth, a vast array of food. Having avoided dinner the night before by pleading exhaustion, she had partaken of a hearty meal this morning, although some of the English dishes had seemed strange fare for breaking one's fast.

There was a silence after her refusal, but thankfully it didn't take the earl long to come to the point. She imagined he was as anxious to get this awkward business out of the way as she was. Just for different reasons, of course.

"Sebastian has told me that he promised you the protection of this family. I assure you that we shall do everything in our power to fulfill that pledge."

"Thank you," she said, the pause he had allowed seeming to indicate he desired some response to that promise.

"He has also told me that since the crown has already awarded your guardian your father's lands and titles, you feel he will now be willing to let you go."

It seemed, then, that Sebastian had talked about her situation at some length. She could only wish she had had the opportunity for such an open discussion with him before she'd been summoned here.

"I can't see why he would continue to pursue me, given that those attributes were what attracted him in the first place."

There was again a slight movement at the corners of the earl's expressive lips. "You will, I hope, allow me to be somewhat skeptical of that claim."

"You may *be* whatever you wish, Lord Dare. I assure you that I am only speaking the truth."

"You must be aware that you are a very beautiful woman, Doña Pilar. As the daughter of a grandee of Spain—"

"My father is dead. Thanks to Bonaparte there are no longer grandees in Spain, not even my fiancé, despite the title he has stolen. I personally no longer have a title. And no possessions, not even the clothing I am wearing."

She had managed to keep all emotion out of her voice as she catalogued her lack of anything that might make Julián—or any other man—desire her.

"And very becoming clothing it is," the earl said.

As she sometimes had with his brother, she believed that she detected amusement hidden beneath those seemingly commonplace words. An amusement directed at her.

"Thank you. It belongs to your sister-in-law."

"I'm not surprised. Anne has a generous and courageous heart."

Generous she would grant, but courageous? The word seemed out of place when used to describe the friendly and unassuming girl who had taken her under her wing. Not that she needed to be taken under anyone's wing, Pilar thought. And perhaps it was time to make that clear.

"I don't believe Julián will come to England to find me, even if he knew where to look, so I wonder if I might impose upon you for...some advice."

"I should be delighted to be of service."

"I believe that I must seek some form of employment."

The statement obviously took the earl by surprise. His eyes had widened slightly, but the reaction was quickly controlled.

"I assure you, Doña Pilar, that as long as you are under my protection, you shall never have to—"

"But I do not wish to be under your protection, Lord Dare. Nor do I believe it is necessary. I thought I had made my reasons for that perfectly clear."

"The fact that you believe your guardian won't come to England to seek you does not, surely, necessitate your seeking employment. Frankly, I fail to see the connection."

"There is none. Other than the reality that having brought nothing of value with me from Spain, I find I must now manage somehow to support myself."

"Usually," the earl said softly, "one's husband might be expected to provide that support."

It seemed Sebastian had held nothing back then in his recounting of their adventures. Obviously the earl was aware of the marriage that had taken place on the docks at Bordeaux.

"Husband?" she said aloud, pleased with the inflection.

"Sebastian. Or is he *not* your husband?"

"There seemed to be some confusion as to which set of laws was in effect in France at the time. In any case, the man who performed that ceremony was not a priest."

"So you consider the marriage to be invalid?"

"I have no idea about the legality of what occurred. All I can tell you is that it was not a mass."

She thought she had rather neatly avoided stating what she felt about that exchange of vows, but Sebastian's brother seemed equally skilled at trying to pin her down.

"And because of that, as far as you're concerned, it was no marriage at all."

"As far as *I'm* concerned," she said, again choosing her words with care, "your brother is free of any conjugal responsibility to me. That is, of course, why I mentioned seeking employment."

"And what sort of...employment did you have in mind, Doña Pilar?"

This time she ignored his use of her title, as well as the ridiculous disappointment that had welled in her chest at his ready acceptance of her opinion concerning her marriage. Of course, that was surely what he had been hoping to hear. He was obviously relieved to be able to move on to a discussion about her future.

"I had thought you might be willing to provide me with a recommendation to some friend who is in need of a governess," she suggested, watching his expression to gauge his response. "I assure you that I have been very well educated, at least according to the standards applied to women in my country. My father had no sons, you see."

"So he had you tutored as if you were one? Sebastian mentioned your skill with a sword."

"My father instructed me in swordplay himself at the beginning of the war. When he joined the fight against the French, he was of necessity away from home for weeks at a time. Although there were always some of his men left behind to protect the estate, he felt that it was important that I could defend myself if the need ever arose. I am also considered to be quite a good shot," she added.

Perhaps if the earl understood she had not been the sheltered heiress he supposed her to be, he might be more willing to help her establish herself in some position away from his household.

"Forgive what is surely unsolicited advice, but I don't believe that is a talent one might wish to tout in applying for a position as governess," Dare said.

There was again that annoying thread of amusement in the warning.

"I speak several languages," she continued, choosing to ignore it. "My singing is merely passable, but I play the guitar with some skill. I was taught both drawing and watercolor. I believe an employer would find no fault with my mastery of those. Perhaps my needlework *does* leave something to be desired, but I'm sure—"

She stopped because the amusement she had heard in his voice was now clearly in his eyes. He was laughing at her. And he was no longer making any attempt to hide it.

"You think me ridiculous," she said.

"You would be surprised at what I think about you, Doña Pilar. Do you really wish to teach someone else's brats to watercolor while you correct their French verbs?"

"There are worse things." *And I have experienced most of them.* She didn't say that, but perhaps it was implied by her tone.

The amusement was suddenly wiped from his face. His lips pursed as the blue eyes, so much like Sebastian's that they made her heart ache, became speculative.

"If you are determined to care for children, may I suggest then that you begin with mine."

"Yours? I wasn't aware… Or are you referring to the child that the countess…?" She paused, uncertain how to finish that statement without seeming indelicate.

"My firstborn. I confess to being particular as to who shall care for him. Or her," he added as an afterthought.

"Here?" she asked.

"And at Sinclair Hall. The household alternates between the two."

The household. Which would include—

"I think it might be better for all concerned," she said, "if you would refer me to some friend."

"Indeed? May I ask why you aren't interested in entering *my* employ? I rather fancy my son having a governess who is considered to be 'a good shot.'"

"You *are* making fun of me," she said, feeling blood rush into her cheeks, a combination of anger and humiliation.

"I am simply offering you what you profess to want—a situation as a governess. I don't see why that shouldn't be here."

Because I am in love with your brother, who married me, by his own admission, only because there was no other alternative.

"Forgive me, Lord Dare, but I find I would really prefer another position." *Any other position.*

"Will you tell me why?"

For a moment she could not think of a single reasonable explanation for that preference. And then she had an inspiration. Something he surely must recognize as logical.

"If my guardian *were* to look for me, it would seem the likeliest place for him to do so..." She paused dramatically.

"Would be with Sebastian," he finished for her.

She nodded, relieved that he had made that lie so easy.

"I don't think that will be a problem," the earl said, destroying that relief. "After all, my brother is of an age now when he will surely wish to settle down and establish his own household. Since there are several quite suitable family properties he may chose from, I doubt he will be under foot much longer."

Settle down and establish his own household. That seemed to imply the earl believed Sebastian would wish to marry soon. And that might prove somewhat awkward, she thought with a spurt of anger, since he already possessed a wife.

"I am simply concerned about his safety should Julián try to find me," she said aloud.

"Oh, I quite understand," the earl said. "And your solicitousness of my brother's safety is quite commendable, of course. There is, however, the remaining problem of your marriage."

"I told you—"

"I understand your objections on religious grounds, Doña Pilar. I'm uncertain, however, as to the legal and moral implications of what occurred in France. You did exchange vows, after all. The minister was ordained by some religion, if not your own. And yours is a religion Sebastian does not share."

"Are you saying that he…that *Sebastian* considers our marriage to be binding?"

"I should think that question might better be addressed to my brother."

"Then may I ask, my lord, why you and I are discussing it?" she asked in exasperation.

He smiled at her, his lips slanting quickly upward in what appeared to be genuine amusement rather than the mockery she had sensed before. His next words confirmed that impression.

"Forgive me. I am too accustomed to looking after the interests of my brothers. An unfortunate habit for which Ian, the most patient of men, has recently taken me quite sternly to task. Perhaps I am again overstepping my bounds as head of the family.''

She said nothing, assessing the sincerity within those blue eyes. It seemed that perhaps a hint of mockery did linger there.

''I would be very grateful if you would apprise me of Sebastian's response to your question when he has had a chance to make one.'' He lifted his hands, palms upward, in a gesture of what was perhaps resignation. ''When that has been ascertained, then we may proceed, I suppose. It may be that, no matter how indifferent both of you are to the significance of the ceremony that took place in France, there remain some troublesome legal problems that will have to be resolved. With your permission, I shall try to determine if that is the case.''

He didn't give a tinker's damn about her permission, and she knew it. The Earl of Dare was used to having his own way. The problem was that she was not perfectly sure in this instance exactly what his way was.

She had come to this interview believing he was concerned about getting rid of her with the least amount of trouble for the Sinclairs. Now he seemed to be implying that even if she didn't consider the vows they had spoken to be binding, it was possible Sebastian did. She wondered how he might have gotten that impression.

''There will be time enough, I believe,'' Dare continued, ''when all of that has been settled to everyone's satisfaction to think about your...employment.

Until then, you will have to make do with my hospitality, I'm afraid."

"Lord Dare—" she began to protest, although she couldn't imagine what alternative she might have.

"*And,* so that your stay with us will be more enjoyable, I shall endeavor to see that my servants are trained to the perfection of those within your father's household," he added. "Unless you might be willing, while you're awaiting the outcome of my inquiries about your marital situation, to undertake that task."

There was no way he could have heard her comment last night. And those who *had* heard it should have had no reason to pass it on to him. Obviously, however, someone had.

"As the alternative to singing for my supper, perhaps?"

"Since your singing is, as I recall, only passable..." One dark brow lifted in inquiry.

"I should think it would be to your advantage to allow me to leave as soon as possible."

"I can't imagine why."

"And I can't imagine why you would wish to keep me here."

"As the head of this family, I feel it incumbent upon me to see to the needs of its members."

"Sebastian—"

"And since you are, at least temporarily, a member of my family," he went on as if she hadn't attempted to speak, "it seems incumbent upon me to also see to yours."

And since you are a member of my family.

The words were more appealing than she wanted

to admit. After her father's death, she had lacked any sort of family bond. Certainly no one could classify the relationship she and Julián shared as familial.

"Whether *I* wish you to or not. Is that what you're saying?"

"Believe me, my brothers frequently wish I would refrain from attempting to see to their best interests. I'm sure they will tell you that those wishes have yet to deter me," he said, smiling at her.

"In any case," he went on, "I'm sure my inquiries will take no more than a few days. I hope you will be able to endure the Sinclair hospitality that long. And if at the end of that time you still feel so strongly that you need to get away, I promise I shall not only *not* stand in your way, I shall try to speed you along it."

"May I have your word on that?" she asked.

"Do you need it?"

"Yes, my lord, I believe I do."

"Then you have it, of course," he said, getting to his feet.

She took that to mean that the interview was at an end. And all in all, she didn't feel that she had acquited herself too badly. She rose, also, and this time she gave him her hand. He touched his lips to the back of it, and when he straightened, his eyes found hers.

"Be warned that we don't take marriage lightly in this family," he said. "Nor do we take it for granted. May I suggest that you have a frank discussion with Sebastian as to his feelings about yours."

"You are quite free to suggest whatever you wish, of course."

She made no promise to act on that suggestion. She would talk to Sebastian, but she didn't want it to appear that their discussion had come about because the Earl of Dare had decreed it. The earl laughed, his eyes softening in exactly the same way she had noticed that his brother's sometimes did.

"I have in the past called into question Sebastian's judgment," he said. "I have actually accused him of acting out of impulse rather than reason. I believe, Doña Pilar, that you may prove me wrong."

She wasn't sure what he expected her to say to that, and so she said nothing. She inclined her head instead, and then she turned on her heel and beat a retreat across the colorful expanse of the Turkish carpet that covered the floor of his study. As she closed the door behind her, she could have sworn that she heard something that sounded suspiciously like laughter.

Deciding that two could play at that game, she finally allowed her own smile. There was no doubt in her mind that, despite his position of power, she had given as good as she'd gotten. And if one could say that about a confrontation with the Earl of Dare, she decided, then one had achieved a victory indeed.

"Your brother suggested that a frank discussion about our marriage might be in order," she said.

From her window upstairs, she had watched Sebastian enter the garden. Although his back was to her, she had had no doubt about her instantaneous identification. She would have recognized the proud set of his head and the breadth of those shoulders among a hundred men.

And he wasn't among a hundred men, of course. He was quite alone. With this close-knit family, that seemed to be the exception rather than the rule. And something she should probably take advantage of, she had decided.

Having made that decision, she had hurried down the stairs, finding her way to the back of the house as much by instinct as through any sense of the direction she should take. When she had opened the tall French door and had found him still alone, she had lifted her skirt and hurried across the lawn.

He was standing in the shade of one of the massive oaks that towered over the manicured grounds, which were actually quite extensive for a house in town. He had turned as soon as she addressed him.

"My *brother* suggested?" He repeated her opening words, the inflection rising in what sounded like disbelief.

This was the first time since the palace reception that she had seen him arrayed in the attire of a proper English gentleman. The contrast between the hardened soldier who had smuggled her out of Spain and the elegant figure before her made him seem almost a stranger.

"The earl," she said. "He seems concerned about the legality of our...marriage."

With the phrasing there had been no other word she might use, but despite her quite open discussion with Dare, she was almost uncomfortable employing the term in a conversation with Sebastian.

"I don't believe the legality of our marriage is the proper concern of my brother," he said.

"He feels he has the right to make it his concern. It and anything else that affects this family."

"This doesn't."

This? And then she realized that he meant the marriage.

"He believes you will soon wish to set up your own household. Establish your own nursery," she added, and wondered even as the words came out of her mouth, why she had brought up the subject of children. The earl had mentioned no nursery other than his own.

"I wonder why he should be under that impression."

"Perhaps because it is the customary thing for a man of your age to do," she said.

He smiled, his lips relaxing for the first time. "I meant to question why he believes *I'm* about to do it."

"You *are* of an age."

"No more than you, I think. Are *you* planning to wed?"

"Not, I assure you, until we have settled the unfortunate problem of our own marriage."

"Problem?"

"Please don't make this any more difficult than it already is," she said.

Almost exactly as his brother's had, his lips pursed before he opened them again. "I see nothing so very difficult about it. We did the best we could under the circumstances. If the legality of the marriage troubles you, then I am perfectly willing to go through another ceremony. If that's what you wish, of course."

"What *I* wish?"

"Forgive me for putting that decision entirely on your shoulders, but *my* name is hardly likely to be blackened by the fact that we were forced to travel as man and wife on our journey home. And it won't be, even if our marriage is eventually proved to have been somewhat irregular."

It was, as he well knew, more than "irregular." But she had to agree with his opinion about the likely response of the respectable people in England to that information. She would be judged little more than a whore. While he...

He would probably be seen as daring. A rake. Perhaps he would even be admired by some for what he had done.

"The only way to avoid having your name blackened," he continued, "will be to maintain that the marriage was a valid one."

"Do you consider it to have been?"

"Legally—" he began.

"I don't mean legally," she interrupted. "Although your brother seems determined to delve into the legalities, I am asking if you, yourself, consider what we did to constitute a valid marriage."

It took him far too long to answer. Long enough that the hope she had not dared acknowledge had time to die a little.

"Are you asking if I consider the vows we made to be binding?" he asked finally.

Despite having posed the question, she wasn't sure that *was* what she'd meant. Part of it, she supposed, but she had been far more interested in his emotional response to having pronounced them.

"Do you?"

"Of course," he said readily. "So unless *you* are

prepared to set up a household or start with someone else the nursery my brother seems so anxious for me to establish, I don't believe you have anything to worry about. At least not until all the legal questions about the ceremony have been answered."

"And the religious questions?" she asked.

His eyes changed. It was subtle, perhaps, but she had been watching them intently.

"The religious considerations must be all yours, Pilar. My convictions don't preclude an acceptance of the authority by which we were joined."

"Meaning that you consider us to be married."

"I believe I have just said that," he said, smiling at her.

"But..." She drew a breath, thinking how promising that seemed.

"I have made no demands on you," he said. "Nor shall I. Nothing about our relationship will change. At least not until Dare completes whatever inquiry he has set in motion."

"And if there proves to be no legal impediment to considering those vows binding..."

"I suppose the next decision is also up to you," he said softly. "Nothing is as yet irreversible. I believe the church provides a remedy for situations such as ours."

"An annulment."

"Leaving you free to marry again," he said.

And so would he be. Perhaps this was what his brother had been trying to suggest to her. That she appeal to the church for an annulment.

But if this were not a true marriage in the eyes of the church, why would she need an annulment?

She wasn't sure of the theology, but the logic made sense to her.

"Since the marriage was never blessed by the church, perhaps in their eyes I am already free to marry again."

"And in yours?" he asked.

It shouldn't be, but she found that was a much more difficult question. And she found that when she searched her heart, her answer was the same as his.

"It seems that once you have repeated those particular words," she said, feeling her way through the confession as a blind man would, "no matter the circumstances, you can't simply ignore them. No more than you would be free to ignore any pledge you had made, whether it was sanctioned by some authority or not. That is the essence of vows, after all—that you intend to keep them."

"Then you consider ours to be binding as well?"

Of course. For some reason the words didn't present themselves at her lips and demand expression.

She didn't want to have been married by virtue of necessity. Not even to him. Not even for all the good reasons for which they had undertaken those particular promises.

And neither of them had addressed the real questions that lay at the heart of this issue. *Do you want to be married to me? If you had been free to choose, would I have been the one you would have chosen?* Or even that which was, by far, the most fraught with danger. *Do you love me?*

She had done what the Earl of Dare had suggested. She had sought a frank discussion about their situation with her husband. And after it, despite the acknowledgment that both of them felt bound by that exchange of vows, she knew that nothing that was truly important had been settled.

Chapter Ten

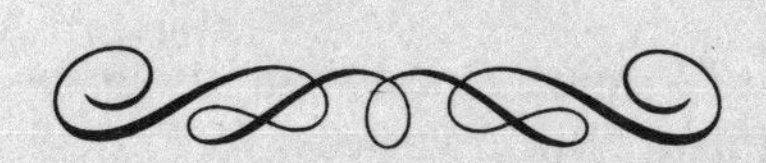

"To Sebastian," the Earl of Dare said from the head of the table, raising his glass in a salute. "The last of the wayward Sinclairs, who has finally returned to the bosom of his family."

"To Sebastian," Ian echoed, raising his own glass.

For the first time Pilar allowed her eyes to rest openly on the face of the man she had married. In the general acclamation of the toast, she felt sure no one would notice. Even as she thought that, those blue eyes found hers, holding there a few seconds before he turned to incline his head, acknowledging the toast that had been proposed by his brother.

"The wayward Sinclair who is very glad to be home," Sebastian said.

"And to Pilar," Anne said, "a most welcome guest."

The glasses were politely lifted again, this time in her direction. She knew kindness had prompted Anne's tribute, but to be included in the homecoming toast made her feel like an impostor. Was it possible no one but the earl had been told the full story of how she came to be here?

"To our guest Pilar. Who is attempting to leave us, I'm afraid."

The focus of every eye shifted from Pilar's face to Dare's. He calmly drank from the glass he had raised as if what he had said was nothing out of the ordinary.

"Leave?" Anne repeated in confusion, turning back to Pilar. "But...whatever for?"

Pilar had suspected the Earl of Dare didn't play by the rules. She had not, however, expected the game to begin so soon.

"Doña Pilar feels that she must go out into the world and earn her keep," the earl explained.

The silence that fell after that was surely awkward enough to satisfy even Dare's desire for drama, she thought. The gazes of those gathered around the table had returned to her face, their expressions varied. Anne and her husband seemed genuinely concerned. The countess's countenance was as serene as the earl's was mocking. And Sebastian's...

"That's hardly necessary," he said.

"I believe it is," she countered.

Why had his brother done this? At table was not the proper place for a discussion of something like this, even if they were, as tonight, *en famille*.

"Why?" Sebastian demanded.

"Because I cannot live upon your family's charity. As soon as certain issues have been resolved..." She paused, glancing at Dare.

"What issues?" Anne asked. "I don't understand."

"That's because we're not intended to understand,'' Elizabeth said. ''A masculine conspiracy, I think. Something at which the Sinclairs excel. Since this one appears to concern Pilar quite as much as Sebastian, however, perhaps a more feminine perspective on whatever is involved might be of some value.''

Her eyes had found her husband's face. She seemed to be waiting for him to explain.

Pilar hoped that he wouldn't. It had been embarrassing enough to be presented last night as a refugee in need of their protection. To be exposed as a woman Sebastian had been forced to marry was nothing short of humiliating.

''In order to be allowed to take Pilar on board the troop transport...'' Sebastian began, without waiting for his brother to speak. And then he hesitated, his eyes still on Pilar's face. ''She was forced to marry me.''

It must have been as obvious to the rest as it had been to her that he had adjusted that wording in mid-sentence. What he had started to say was that *he* had been forced to marry *her*. Not the other way around.

''You're *married?*'' Anne asked.

''But it was not a mass, you see,'' Dare said, his eyes also on Pilar's face, that small enigmatic smile playing about his lips. ''And since no one seems certain what the laws regarding marriage are in France these days, perhaps it was not even legal.''

There was another silence. She could imagine the thoughts that were forming in their minds in response to Dare's revelations. Last night they had courteously ignored the fact that she had traveled from Spain in the company of two men, neither of whom was related to her.

Now they had been informed that she was married to one of them, which, depending on their individual impressions of her, had either relieved or exacerbated their dismay. And Dare was insinuating the marriage that had taken place between her and Sebastian had the blessings of neither the church nor the state.

"If that is the case," the countess asked her husband pointedly, "why ever should you feel it necessary to discuss the subject at dinner?"

The earl smiled at her before he answered. "Because I am hoping for your aid, my dear, and Anne's as well, of course, in convincing Doña Pilar to stay with us. At least until the question of this marriage can be fully resolved."

Elizabeth held his eyes a long moment. Then she turned, smiling at Pilar.

"You mustn't let him ride roughshod over you, you know. It's quite the worst thing you could do where Dare is concerned. It is *possible,* however, that in this situation he may be right."

"Where should you go if you leave?" Anne asked. "Or do you have friends in England?"

"I have no friends," she said.

No acquaintances. No family. And nowhere to go. Dare was very well aware of that. She had asked for his help, and instead—

"It isn't necessary for *you* to leave," Sebastian said. At the quiet conviction in those words, the attention of everyone at the table shifted yet again. His eyes, however, were locked on Pilar's face as he continued.

"I shall be rejoining Wellington as soon as he arrives from Paris. After that, as you know, I have some...unfinished business. You are free, therefore, to stay here without the inconvenience of my presence. Anne and Elizabeth will look after you. And now, if you'll all excuse me."

He began to rise, the startled footman hurrying forward from his place against the wall to pull back his chair. Although his voice and face had been perfectly composed, the abruptness with which Sebastian flung his napkin down onto the table revealed that calm to be the result of a precariously imposed control. Even from where she was sitting, Pilar could see that his hands were trembling.

"Whatever Dare is playing at," Ian said to his younger brother, "it isn't directed at you. Since Wellington hasn't yet returned to London and seems unlikely to do so tonight, there's no need for you to leave, either. This *is* a celebration of your homecoming after all."

"Is it? I had somehow thought that, like last night, it was an inquiry into my actions."

"No one is questioning those, I promise you," Ian said soothingly.

Sebastian considered the face of the man at the head of the table. "Is that true, Val? Are you or are you not questioning what I did in France?"

"Whatever occurred in France is your concern. *Mine* is what occurs here."

"Here? In *your* house, do you mean?" Sebastian asked, seeming confused by the earl's comment. And then his face suffused with color. "If you're implying—"

"I'm implying nothing," the earl interrupted. "Except that I don't wish Doña Pilar to leave. For one thing, I'm not convinced it's safe for her to do so. That *is* why you brought her here, isn't it? To protect her?"

"As well as to introduce your wife to your family, I should hope." That was Anne, of course, smiling at her as if this familial contretemps wasn't embarrassing to them all.

"The ceremony that took place in France was purely a matter of expediency, I assure you," Pilar said. "As Sebastian said at the time, there was really no other alternative available to him."

The crease she had noticed before formed between his dark brows. He opened his mouth, but the earl intervened.

"Whatever the two of you feel about the validity of those vows—"

"Whatever the two of us feel is of absolutely no concern to you," Sebastian said angrily, turning his attention back to his brother. "Nor to anyone else at this table. While I recognize your right as the head of the family to investigate the legality of our marriage, I deny your right to offer either advice or an opinion about our feelings. I'm sure the conduct of yours and Ian's courtships and your marriages enjoyed the approval of everyone in London. That doesn't grant you the freedom to concern yourself with whatever irregularities you may find in mine. And now, if you will excuse me, I shall bid you all good-night."

Sebastian's eyes met hers again briefly. It seemed there was some message hidden in the glance. Whatever it might have been, she was unable to decipher it before he turned and stalked out of the room.

Silence settled over the table as the door slammed behind him. Whatever Dare had been hoping for when he had begun this, Pilar thought, surely it wasn't what had just occurred.

"Oh, dear," Anne said, the words very soft.

"I'll go to him," Ian offered, beginning to rise.

Before he could get to his feet, Pilar had already risen, looking at the man at the head of the table. At least the mockery had been wiped from his eyes, she noted with satisfaction.

"He's right," she said. "This is *not* your concern. It's not the concern of any of you, whether you are his family or not. Whatever Sebastian has told you about me..."

The memories of everything that had happened since her father's death bombarded her. And suddenly she knew that she couldn't possibly make these people understand the evil of someone like Julián Delgado.

Here in the safety and splendor of this London town house, his depravity seemed almost unreal, even to her, who had lived through it. They had probably never in their sheltered lives been exposed to the kind of evil of which Julián was capable.

"Whatever he told you, it won't have been the whole," she finished quietly. "The judgment you make or have made about your brother's actions—or about mine—is flawed by your lack of knowledge about the kind of opponent we faced."

No one responded. And the guilt she had expected to see in their faces over the lack of understanding she had just accused them of didn't appear.

The gap that lay between their lives and what she and Sebastian had faced in Spain must indeed be too wide to be breached by mere words, no matter how well chosen. Having reached that conclusion, unconsciously she raised her chin, defying them to judge either her or her husband.

Then, with the breeding and culture of a thousand years behind her, Pilar straightened her spine. She lifted her skirt in one hand and swept from the room like the daughter of a Spanish grandee she had been since birth.

"I assume," the Countess of Dare said into the equally stunned silence that had fallen after Pilar departed, "that was exactly what you intended when you began this."

"Slightly more spectacular than I'd anticipated, I confess. It seems our brother has met his match," the earl said, no longer bothering to hide his amusement.

"I have a feeling life in that household will never be dull," Ian suggested with an answering smile.

"Do you think someone should explain to them..." Anne began, and then she hesitated, her eyes troubled.

"Someday," Ian said. "But not tonight."

"Definitely not tonight," Elizabeth agreed. "There will be time enough for explanations when they have had a chance to comfort one another. There's nothing like opposition to force two people together, united against the world that doesn't understand them."

"How well you know me," her husband said. "By the way, I have offered Doña Pilar the position of governess to our son or daughter. I hope that meets with your approval."

"Given the Sinclair propensity for attracting excitement, I had rather been hoping to introduce a calming influence into the nursery. *Your* father must have employed a series of Amazons as wet nurses.''

''Then if Pilar accepts, we shall simply be carrying on a family tradition. What could be better than that?''

''Nothing short of employing the entire Mongol horde,'' Elizabeth said with a perfectly straight face.

The logical place to seek a man who had just announced his intent to leave home would probably have been in his rooms, where he might be expected to be engaged in gathering together his belongings. For some inexplicable reason, that wasn't where Pilar went to look for Sebastian.

And as soon as she stepped out into the moonlit garden, she knew she had not been mistaken. The faintest scent of tobacco smoke was carried to her on the night air. She lifted her face, breathing in the smell of it as if it were some exotic Eastern perfume.

When she lowered her eyes, they had adjusted enough that she could see him standing where he had stood this morning, his figure shadowed by the same oak. She watched as he brought the cigarillo to his mouth, the tip glowing redly in the darkness. She started toward him, knowing that he would recognize the paleness of her cream-colored gown long before he could distinguish her features.

''My apologies for my brother's rudeness,'' he said as she approached. ''He fancies himself the family patriarch. And I, as you may have guessed, have been cast in the role of the willful, prodigal son.''

''I imagine yours is no different than most families.''

She wasn't sure on what basis she had made that judgment, never having had siblings of her own. With Anne's eager friendship, however, for a little while it had almost seemed as if she had.

"It isn't that I haven't provided them with ample justification for assigning me the role," he admitted. "And if one didn't understand the situation we were in, then what I did in Spain might very well seem the same kind of reckless behavior in which I've indulged in the past."

"What choice did you have?" she said, offering the question as condolence.

"I suppose I could have left you in France along with the other women."

Despite his previous anger, it was obvious from his tone that he was teasing her. Or perhaps…

He was flirting again, she realized. And at the thought, her heart began to beat a little faster.

"I find that I'm very grateful you didn't."

"In spite of tonight?"

"Are they always like that?"

"Like what?" And when she didn't answer, afraid of giving offense, he added, "I would really be interested in your impressions. I don't know if it's the time I've been away or the fact that I've become accustomed to not being treated as anyone's little brother, but I feel almost a stranger among my own family."

That was undoubtedly her fault. They couldn't have been pleased to have been presented with this questionable marriage as a fait accompli.

"The earl seems…a trifle controlling."

Sebastian laughed. "To say the least."

"I'm sure it's natural that they would want some say in the choice of your bride."

Malford had suggested that the Sinclairs were both extremely wealthy and extremely influential at court. Still, even successful families welcomed the influx of money that came with marriage settlements. That was one way they remained wealthy and influential.

The Sinclairs were doubtless disappointed that the youngest brother's wife had brought them nothing. And that was probably why Dare was so set on investigating the legality of the marriage himself, she realized belatedly.

"Perhaps they had hopes that you would marry someone who could…add to the family's prestige."

She had amended that thought at the last moment. It would be better not to mention the financial aspects of what she had been thinking. After all, these were his brothers. While he might feel free to criticize them, he would resent anyone else painting such an unflattering, money-grubbing portrait of them.

"You think they're regretting your lack of dowry," he said accurately, his voice mocking.

"My lack of a dowry. My lack of title. My lack of everything, I should think."

"I know it must seem like that to you, but despite Dare's performance tonight—" He stopped, the crease forming again.

"What is it?"

"My brother never does anything without having thought through all the consequences. That's probably why he believes me to be impulsive—because he never is. And I've been trying to imagine why he would bring this subject up at what was supposed to be a celebratory dinner."

"And have you?"

His lips pursed and then tightened. She waited, knowing he was trying to decide about his brother's motives, something she obviously couldn't help him with.

"Not yet," he said finally, "but the more I think about it, the more sure I am that that *was* a performance. Dare may occasionally be rude, as he was to you tonight, but it's always deliberate."

"Deliberate?"

"I assume you confided in him privately that you wished to leave. Making that information public wasn't, I assure you, a slip of the tongue."

"I asked for his help in securing a position."

"Doing what?"

She knew, even before she told him, what his reaction would be. "I asked him if he knew of anyone who had need of a governess."

His shout of laughter was less subtle than Dare's mockery, but the import of both was the same. It seemed neither believed that to be suitable employment for her.

"A governess?" Sebastian repeated disbelievingly when his laughter had died away. "And what did Dare say to that?"

"His initial reaction was the same as yours, I'm afraid. And then he offered me a position in his own nursery."

There was a great deal of satisfaction in telling him that, at least until he laughed again.

"Now *that* I should like to see," he said.

"Indeed?" she said stiffly.

It seemed he couldn't imagine her caring for children. The truth of it was she never had. Except for Magdalena's baby, she remembered.

As she had held that solid little body cradled in her arms, his rosebud mouth had made suckling noises as he had nuzzled fruitlessly against her breast. And it had felt wonderful.

"What is it?" Sebastian asked. Like his voice, his eyes had softened.

Embarrassed, she shook her head, knowing she could never confess what she had been thinking.

"You were thinking about something just then. Something that seemed to transform your face."

Again she shook her head. "It doesn't matter," she denied, her voice unexpectedly husky. "You're right, of course. I suppose it's amusing to think of someone like me presiding over the earl's nursery. I've never cared for a child, but I couldn't think of any other position for which I might be even remotely qualified. It seems there aren't many things a woman can do to support herself. Not even in England."

A woman such as herself attempting to seek employment in Spain would be far more unthinkable. Women of her class went from being daughters to being wives. There was nothing else.

"Women aren't supposed to have to think about supporting themselves," Sebastian said, his voice still lightened.

"We're all supposed to marry, of course."

Dare had said that as well, she remembered. Husbands were supposed to provide for their wives.

"But surely there must be those who, for one reason or another, don't marry,'' she said. ''What do they do?''

His answer was so long in coming that she wondered if he had never before considered the question.

''Live with relatives, I suppose. Become companions, hired or otherwise. Or governesses,'' he conceded. ''Some may even end up as shop girls, depending upon their station.''

''Companions?'' she asked, never having heard the term, at least not in any context that made sense of what he seemed to be suggesting.

''Women who provide companionship, mostly to older ladies. They read to them. Fetch their shawls when they feel a draft. Run endless errands. As I said, some are hired and some are simply poor relations forced by their circumstances to assume the position.''

A far more distasteful way of singing for one's supper, but beggars couldn't, after all, be choosers.

''Would you find it less amusing if I sought a position as a companion?'' she asked.

''I can think of no one less suited to that role.''

''Then—''

''Is that what you really want? To fetch and carry for some irascible old woman? Or to spend your life wiping the noses of someone else's children?''

''My situation would be worse in Spain,'' she admitted.

She wasn't thinking of Julián. She could never go back to that. It was only with the heady freedom of the past few days, as full of peril as they had been, that she had realized the reality of that.

No matter what happened, she would never again exist in that kind of bondage. And as for making her own way in the world, her chances of doing that were much better here.

"There *are* other alternatives," he said.

The word reverberated. "Alternatives other than finding employment or returning to Spain? If so, what are they? I would like to hear them. After all, I really *can't* live with your family indefinitely."

"As my wife you could."

"The marriage—"

"The *marriage,*" he interrupted, his voice raised to override hers, "is whatever we choose it to be."

"I'm not sure what that means."

"I understand your religious concerns, but you've admitted that those vows meant something to you when you made them. They did to me as well. It seems that should be the important part."

"And if it turns out that those so meaningful vows weren't legal?"

"Does that really matter? *If* we both consider them to have been morally binding?"

"It seems to matter to your brother," she reminded him.

"To hell with my brother."

"You don't mean that," she said. "You're angry with him because he has questioned your actions, but...he is part of your family. You don't really wish to be estranged from him."

"Of course not. But I also don't intend to let him tell me how to live my life."

"Somehow I think he'd have a difficult time of that," she said.

However Sebastian's family saw him, she had always known him as a man capable of making his own decisions, even if he was forced to make them quickly and under dangerous conditions.

He laughed again, the sound pleasant in the darkness. He drew once more on the cigarillo he held before he dropped it to grind it under his boot.

"That won't stop Dare from trying."

"Probably not," she agreed, smiling at him.

Somehow, in this very different setting, the same kind of ease she had felt aboard ship that night had stolen over her. Despite what Sebastian had suggested about the possibility of maintaining their marriage, she didn't feel under any pressure to make that decision. At least not under the same kind of pressure as when she had had to make it in France.

This had been an invitation. Or, and the thought was disconcerting, a proposal, perhaps. The word conjured up the kinds of romantic images that had not been part of their hurried marriage on the docks.

"You don't have to leave," she said, admitting to herself how reluctant she would be for that to happen. "Not on my account."

"Nor do you. Not on mine. But if we are going to continue to reside together under one roof, then perhaps it might be wise if we bow to the dictates of society."

"Are you suggesting we should live as man and wife?"

"I'm suggesting that as far as I'm concerned, we *are* man and wife."

Her throat was impossibly tight. She swallowed against the force of the emotion that suggestion had evoked because there was one other question that had to be answered.

"I know you felt you had no other alternative—"

"You said that before," he said. "At dinner. I meant to tell you then, but something Dare said distracted me."

"You meant to tell me what?"

"I can't remember looking very hard for another alternative. The one that presented itself seemed so perfect."

The one that presented itself...

"Are you saying that...you wanted to marry me?"

"I must have," he said, smiling at her. "I leapt at the chance, didn't I. You're the one who had to be convinced."

"If you had told me how you felt, perhaps I might not have had to be convinced," she said, pushing the words past the knot in her throat.

Of all the things she might have expected him to say, this was the last. She had been living with the idea that he had been coerced to marry her both by her circumstances and his notions of honor. It was very difficult to accept that instead it was what he had really wanted.

"I'm not sure I knew how I felt. Not at the time. The situation had to be dealt with immediately. There wasn't time to consider anything other than staying one step ahead of your guardian. But...I know now that if I *had* had the luxury of considering what I felt, I wouldn't have done anything any differently."

Nor would she, she realized. She had trusted him from the beginning. Considering her experience with the results of her father's misplaced trust in Julián, that in itself had been remarkable.

"I'm not asking you to decide tonight," he said.

"It may be that the thought of being at the beck and call of some old lady is a more enticing prospect than really being my wife. Only you can make that decision. And if the other is what you want, I won't stand in your way. Despite Dare's antics, he'll help you to find a position if you are determined to do so. Be warned, however, I will *never* allow you to go back to Spain."

She could see no reason not to reassure him about that, at least. Her thinking was unlikely to change, no matter what happened between the two of them.

"I didn't realize until I was away from it what a terrible prison of guilt Julián had created for me."

His face changed, the angles and planes hardening before her eyes. Of course, she knew how he felt about her guardian.

"Don't think about it," he advised. "Or about him. That's over. The only thing you must think about now is with what you wish to replace that prison."

"Marriage or...singing for my supper," she said, smiling.

"I beg your pardon?"

"Something your brother suggested."

"Dare? That arrogant bastard."

"A family failing?"

His laughter was relaxed and unstrained. "Perhaps. Ian, however, really *is* the best of brothers. Steady and kind and incredibly generous of heart."

As was his wife. And once again that sense of longing for the embrace of family was so strong as to be a compelling argument by itself for accepting what he had just offered.

Sebastian, however, deserved more than that.

More than someone who had agreed to be his wife in order to be safe or to acquire a family.

"I feel I must warn you about something else."

Her eyes, questioning, came up to meet his. "Warn me about what?"

"If I'm lucky enough that you decide you prefer this marriage to a nursery full of children not your own or to the incessant demands of some old woman, then..."

For the first time, he seemed to be having difficulty saying what he was thinking. She didn't prod him, letting the silence expand. The tension built as it did.

"I should probably clarify that I'm *not* offering you a marriage of convenience," he said. "I don't care about settlements or titles or whatever you may believe you lack. I care very much about the rest."

"The rest?" she repeated, knowing full well what he meant.

Still, after thinking he had married her only because he had no choice, she had very much needed to hear him say those words.

"You," he said softly.

You. She had nothing else to offer him, but this she could give with a free and open heart. A heart which had, she acknowledged, belonged to him for a very long time. Long before she had known it did. Perhaps even from that first day when she had stolen his sword and pressed it against his throat.

Her eyes fell to the strong brown column of his neck. She wondered if that tiny scar, along with those Julián had so cruelly cut into his face and his chest, would still be visible.

If she agreed to what he was offering, the lean,

muscled body she had glimpsed that day would lie beside her every night for the rest of her life. There would be no unanswered questions between them. Nothing about either of them would remain secret or hidden.

"Does that frighten you?" he asked. Again it was almost as if he had read her mind.

"No," she whispered.

It didn't. She had been horrified at the thought of Julián touching her. Thank God, he never had. This, however...

Only when his thumb brushed along her cheekbone did she look up. He smiled at her, the fingers of that same hand drifting lightly down the side of her throat.

He waited, as if giving her an opportunity to deny his right to touch her. When she didn't, he moved his hand to the back of her neck to draw her to him. As his head began to lower, his lips parting, hers opened to him as naturally as if she had kissed him a thousand times.

And when his mouth closed over hers, the sensation was exactly that. As if this were right. Long desired. And too long delayed.

It wasn't until his lips made contact—the feel of them against hers warm and sensual—that she knew this was what she had longed for since the last time he had kissed her. That night in the king's garden.

Then, remembering the sensation of his body pressed along the entire length of hers, she took the half step that would bring them back into that same physical contact. His arms closed around her, pulling her into an embrace that was hungry enough to rout any doubts that might have remained in her heart.

She had known the first time he'd held her that he was far more experienced than she. Now his mouth ravaged with an expertise that left her breathless, aching for something more. He kissed her a long time, his hands moving against her back and hips, urging her body closer and closer to his.

Her father had raised the magnificent Spanish Barbs like the one Julián had ridden that day down the slope to the river. Because she was her father's heir, he had made sure that the process involved in breeding those beautiful animals had been familiar to her since childhood.

She had known that night in the garden what was happening to Sebastian's body. And she had been made uneasy by the sheer power of his arousal. Tonight the effect that being close to her had on him was anything but frightening.

From the moment she had seen him beside the river, his body naked except for the clinging knit drawers, she had been aware of him as blatantly, undeniably male. That awareness had only increased in the days they had spent together.

Tonight the barricades between them had been breached. He was her husband. And she was his wife. Despite the unconventional ceremony that had joined them, they had both acknowledged the reality of that relationship.

His lips eventually found her throat, tracing downward until they encountered the low neckline of her gown. The feel of his mouth, moist and hot and worshipping, as it moved over her skin set off a shivering reaction.

A wave of heat built until it invaded the very core of her body, centering low and deep within it. Sweetly aching.

When his callused fingers pushed aside the fabric, allowing his lips access to the rounded curve of her breast, she gasped. Her fingers dug into his back, gripping the material of his jacket as if she were afraid to let go.

She almost was. She no longer felt connected to the earth. She was grounded only by the feel of his hands and his mouth moving possessively against her body.

As soon as he heard that reaction, however, Sebastian lifted his head. She felt the slow breath he released, sighing out over the moisture his lips had left on her skin. She shivered again, uncontrollably, and his hand soothed across her back, holding her gently against his chest.

"There's nothing to be afraid of," he whispered, his mouth moving now against the thin, fragile skin of her temple. The words were as soft as the breath he had taken.

"I'm not afraid," she said. "Not of you. Not of this."

He held her a moment more. And then, putting his hands on her shoulders, he set her away from him so that he could look down into her face. In his eyes were promise and hunger. And she wanted them both.

"I didn't intend for that to happen," he said.

"What did you intend?"

"Only to kiss you. And to convince you to think about what I suggested."

"That's what you did."

He smiled at her before he nodded.

"I had no idea you'd respond that way. I should have, I suppose. You have always managed to surprise me."

"What if I have already thought about your suggestion?"

He hesitated, drawing another deep breath. Somehow, without seeming to move away from her, he had increased the distance between their bodies minutely.

"Tomorrow," he said.

"Tomorrow?"

"I want you to be very sure. You know the problems we'll have to face. It may be that this marriage will never be sanctioned by the church. Only you can decide how much that will matter in the years to come.

"Sebastian—"

"That isn't a decision that should be made in the moonlight. Or after a kiss. Certainly not after that one. Nor should it be made as the result of a justifiable anger over the interference of my family. This is something that must be carefully thought through, because I warn you, my darling, once you're mine, I'll never give you up. Not for any reason. You must make no mistake about that."

There was nothing he could have said that would have made her more certain of her decision. Or more convinced it was the right one.

However, morning *would* be time enough to tell him that. They would both be more in control of their emotions. And, she decided, better prepared to deal with his brother's machinations.

"Sebastian?"

Speak of the devil, she thought.

At the sound of the earl's call, they both turned, almost guiltily, peering through the darkness toward the town house. A dark figure stood on the balcony, silhouetted against its lights. Too reminiscent of Julián's appearance at the palace that night, she decided, shivering again for a very different reason.

"Dare," Sebastian whispered, taking her arm and pulling her into the deeper shadows. "I can imagine what he'll have to say if he finds us together."

"He'll know you're here," she warned. "I could smell the smoke. Go to him before he comes to look for you."

His eyes found hers, holding a long moment.

"Tomorrow," she promised, smiling at him.

He nodded, dropping a quick kiss on her forehead before he turned and hurried along the path that led to the back of the town house.

Mindful of the betraying paleness of her gown, Pilar shrank farther into the shadows, watching as he ran lightly up the stairs, taking them two at a time. In the stillness she could hear the murmur of his and his brother's voices, but the distance was too great to distinguish what they were saying.

She hoped the earl had come to seek a reconciliation rather than to add more fuel to the fire of Sebastian's resentment. After a moment, she was relieved to see Dare, distinguishable because he was the taller of the two figures, put an arm around the shoulder of his brother.

Then they walked together, still talking, toward the open door. She watched until they had disappeared inside.

Unconsciously, her lips curved into a smile. It

seemed that everything she had worried about since her arrival might be resolved in the course of the next twelve hours. She would give Sebastian her answer and hopefully Dare would give them his blessing.

She glanced upward, her eyes seeking a glimpse of the stars that had spangled the sky above the sea the night Sebastian had told her about his family. The spreading branches of the oak blocked her view.

She moved back a step, trying to peer up through an opening in the canopy of leaves. As she did, she collided with something solid.

There was no sense of alarm. Not until a man's hand closed over her mouth and his other arm locked around her chest, pinning her arms to her sides as he dragged her backward.

She had begun to struggle as soon as she realized what was happening, but no matter how frantically she twisted and turned, it had no effect on the muscled arm wrapped round her body.

She tried to scream, in spite of the palm that was pressed so tightly over her mouth and nose that it was hard to breathe. The sound that emerged was too muffled and the distance too great for anyone in the Earl of Dare's elegant London town house to hear it.

As her assailant half dragged and half carried her from the garden and threw her into the waiting coach, she realized that none of the Sinclairs could possibly be aware of what had happened to her. And they might not be for hours.

Chapter Eleven

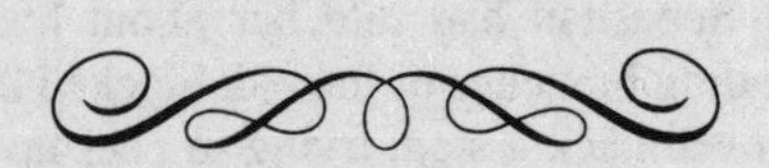

"I hope you'll both agree that it's time to resign my commission," Sebastian said. "With Wellington's approval, of course."

"Obtaining that shouldn't be a problem," Ian offered. "Now that Bonaparte is contained."

The knock that sounded on the door of Dare's study was unexpected, certainly at this hour. Even more unexpected was the fact that it opened without permission having been given. When Anne Sinclair stepped through the doorway, however, none of them thought to question her right to invade what had been a very masculine conclave.

"Oh, please don't get up," Anne protested as the three of them began to rise. "I'm looking for Pilar. In light of something she said to me this morning, as well as your remarks at dinner, Sebastian, I decided someone should tell her the truth about the previous Sinclair courtships and marriages."

For some reason, the smile with which Ian had greeted his wife's arrival faded at the last phrase, although his eyes continued to hold hers with such a look of intense love and concern that it was almost embarrassing. At least it would have been embarrassing, Sebastian admitted, had he not recently learned what the emotions reflected in Ian's face felt like.

''Obviously, however, she isn't here,'' Anne added, smiling at them in turn.

''I assume you've looked for her in her room,'' Dare said.

It had been long enough since he'd left Pilar in the garden that she *should* be upstairs, Sebastian decided, glancing at the clock on the mantel. It was a shock to realize he and his brothers had been talking for more than an hour.

Time well spent, he admitted, because their attitudes seemed to have undergone a transformation since their previous discussion. Especially Dare's. The earl had been able to consider the possible ramifications of Sebastian's actions on the continent without provoking in his youngest brother the anger created by last night's interrogation.

''According to her abigail, she never came up,'' Anne said in answer to Dare's question.

''Perhaps she's with Elizabeth,'' Ian suggested.

''Elizabeth hasn't seen her since dinner. I confess to being concerned enough that I've asked the servants to search the house. You don't suppose she really *has* left us to seek employment?''

''She was in the garden,'' Sebastian said. He had already gotten to his feet. ''I'd gone outside for a breath of fresh air and she joined me.''

Nothing could have happened to her there, he reassured himself, despite the sudden increase in his heart rate. The years he had spent at war, combined with the events of the past few weeks, had made him unnecessarily wary.

After all, this wasn't Iberia. This was his brother's home, located in one of the most fashionable neighborhoods in all of London, which was surely the safest and most cosmopolitan city in the world. What did he imagine could possibly have happened to Pilar *here?*

Despite that reasoned argument, all his well-honed instincts for danger were in full force. He had left the woman he loved alone in a dark garden from which it seemed she had disappeared.

"And when you came in with me?" Dare asked.

"She stayed behind," Sebastian confessed, adrenaline flooding his body.

He fought for calmness, telling himself that there had to be a logical explanation for Pilar's disappearance. One that had nothing to do with what had happened in Spain.

"You left her there?"

The earl had also risen. His face was composed, but there was something in his voice that made Sebastian know he was thinking the same thing he was.

"I never even considered there might be any reason not to," he said, heading toward the door. As he ran down the hall, he was aware that they were following.

He was a fool, he thought as he flung open the French doors. Pilar had warned him again and again not to underestimate her guardian, and yet once they had reached London, he'd let down his guard, putting the dangers through which they had passed out of his mind.

After all, Delgado was in Paris, serving as ambassador for his king. The war was ended. He was home. For all those very good reasons, he had foolishly believed them to be safe.

"If you've searched the house, then she must still be out here," he said, throwing the comforting words over his shoulder at Anne as he ran across the balcony. "Pilar?"

He stopped at the top of the steps, his eyes searching the darkness as he waited. The peaceful, cloud-dappled moonlight drifted over the close-cropped lawn and silvered the ornamental shrubs. His eyes examined each patch of shadow, praying that his gaze would find the pale gown she had been wearing or that she would step out of the shade, coming toward the sound of his voice.

"Pilar?" he called again.

"Sebastian," Anne said, stepping up beside him to put a warning hand on his forearm. He looked down into her face and was even more frightened by the sympathy he saw in her eyes. "I've already looked here. *Before* I came to find you."

"Ian, would you rouse the servants and have them conduct a thorough search of both the house and the grounds?"

Dare's voice had come from behind him. Without a word, Ian turned and limped quickly toward the door. Sebastian started down the steps, but Dare's hand on his shoulder prevented him.

"They'll bring torches," Dare said. "It will be quicker."

"She was here when I came inside," he said, as if that made any difference now.

"But if she were *still* here, don't you think she would have answered you?"

The possibility that Pilar was somewhere safe was rapidly diminishing. And if she weren't, the fault could be laid at no door but his.

"Then where the hell do you think she is?" he asked, pulling free from the grip of his brother's hand.

He ran down the shallow steps, but it took only a few minutes to confirm what he had known in his heart and refused to accept. The garden was empty.

Resisting the urge to smash his fist into the oak under which he'd kissed her, he turned instead, heading back to the town house. He could see his brother and Anne still standing at the top of the steps.

"She isn't here," he said when he reached the bottom.

"I take it that...you don't believe she left voluntarily," Anne said. Her eyes were wide and very dark in a face that seemed to have lost all color.

"I don't know how that bastard could have found us," he said to Dare, making the obvious leap from Anne's question.

Even as he offered that excuse, he knew he should have expected Delgado would come after them. *He's not a man,* Pilar had said. But even a mere man could have easily found out the identity of the officer on Wellington's staff whose face bore the distinctive scar the Spaniard himself had cut into his cheek.

Then, with a few questions to the right people, perhaps to someone in the Horse Guards here in London, Delgado would have been able to trace

Captain Sebastian Sinclair's family. It wasn't as if the Sinclairs were unknown. Or as if the King of Spain's accredited ambassador wouldn't have been shown every courtesy, he thought bitterly.

"Where would he take her?" Dare asked.

He had no way of knowing, Sebastian realized. It would depend on whether Delgado's mission to Paris had been completed, he supposed, but given the speed with which her guardian had tracked them...

"Paris," Sebastian said, praying he was right.

"If a more intensive search of the grounds proves to be unsuccessful..." the earl began.

Sebastian knew what was coming. "He'll have had more than an hour's start."

"He doesn't know the country. Nor does he have my stables," Dare said, that habitual arrogance somehow comforting in this instance. "We'll catch him."

"There are probably a dozen places to which he could be headed," Sebastian said.

"To take ship to France? Gravesend," Dare advised decisively.

"Or some freebooter's cove."

"An Englishman perhaps. Not a Spaniard. In this case, we have no choice but to go with the most obvious."

"*I* go," Sebastian corrected. "You and Ian—if you're willing—should investigate the most likely points of departure in case Madrid and not Paris is his destination."

For a moment he believed his brother was about to refuse, and then the earl nodded. "Take the grays," he offered.

"And Father's pistols," Sebastian requested.

Again the blue eyes held a fraction of a second too long before Dare nodded. "Of course," he said simply.

"A Spaniard," Sebastian said. "Seeking a passage to France tonight. He has a woman with him, but he may have kept her hidden."

Sebastian had stopped at the last public house before the docks, believing that someone inside it would have the information he needed. It was late enough that the place was almost deserted.

"Do you have any idea how many ships bound for France leave here every day?" the man asked.

"I'm only interested in those leaving tonight. Or possibly tomorrow. How many of those?"

The innkeeper shook his head. "Half a dozen, perhaps."

With the help of Dare's grays, Sebastian had cut the time by which they could be ahead of him at least in half. An optimistic estimate, perhaps, but he had pushed the team for all they were worth. And they were worth a great deal.

"I will tell you this," the man went on, "if you want to prevent this Spaniard from leaving tonight, you've got your work cut out for you. Those ships will sail with the tide, and it goes out in less than two hours."

You've got your work cut out for you. It seemed there was no way to do that work other than to try to physically go from ship to ship, questioning their captains. A near impossibility in the time frame he'd just been given.

Fighting both fear and frustration, he nodded his

thanks, laying a crown before the host. The man's eyes widened as he picked up the coin. Sebastian had already begun to turn away when the innkeeper's voice stopped him.

"The launches would have been stowed at sundown."

Sebastian turned back, trying to decide why the innkeeper thought that was important. Launches were the small boats used for ferrying passengers to and from the ships that anchored in the estuary. When their work was done, they were raised over the side and stowed away to be used in the next port of call.

If the ships in the estuary were catching the dawn tide, then their launches would have long since been taken on board. So anyone who wanted to be ferried out to one of those ships tonight...

Just as he'd mentally reached that point, the innkeeper said it for him. "If your Spaniard arrived in the last half hour, as you say, then he would have had to hire a tender to take him out."

"Where would he have found one?" Sebastian asked.

"There be plenty of those lining the pier. Always ready for the late passenger or a forgotten cargo."

"Thank you," Sebastian said sincerely, laying down another coin.

"Good luck," the man called as he crossed the public room on the way to the door.

When Sebastian stepped out onto the street, he pulled his frieze cloak more closely around him. Despite the fact that it was June, the wind off the Thames was damp and cold.

The same moon that had provided enough light

in the garden to allow him to read the emotions in Pilar's eyes illuminated the masts and furled sails of the ships waiting in the estuary to catch the outgoing tide. And just as the innkeeper had told him, lining the pier that extended into the water toward them, a dozen skiffs bobbed gently on their mooring lines.

All he had to do was to find the one that had taken a Spaniard and a woman out to one of those ships. And as soon as he had identified which one—

First things first, he told himself, tamping down the anticipation. It was always possible his speculation about Julián's destination had been wrong. It was always possible that even now Delgado was making for Plymouth or one of the southern ports, planning to take ship there for the much longer voyage to Spain. If that were the case, Sebastian would have to rely on Dare or Ian to stop Pilar's guardian.

Fate can't be that cruel, he thought. He wanted the pleasure of killing that bastard himself.

Besides, he knew they were here. It seemed he could feel the malevolent force of Delgado's evil, as rank as the miasma that drifted up from the waste carried by the river from the sprawling capital upstream.

By now he had reached the beginning of the long pier. Before him in the moonlight lay what seemed to be a fleet of small boats. He would have to rouse the owner of each until he found the one that had carried the man and woman he sought.

The stench rising from the river was almost a physical assault as he worked his way along the dock, asking the same question of each captain. And receiving the same answer.

No one had carried a Spaniard and a woman out

to any of the ships. No one, it seemed, had carried any passengers at all in the last half hour.

Of course, if they had been detained during the journey for some reason or if the abduction had occurred later than he'd believed, it was possible they had arrived at the port only minutes before he had. His eyes lifted again to the masts silhouetted against the sky and then fell to search the dark water that lay between. No skiff was making its way across that empty expanse.

Then where the hell were they? he wondered, fear that he had been wrong knotting his stomach. He turned, his gaze tracking the length of the pier jutting out into the sea.

She was standing at the end of it, the wind off the estuary whipping strands of midnight hair free of the low chignon in which it had been confined at dinner. A dark cloak now covered her gown. Still, there was no doubt in his mind that the figure staring out toward the sea and the waiting ships was Pilar.

There was nothing else there. No one else. There were not even any of the numerous tenders that crowded the port end of the dock.

There was only the moonlight, lining the distant sails with silver, and the open sea and sky, which seemed to dwarf the solitary figure. The same icy finger of premonition that had touched his spine the day he met her brushed along it again.

And suddenly, the memory of Harry's sightless, slowly glazing eyes was in his head. Wetherly's death had given him a warning he could not ignore.

Julián had used this same trap before, he thought, remembering the forgotten cloak, lying dark and abandoned against the barren earth of that graveyard. That time Delgado had employed Pilar's maid as the bait. This time he might have had his pick of any of the dark-haired strumpets who plied their sad trade along the streets and alleys of the port.

He choked back the almost irresistible urge to call her name so that she would turn and he could see her face. Despite what his senses had told him when he'd first seen her, he assured himself that this wasn't Pilar. It couldn't be.

His hand closed around the butt of the dueling pistol he had concealed in the inner pocket of his cloak. He couldn't see where Julián or his men might be hidden. There was literally nothing at the end of the pier but the woman and the unbroken panorama of sea and sky.

Still, he knew Delgado was here. He could feel him, waiting in breathless anticipation for Sebastian to do whatever it was he wanted him to.

He had no way of knowing how many men he might be facing, but Delgado wouldn't have come to England alone. Just as he had taken part of his troop to Paris, he would have brought them here to help him retrieve his fiancé. *Who is now my wife. My wife.*

It seemed to Sebastian that there was now only one way to find her. He must spring Delgado's trap.

He began to walk toward the figure at the end of the pier. In the eerie silence his boot heels echoed more loudly on the wooden planking than they had before. At that sound, the woman turned, looking toward him for the first time.

Whatever Delgado intended, there could be no more doubt about the bait he was using. The moonlight fell across the perfect oval of her face, giving her skin a luminescence that was almost spectral.

And then he saw her eyes, which had, only hours ago, been full of fire and life and joy. In contrast, they were now strangely flat, black and lifeless.

"Pilar?"

He spoke her name because he could not help himself. The questioning inflection was a reaction to the profound change reflected in her eyes. For a heartbeat he doubted his identification, his gaze again sweeping over her face.

His footsteps had not slowed. And gradually, as he came closer, her features began to become more distinct. To arrange themselves into a pattern that was familiar. Beloved.

"What's wrong?" he asked.

The hair on the back of his neck had begun to rise. There was still no one else around them. No footsteps followed his across the betraying surface of the pier. He fought the impulse to glance behind him, expecting at any second a musket ball to explode against his spine.

"Don't come any closer," she said. "You must understand that I'm not going back to London with you."

She had not raised her voice, but the words were clear and precise, each of them dropping with the coldness of a stone onto the surface of his heart.

"Why not?" he asked, listening to the water-lapped silence around them.

Every nerve was attuned for the least suspicion of a sound. For any movement. For anyone drawing breath or a weapon.

There was nothing. It seemed there was no one

else in the whole world. Only the sea and the sky. And the two of them.

"I am returning to Spain with my fiancé." Her voice was perfectly calm, the words spoken without any trace of emotion.

"You don't have to be afraid of him," he said. "I told you that."

Delgado was forcing her to say these things. Like a puppet master, he was somewhere behind the scenes, pulling the strings for what Sebastian recognized, as he had with Dare tonight, was merely a show.

Pilar said nothing for a moment, and then her lips tilted. "You don't understand, Sebastian, and you must. I'm going home. I *want* to go home. To my country. To my people."

"I understand that he's forcing you to say this."

"No. No, he's not," she said. "I asked him to let me tell you myself. So that I could try to explain how—"

"There's nothing to explain," he broke in, his voice savage with the force of his anger. "Whatever he's threatened you with, you don't have to be afraid. He can't hurt you. You're in England now."

Delgado had just taken her from under the very noses of the Sinclairs. He wondered after he said them if those words sounded as ridiculous to her as they had to him. All along, he had promised her protection, and yet, with her sheltered in the very heart of his family, he had not been able to provide it.

"You are no longer bound by the promises you made," she said, her voice unchanged. "Not by any of them."

He examined the words, wondering which promises they were intended to free him from. And why, if she really wished to return home, she had felt compelled to tell him that.

Except she didn't want to return. He knew that she didn't want to go back to Spain and Delgado, no matter what was in her voice or her eyes.

"And if I don't wish to be freed from those promises?" he asked, taking a step closer to her.

"Don't," she said, moving back to the edge of the pier.

From where he stood, he could see that she was poised on the very last board. Another step would send her tumbling into the dark water below.

"What has he threatened you with this time?"

For a moment it seemed that something gleamed in those lifeless black eyes. Then she blinked, and whatever it had been was gone. A trick of the moonlight or...?

"Why are you crying?"

That's what he had just seen. Tears. And as a result, he took another step toward her. An unthinking reaction to her distress.

She turned her head, glancing at the dark water before she looked back at him. "Please, Sebastian. Don't come any closer, I beg you."

Whether it was the change in the angle of light or the fact that he was now much nearer, for the first time he could see the bruising that was beginning to darken the fragile skin at the corner of her mouth. A wave of incredible fury roared through his body.

Whatever Delgado had threatened her with, it was obvious he had already struck her. To force her to tell these lies? To force her to become the bait for his trap.

His trap. He had to remember that this was Delgado's game, carefully orchestrated to make him react exactly as he almost had. Whatever was going to happen, he knew now that he was supposed to take those final steps, the ones that would bring him to Pilar.

Delgado intended him to take them—whether in rage or fear or desire. That's what he was supposed to do. To approach her so that Delgado could kill him. The only question was, if Pilar's guardian was in position to do that, why hadn't he done so already.

"What bargain did you make with that devil this time, my darling?"

She had begged for his life once before. That day by the river. She had knocked his pistol away, leaving him helpless to prevent what had followed. She had done it then because she believed that otherwise Delgado would kill him. This...this, he knew, was no different.

For a second or two, he thought she would refuse to answer him. Then she said, "It doesn't matter."

"It matters to me. It matters a great deal to me."

The breath she took lifted the slender shoulders under that dark cloak. A strand of hair blew across her face. One small white hand was lifted to brush it away, holding it out of her eyes so that her gaze rested undisturbed on his face.

"It matters to me because I love you," he said, realizing only now that he had never told her. Perhaps he had assumed she knew.

"If that's true, then know that this is right," she said. "For both of us."

And then she watched his smile form before she lifted her eyes again to his.

"There is nothing *right* about this," he said softly.

"They will never accept me as your wife," she said. "Even if you could somehow convince them you married me because you wanted to."

"Why else do you think I married you?"

"Because you had no choice. Neither of us has a choice."

The tense was wrong. *Neither of us has a choice.* Which implied...that she wasn't talking about what had occurred in France.

"Tell me you don't love me," he demanded. "Make me believe it."

"I can't make you believe anything but what you want to believe."

"At least let me hear you say it."

The ultimate test, he acknowledged grimly.

Her eyes seemed to focus somewhere behind him. When they came back to his face, they were as cold as the water flowing beneath the pier. And her voice, when she spoke, was raised so that the words rang out clearly in the nighttime stillness.

"I don't love you, Sebastian Sinclair," she said. "I have never loved you."

There was only one thing that could force her to say that. One thing that could have induced her to deny everything that had been between them. It seemed that Delgado could be depended on to reuse again and again the tricks that worked.

This one wouldn't, he vowed. It was time for a deception of his own.

He wasn't going to give the bastard a chance to shoot him. Instead he was going to make it seem he was giving Delgado what he wanted.

The Sebastian Sinclair who had held his murdered friend in his arms would have closed the distance between them, pulling her away from the edge and forcing her to come with him. The one who loved the woman at the end of this pier more than his own life was going to walk away from her.

Retreat was often the better part of valor. He would watch for Delgado's next move and arrange things so that when the inevitable confrontation occurred, Pilar wouldn't be in the line of fire.

His lips tilted as he thought how pleased Dare and even Wellington would be to hear that for once he was being ruled by his head and not his heart. Without taking his eyes off her face, he inclined his head politely, almost as if he were turning her over to her next partner after they had finished some sedate ballroom set.

Then he turned and began to retrace his steps along the echoing boards of the dock, walking away from her. Back along the way he had come.

He had transversed less than half of the distance when the ball struck him, the sound of the shot a heartbeat behind its impact. As his shocked brain managed to put those two unexpected events together, he heard Pilar begin to scream.

Chapter Twelve

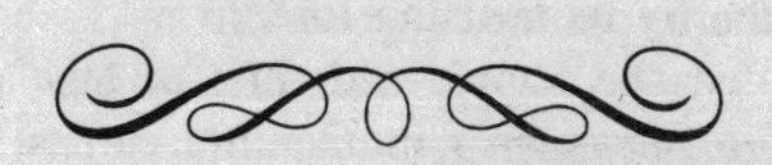

"No!" When she saw that telltale check in Sebastian's stride. Outrage at her guardian's treachery drew out the single syllable until it became a crescendo of sound that echoed off the water as loudly as had the shot. "You *promised.* You *promised* me."

She'd done everything Julián had told her she must do, and he then had reneged on their agreement. She should have known better than to trust him.

After all, he had told her at the beginning that this time he wouldn't leave Sebastian alive to cause trouble. Then, after she had given him all the valid reasons why he didn't want to face the Sinclairs, who would be out to avenge their brother's death, he had pretended to relent.

Seared by guilt at her own culpability, she was stunned as Sebastian turned and began running toward her. Another shot rang out, but she heard the splash of the ball as it hit the water harmlessly behind her.

Suddenly Sebastian was beside her. Without

breaking stride, he wrapped his arm around her, dragging her with him.

Toward the end of the pier. Toward that cold, dark current she had watched race beneath the boards she was standing on. It had been strong enough to carry the occasional piece of flotsam, which had bobbed to the surface only to be carried down again by its swirling force.

It seemed she hadn't had time to take a single step before Sebastian's momentum carried both of them off the end of pier. She had a split second to look down at the water before they hit it, plunging beneath the surface.

At some point she must have instinctively drawn breath. And despite the shock of their submersion into the cold water, she managed to hold it.

After a few seconds she became aware that Sebastian's arm was still firmly around her, holding just beneath her breasts. He was pulling her along as he swam, the powerful muscles in his legs propelling them away from the danger. The weight of the cloak Julián had wrapped around her acted like an anchor, making progress difficult.

The slow seconds ticked by as Sebastian continued to tow her, deaf and blind, through the black void. They had been under so long that her lungs had begun to ache. The urge to breathe in the brackish water was almost overwhelming. She began to struggle against Sebastian's hold, her fingers prying at the arm around her chest.

She had to escape. She had to get to the surface. She had to breathe. And eventually the litany of that need drowned out any other fear.

Panic lent her strength. Or perhaps Sebastian finally understood what she was trying to tell him, because suddenly she was free.

She fought her way to the surface, not worrying about who or what might be waiting there. Two of Julián's men had been in the rowboat hidden beneath the pier. She had no idea where that boat was now.

Her head broke the surface and immediately her mouth opened to pull in life-giving air. She took two or three whooping inhalations, the noise magnified by the eerie quietness around her. She was aware that Sebastian had surfaced nearby, but she couldn't seem to concentrate on anything but her need for air.

Something hit the water beside them. It took her too long to realize the sound meant someone was shooting at them again. When Sebastian's hand closed around her arm, all she really understood was that he intended to pull her under.

She jerked away, although another ball struck the water nearby. And by now, she understood what was happening. Still, the notion that she would rather take her chances on getting shot warred with her horror at returning to that cold, silent world below.

Finally, unhappily, she recognized that she had no choice. This time, however—

"Wait," she said, the word as breathless as she.

Her trembling fingers fumbled with the fastenings of the cloak. After what seemed an eternity, the wet cords finally loosened enough for her to untangle them. She pushed the heavy garment free, letting it sink beneath the surface.

Then she drew another breath. Almost before she could close her mouth, Sebastian's hand had fastened around her arm, pulling her once more under the water that had swallowed the cloak. Only as it closed over her head, did she think about the too-revealing paleness of her gown.

She gave herself over to Sebastian's guidance, praying that his sense of direction was better than hers. She had lost all orientation to the pier or the shore or the ships.

She realized that he was using the flow of the current to help propel them, which must mean they were heading out into the estuary rather than back to shore. In her head she allowed the image of those tall-masted ships, gently drifting on the swells, to form. As it did, she tried to evaluate the distance to them.

Too far away, she thought, feeling a growing sense of panic. Too far. Too far.

The men in the rowboat would find them before they could swim there. Or their stamina would fail.

Already the cold of the water was seeping into her bones, draining the strength from her limbs. She could no longer feel her feet. And Sebastian—

Sebastian had been shot. Or was it possible…

She allowed herself to focus again on that terrible moment, watching in her mind's eye as his body reacted to the impact. How much longer could he continue the exertion necessary to get them away from the pier?

Even as she questioned his strength, he began to urge her upward. Although her lungs were beginning to burn, she wasn't at the point of a desperate need for air as she had been before.

She made no objection, however, when they

broke the surface together. She simply breathed, trying to control the volume of the sound she made.

"There," he said softly.

Moving her hands and her feet to stay afloat, she turned toward the sound of his voice and then in the direction he was facing. Revealed by the moonlight was an island, little more than a bar or shoal, sparsely covered with rocks and vegetation. At high tide it would probably be almost completely submerged.

"Can you swim?"

Sebastian's question brought her gaze quickly back to his face. He looked exactly as he had the day she'd met him. The black hair was plastered to his skull, rivulets of water streaming downward over the sun-darkened skin. Dark lashes spiked with moisture framed his eyes, which seemed as calm now as they had then.

"A little," she said.

Her father had taught her to swim in that same river during one long hot summer when she was a little girl. Although that had been years ago, she believed she could make it as far as that narrow bar. After all, the only other choice...

Perhaps it was better not to think about the other choices, she acknowledged, her eyes lifting toward those distant ships.

Without another word, Sebastian nodded. He released her arm and began to swim away from her. She glanced back the way they had come, surprised at the distance they had managed from the pier.

Something was moving through the darkness between them and the lights of the port. Blinking to clear the water from her eyes, she saw that it was a boat, obviously the one that had been hidden beneath the pier. The men on board were pulling hard against the oars, causing the craft to surge forward over the surface.

Three men, she counted. Only two were rowing. The third was sitting imperiously at the bow, gazing out into the estuary. Although she knew it was impossible, given the distance, he seemed to be looking directly at her.

Julián. The men in the boat must have waited for him to come to the pier from the vantage point from where he had fired that shot. Why hadn't she realized what he planned when he'd sent her out with the others?

She turned, intending to call a warning to Sebastian. He had also turned, she realized, perhaps to gauge her progress. And he, too, was watching the rapidly approaching boat.

Glancing back at it, she was surprised at how quickly it was closing the distance between them. Filled with a different sense of panic this time, she began to swim toward Sebastian, trying to remember those long-ago lessons and her father's kind, patient voice.

The same father Julián had murdered for inconveniently being between him and his goal. Just as Sebastian was tonight.

There was less cover on the island than he'd anticipated, but Sebastian had realized that only after they'd pulled themselves on shore. Of course, any cover was better than being exposed and helpless in the open sea.

Keeping low, they had run across the shingled

beach and slipped into the salt-crusted line of rocks and scrub. Then, lying prone, they watched the inexorable approach of Julián and his men.

Sebastian wasn't sure whether he and Pilar had been seen or whether Delgado had decided he couldn't afford to move on without searching the island. In any case, it was obvious the men in that boat were coming here. And obvious, too, that the advantages were all on their side.

He touched Pilar's arm. Her eyes reluctantly abandoned their focus on the boat that was drawing nearer and nearer.

"Stay here," he whispered. "Whatever happens, don't move. Not until I come back for you."

He had begun to push himself up from the ground when her hand closed around his wrist. He stopped, but that was more the result of a sudden lightheadedness than because of its restraint.

The wound was high on his chest. He had enough experience with battlefield injuries to know that the ball had struck neither bone nor anything vital. If it had, he would never have made it this far. Due to his exertions, however, it was bleeding more than he liked.

There was no time to do anything about that. And, he acknowledged, glancing again at the boat, the loss of blood was probably the least of his worries.

"I'm sorry," Pilar said, bringing his eyes quickly back to her face.

"For what?"

"He said that if I could make you leave, he'd let you go. He wouldn't kill you. I didn't mean any of what I said back there."

"Don't you think I knew that?"

"Did you?"

"I knew he'd done the same thing he always does. He threatened to hurt someone else to force you to do what he wanted."

"And like a fool, I believed him. Even when he told me he'd let you go."

"You had no choice. No one does in that situation. Whether you believe him or not. Besides, I knew you were lying," he said, smiling at her. "Especially when you said you didn't love me."

There was a small silence before her lips curved into an answering smile. "Typical staff officer arrogance," she said.

Hearing the teasing note in her response, he felt a wave of love and admiration for her unquenchable spirit. Perhaps she hadn't reacted as he might have to her guardian's threats, but she had done what she felt she had to do in order to survive and to protect others. No one could fault her for that.

He leaned toward her, propping his upper body on his forearm. He brushed his lips against the corner of her mouth, near the place where he had noticed the bruising.

"I won't ever let him hurt you again," he said.

He had no idea how, outnumbered three to one, he imagined he would be able to keep that promise, but he gave it anyway.

Her hand released his wrist, lifting to cup his cheek. She turned her head slightly, aligning her mouth so that it was just under his. He didn't resist the invitation.

They had no time for the long, unhurried kiss they shared. Both of them understood, however, that it might be their last. Their lips clung. Caressing. Cherishing. Reluctant to release.

Finally Sebastian broke the contact, lifting far enough to look down into her eyes. And instead of saying any of the things he wanted to say, he simply gave his order again. "Don't move."

Then he pushed up into a low crouch and disappeared into the darkness.

His father's dueling pistol rested somewhere at the bottom of the Thames. He thought briefly about Dare's possible reaction to its loss, and then put it from his mind.

He had more pressing things to think about—such as facing three armed men without a weapon. No weapon *other* than his intellect, he amended. His intellect, his experience and his determination that Pilar would not be forced to return to Spain with Delgado.

He watched as the oarsmen pulled the skiff up onto the beach. The King of Spain's ambassador didn't deign to step out of the boat until there was no longer a possibility that he might get his feet wet.

I'll wet them for you, you bastard, Sebastian vowed. *In your own blood.*

He deliberately loosened the grip of his fingers around the thick branch he'd selected, and then tightened them again, one by one, making sure of his hold. Armed only with a limb and about to face a couple of pistols, a sword and God-knows-what-else, he had to be prepared to make the most of every opportunity.

Surprise was his only advantage. He doubted the Spaniards would expect him—weaponless and wounded—to attack *them.* Delgado was a good enough shot that he must be reasonably sure he'd hit his target, even if not dead center.

A poor choice of words, he acknowledged with grim humor.

He still felt light-headed, but he was anxious to begin the attack. His muscles were tense in expectation of the spring that would bring him near enough to his enemies that he could use his makeshift club.

As the three came closer and closer to his hiding place, he could distinguish Delgado by his size. The count had taken the lead, the others following in a single file behind him.

He let them walk by his hiding place, close enough that he could have reached out and touched them. Almost faint from the combination of blood loss and anticipation, he knew he would have only one chance. He had to make the most of it.

Only when they had all passed him did he allow the tension that had been building in the coiled muscles of his legs to release. He sprang upward, right behind the last man. The branch was already raised above his head, poised to strike.

When it did, all element of surprise was lost. The hollow sound the wood made impacting on the Spaniard's skull assured him that he'd lowered the odds in his favor.

The man toppled to the ground like a felled tree. As he did, the pistol he carried fell from his hand, to be lost in the darkness.

Sebastian cursed its loss, but he knew there was no time to search for it. At the sound of his blow, the next man in that single file had turned, rushing toward him with his sword drawn.

Sebastian changed the position of his grip, swinging the club sideways. The end of the branch hit the man's sword, rebounding off metal and bone powerfully enough to cause his hand to tingle.

The Spaniard let out a yelp, but unfortunately he didn't drop the sword. And by that time, Delgado had realized they were being attacked.

He was carrying the rifle he'd used at the pier. As Sebastian warded off the attempts of the other Spaniard to slash him with the sword, he was aware almost subliminally of every move Pilar's guardian was making. The halt in his forward motion. The moonlight glinting off the chased metalwork on its stock as he began to bring the rifle into firing position. The exact moment when he began to train it on his target.

Still the swordsman thrust and parried at the branch, which Sebastian was finding an unsatisfactory foil. He had not been given the opportunity for another of those broad swings that might have disarmed his opponent. His entire attention had been devoted instead to keeping the blade away from his heart.

His eyes flicking from sword to gun, Sebastian had watched as his enemy raised his weapon and sighted along the barrel. Now the rifle was fully extended, prepared to fire. The swordsman fought on, his rapier harrying and darting, coming closer and closer to the same target at which his master aimed.

Sebastian had looked death in the eye on dozens of occasions. Never before had he felt its cold breath as strongly as he did now. And too conscious of the rifle drawing a bead on his heart, he let the blade slip in under his guard.

He felt the cold steel more as a blow than a cut. He had been able to partially dodge the blade by a reflexive twist of his body. Although he had been successful in pulling away from the point that had been embedded in his chest, he could feel the rush of hot blood that followed its removal.

Furious with himself for allowing his attention to be distracted by what Delgado was doing, he renewed his attack through the simple expedient of driving the end of the branch into the swordsman's solar plexus.

The move seemed to take him by surprise. He doubled over, letting down his guard.

Sebastian pulled back the limb and brought it down against the side of his adversary's neck in what had been a nearly unconscious physical sequence. His body seemed to react without the direction of his mind, guided perhaps by its memory of the countless battles in which hand-to-hand combat had played a role.

The sound of that blow was not so solid nor so satisfying as the first had been, but the man fell to one knee, and then, dropping his sword, toppled sideways.

Two down, Sebastian thought, turning his attention to the last man standing. His eyes were drawn first to the black eye of the rifle's muzzle, which was pointed directly at his heart. He had to force them to lift and focus on the face behind it.

"So...we meet again, Captain Sinclair," Delgado said.

Breathless, weak, light-headed—Sebastian felt a

ridiculous impulse to laugh at the melodrama inherent in that. The man could probably make a decent living at the Haymarket.

He sobered quickly, however, as he watched Delgado's face change. The dark features took on a look of malevolent triumph as his finger began to tighten over the trigger. His lips were arranged in a sneer of satisfaction.

Sebastian knew he couldn't let the Spaniard win. Or if he did—and with a rifle trained at his heart, it seemed likely Delgado would—then it could not be because he'd simply stood here and let the bastard shoot him down like a dog. Sinclairs didn't die that way.

He dropped his makeshift weapon and with a roar of fury that encompassed everything Delgado had done, he began to sprint across the distance between them. It seemed he had taken no more than a step or two when he heard the shot.

This time, surprisingly, he had been aware of the sound before he felt the impact. That thought had formed before he watched Delgado's eyes widen.

Then the Conde del Castillo took a staggering step backward. The rifle he held discharged, but when it did, it was no longer directed at its target.

By the time Sebastian reached him, the black eyes were beginning to glaze, exactly as Harry's had done. He was dead before he hit the ground.

Only through the greatest effort was Sebastian able to stop before he'd run into the dying man. Trembling in reaction, he slowly turned.

Standing in the spill of moonlight behind him was Pilar. The pistol the first man had carried was in her hand, and it was still aimed at the place where her guardian had stood.

Swaying drunkenly, shocked to discover he was alive, Sebastian could do nothing but stare at her. Finally she lowered the gun and then let it fall to the ground. It bounced once as it hit the sand. Then she began to run.

It was only by sheer force of will that he didn't go down when she threw herself against him. After a second or two, she seemed to realize how badly he needed her support. He leaned into it gratefully, his forehead resting on the crown of her head.

"I don't suppose you can row a boat, *too,*" he said after a moment, the words punctuated by gasps as he tried to catch his breath.

"Are you expecting me to do *everything?*" she asked, that same teasing quality in her tone once more.

"If you don't..." he began, and realized midway through the sentence that he really might not have breath to finish it.

Despite her arms locked around his waist, his legs gave way as if the bones had suddenly turned to water. She went down with him as he fell, helping him slow that ungainly descent. And when he was on his knees in the sand, still she held him, putting her hand against the back of his head and pulling it against her shoulder.

"My poor beautiful Sebastian," she whispered.

"Hardly...beautiful," he said, closing his eyes, mainly to keep the world from spinning around him.

"*So* beautiful," she said again, her lips moving against his hair. "And the answer is yes."

There was a long silence.

"Forgive me," he said truthfully, "but...I seem to have forgotten the question."

She laughed, despite everything.

"It *has* been several hours since you asked me. I knew the answer then, but you wouldn't let me tell you."

"*That* question," he said, finally understanding. "And you are saying yes?"

"I don't want a marriage that has been arranged or bartered or contrived, but I very much want *this* one. Legal or not. Blessed by the church or not. Approved by your brother or not."

"Consummated or...not?" He was relieved to find that his voice seemed stronger. Perhaps not *that* strong, he acknowledged.

"I don't want a marriage of convenience, either, my darling. *That,* I assure you," his Spanish bride said softly, "was never an alternative."

"Then we bribed Julián's men to row us back. You had given Sebastian the money, I think."

"I'm delighted he found it useful," the Earl of Dare said with a small bow. Pilar acknowledged the gesture by inclining her head. "I confess I'm surprised that you found them amiable to bribes."

"At one time they had been my father's men. I knew them both. I think they were embarrassed by what they had helped Julián do. And sorry for it. Their loyalty to him was always based on fear. With Julián dead..." She shrugged.

"Of course," the earl said, as if everything she had told him, including the fact that she had shot and killed her guardian, was not in the least extraordinary.

All in all, she admitted, Dare had proven to be a most satisfactory ally, in spite of the objections she believed he still harbored about her marriage. She certainly could not have asked for anyone more efficient at disposing of the inconveniences of their current situation.

She didn't mean Julián's body. The outgoing tide had carried that away as surely as it had swept up the ships bound for France. And she thanked God she had not been aboard any of them.

As soon as they'd returned to Gravesend, she had sought out the innkeeper Sebastian had directed her to. In a matter of minutes, her husband had been ensconced in the inn's best chamber, one of the kitchen boys had been dispatched to bring a surgeon and the groom sent to London to fetch the Sinclairs.

The earl, however, had not arrived until this morning. That had been due, she now understood, to his own efforts on her behalf.

He had immediately lent his support to her strong objection that Sebastian should be bled. He had rather rudely sent the local surgeon on his way, although he had given him a gold coin for his trouble. Then he had sent to London for his own physician, who was with Sebastian now.

"May I ask what your plans are," Dare continued, "now that you are free of the danger your guardian represented?"

She *was* free, she realized. There was nothing to prevent her from returning to Spain. With Julián dead, it was possible the king might even see fit to restore her father's lands to his rightful heir. Which could, she realized, make her more acceptable to Sebastian's family.

Of course, it didn't matter whether they found her an acceptable wife for a Sinclair or not. Her name and her heritage were as old and honorable as theirs. Perhaps the exchange of vows between her and Sebastian had been unconventional by their standards—

Actually, she admitted, they were even more unconventional by her standards. However, they *were* vows, and since they both intended to keep them…

"To live in England with my husband, of course," she said.

She held Dare's eyes, expecting to see some indication of disappointment or perhaps even anger within them.

"I take it then that I will be forced to continue my search for a suitable governess for my son."

"I thank you for your kind offer, my lord," she said, suppressing an inexplicable inclination to smile at him, "but I regret that I will be unable to accept that position. My husband has informed me that he intends to set up his own nursery very shortly. He is of an age, you see."

"What a pity," the Earl of Dare said, with what she could have sworn was a twinkle in those Sinclair blue eyes. "Not Sebastian's nursery, of course. He is, as you say, of an age."

She expected him to explain, but he watched her instead, that small enigmatic tilt at the corners of his lips.

"Then…a pity, my lord?" she prompted finally, giving in.

"I rather fancied my son having a governess who is considered to be 'a good shot.' Even in the moonlight,'' he added, ''*and* using a pistol with which she was unfamiliar.''

There was an unmistakable admiration in the last, and despite their rather difficult relationship, Pilar found she was flattered to hear it.

''I'm sure there are few women who could have fought so well as you did last night, Doña Pilar,'' he went on. ''Fewer still who wish to become governesses.''

Pilar laughed aloud and was surprised when her brother-in-law's laughter joined hers. It was reflected in his eyes, she realized, just as Sebastian's often was.

''There are probably more of us than you imagine,'' she said. ''Perhaps the others have been advised that being a good shot is not a skill one should tout when seeking employment.''

She was rewarded again by his laughter. Before she had time to respond, the door to the inn's parlor, which the earl had made his own, opened to reveal the Scots physician who'd been brought out from London.

''He'll do,'' Dr. McKinley said. ''Constitution of a horse, despite those years of war. Or perhaps because of them. If you're Pilar, he's asking for you,'' he added, glancing at her for the first time.

''Is it all right for me to see him?''

''If you hurry. I've given him something to make him sleep. That's the best remedy for blood loss. Lets the body replenish the supply. Go on,'' the doctor advised. ''Unless, of course—''

He looked at the earl, his brows raised in question.

''Doña Pilar is my brother's wife,'' Dare said.

"It's quite acceptable for her to visit him, I assure you."

"You don't have any other brothers who are likely to be shot, stabbed or bludgeoned, do you, my lord?" she heard McKinley ask as she began to make her way across the room. "If so, I had thought I might move into your household. Save us both a deal of to-and-fro-ing."

"I'm sure you'll be pleased to hear that Sebastian is the youngest. Pull him through, McKinley, and you will have seen the last of the Sinclairs. Except for confinements, of course. I have a feeling there will be a number of those in the next few years. Perhaps you should move into Sinclair Hall after all."

"Frankly," the Scotsman said, "I prefer a less volatile practice, but I shall keep your offer in mind, my lord. Do call on me at any time. I shall be fascinated to see if the next generation of Sinclairs proves as interesting as this one."

"I think you may be assured of that," Dare said.

"That you'll call me or that the upcoming generation of Sinclairs will be interesting?"

"Both, I should think," the earl said. "In fact I'm absolutely sure of it."

"You're awake," Pilar said as she eased the door open.

He had been, thinking about all that had happened, while the drug coursed soothingly though his system. Despite the doctor's prodding and poking, the pain was even beginning to ease.

"For the time being," he said truthfully. "There's

no guarantee how long I'll manage to keep awake. Stay with me?"

That had sounded like a plea. Perhaps she would blame the weakness of will that prompted it on the laudanum, but in truth, he wanted her where he could see her. He had been far too complaisant before, and they both had paid the price. He didn't intend to be careless again.

"Of course," she said, crossing the room to take the hand he held out to her.

"Is Dare still downstairs?"

"He's taken over the inn. No one seems to object. I suspect he has paid well for the privilege."

"He always does," Sebastian agreed, deciding as he looked up at her face that he didn't want to talk about his brother.

The effects of the sleepless night she'd spent were evident. The skin beneath her eyes was smudged with exhaustion, her skin almost gray beneath the touch of sun.

He wanted to take her into his arms and cradle her against his body while she slept. He had done that, he remembered. The night he'd abducted her. The night he had known that he was falling in love.

"He gave me permission to come up to you," Pilar said.

Distracted by the memory of holding Pilar in his arms, for a moment he didn't understand who she meant. Only when he had put the pronoun together with what they had been talking about before, did he understand.

"Dare gave you permission?" he asked in disbelief. Not that his brother would permit her to come to him, but that he might think it was his right to decide something like that.

"As your wife. Apparently the earl has accepted our marriage."

"He had better," he said, deciding he'd bloody well had enough with trying to please his brother.

At the moment it seemed almost too much trouble to worry about his family and their reaction to the steps he'd taken to protect Pilar. That was his business and his alone. And if he had no regrets…

He didn't, he decided, looking up into those dark eyes. Perhaps what he had done had been as rash and impulsive as Dare and Ian always accused him of being, but in this case, that recklessness had stood him in good stead. He would never have found anyone better suited for him than this woman.

"Lie with me," he said, using the hand he held to pull her nearer.

Her eyes widened, and he realized what she must think.

"You're exhausted," he explained. "You need to rest."

"Lie down with you to sleep," she said, the inflection questioning and relieved.

"For now," he acknowledged.

"And for later?" she asked softly.

"We are husband and wife. *With* Dare's blessing. There are *some* conventions I assure you I don't intend to flout. For now, all I want to do is hold you close against my heart," he added.

The dark eyes were briefly touched with moisture, which was quickly controlled.

"Against your heart. How very strange," Pilar said. "That is exactly where I have been longing to be, *mi corazón.*"

Epilogue

"And tonight, we are privileged to celebrate yet another homecoming," Dare said, raising his glass toward his younger brother and again then to Pilar. "And if it were not for you, my dear..."

"Hear, hear," Ian said, raising his glass to join in that salute.

"Hear, hear," Sebastian repeated softly, his eyes meeting hers. "Thank you seems completely inadequate in the situation, but...thank you for saving my life."

"It was quite self-serving, I assure you," she said, returning his smile before she looked around the table. "I have been more than repaid by your many kindnesses. I don't suppose any of you can understand what it means to someone who has lost every member of her family to be welcomed so warmly into another."

"To the Sinclairs. Rogues and scoundrels all," Anne said, her gaze touching on the earl's face before it returned to Pilar's. "Believe me, I know exactly how you feel. I, too, was an orphan, and they took me in,'' she said, turning to smile at her husband.

''I had no choice,'' he said. ''You were practically left on my doorstep.''

''Which is why, I suppose, you drove halfway across the country in a snowstorm to fetch me home,'' Anne said with spirit.

''A simple case of doing my duty,'' Ian said.

''He thought I was four, you see,'' Anne explained to Pilar. ''And in need of a trinket in my Christmas pudding.''

''He thought you were four?''

''How Ian and I met doesn't matter, I suppose. I've thought from the beginning, however, that you really should be told the truth about the previous Sinclair marriages. You seem to have the idea that—''

''I'm sure Pilar isn't interested in the dull details of our courtships,'' Dare interrupted.

Despite the earl's tone, which had clearly been intended to quell the discussion she proposed, Anne seemed undismayed by his objection and certainly undeterred from her intent.

''She might be interested. *If* she knew that they were as irregular as hers,'' Anne said. ''Perhaps even more so.''

''You said something to that effect the night Pilar was abducted,'' Sebastian said. ''I confess *I'm* curious, whether she is or not. Especially since I've always been considered the black sheep of this family.''

''You still are,'' Dare said crushingly.

''No, Anne and I are the black sheep of this family,'' Elizabeth said calmly. ''At least according to the beau monde.''

''Black sheep?'' Pilar questioned, not sure she understood the term in this context.

''Social outcasts,'' Elizabeth explained, smiling at her.

''But...'' Sebastian looked from one of his brothers to the other, obviously hoping for clarification.

''I was dealing faro in a gambling hell when Dare found me,'' the Countess of Dare said. ''He won me on a hand of cards.'' Her face was perfectly composed as she told that incredible tale.

''And I...'' Anne began, speaking into the sudden silence that had fallen, her eyes again on her husband's face. ''My father was a coward whose actions resulted in the death of many good men on the Peninsula. Ian was almost one of them. Despite that, and despite even—''

''Anne,'' Ian said softly when the flow of words faltered.

''Despite the fact that he was my guardian, he proposed to me.'' she said. It was obvious to them all that was not what she had started to say. ''I accepted, of course. We were married in Scotland.''

''Do you mean...an elopement?'' Sebastian asked, clearly relishing the scandal of that. ''*Ian* took you to Scotland? Major Ian Sinclair, the steadiest officer and the finest gentleman in His Majesty's army, spirited his own ward across the Border?''

''The course of true love,'' Ian said without a trace of embarrassment.

Actually, Pilar decided, he was looking quite pleased with himself.

''By the way,'' Sebastian said, ''there's something I forgot to tell you. Wellington sends his congratulations. Those were given me along with his advice that I should try to emulate you in all things. I'm fairly certain when he said that he hadn't heard about your elopement."

"So you see, Pilar," Anne said, ignoring the brotherly teasing, "whatever...unconventional path led Sebastian to you or you to him, none of us are in any position to criticize it. Nor do we have the slightest inclination to do so. I thought you should know."

"Thank you," Pilar said, wondering what she could possibly say in light of those confessions.

It seemed that the Sinclair brides had created a tradition of unusual courtships. It also seemed that she had been worrying unnecessarily about their husbands' willingness to accept hers.

"Perhaps, given your generosity, I should share something of our courtship," she said, feeling far more willing to do that now. "Sebastian rescued me from the man who murdered my father. In reality, he rescued me more than once, each time at great personal cost to himself."

"And in a fit of gratitude for my many sacrifices," Sebastian said, his voice teasing but his face touched with a slight blush along the cheekbones, "she finally gave in and agreed to marry me."

"No," Pilar corrected seriously, "I *married* you because you assured me that was the only way I might safely leave Spain."

The silence that fell this time slowly filled with tension. No one broke it until Sebastian said, "But now you've decided to honor those vows because...?"

"Because I love you," Pilar said readily. "And because Anne has assured me that Sinclair marriages are magical. I have yet to put that to the test, of course."

"Is that a challenge?" Sebastian asked.

"I believe it might be," she agreed.

"Then I believe I accept," he said. He stood, again taking the footman by surprise. "Come, my dear. It's past time you became a Sinclair *wife.* You will excuse us, won't you?" he asked politely, raising one dark brow in imitation of his oldest brother.

"Of course," the earl said with equal aplomb. "With your recent wounds, we all expected you'd make it an early night."

"I find that I am fatigued as well," his countess said, feigning a graceful yawn behind the tips of her fingers. "Perhaps an early night would not come amiss for us, my love."

"I have *never* found an early night in your company to be amiss, Elizabeth," Dare said, rising with alacrity. "Ian? Anne? With your kind permission."

"Of course," Ian said.

And almost like Anne's promised magic, in a matter of seconds the dining room had cleared except for Ian and his wife, who still sat across from one another at the table.

"Do you really believe Sinclair marriages are magical?" he asked.

His tone had been as light as Sebastian's, but Anne's, when she answered, was contemplative.

"I believe *love* is magical. And when two people vow to love forever, despite any and every obstacle that may be thrown into their path—" She stopped, the words a little too abruptly cut off.

After a moment, Ian pushed up from his place and walked around the table to hold out his hand. Smiling, Anne put her fingers into his.

"Most beloved of wives, this seems a night for making magic. At least my brothers think so. Shall we join them?"

"I have, it seems, more than my deserved share of magic in simply being your 'most beloved of wives,' but I think that your brothers, as much as I hate to admit it, have the right idea."

"If they do," Ian said, returning her smile, "it will almost certainly be the first time.

"At last," Sebastian said, his lips trailing over her throat.

Despite the long hours they had spent together at the inn, this was the first time she had truly felt as if they were married. There had been something clandestine, almost illicit, about going to the bedchamber Sebastian occupied there.

No one had said or done anything to make her feel she didn't have that right. And as long as Lord Dare had stayed, overseeing his brother's care, he had treated her with every courtesy. Exactly as if she were his brother's wife and a member of his family.

It had not been the same, however, as having their own suite of rooms. Or having the right to come to them openly and together, as they had done tonight.

"Did you really not know the circumstances of their marriages?" she asked, lifting her hand to touch his cheek.

"I knew only that they'd both married. As for the circumstances..." He shook his head. "I suppose those are not the kind of explanations one includes in letters."

"Still..."

"Must we talk about my brothers?" he asked.

His lips moved lower, trailing along the low neckline of her gown as he talked. She shivered to feel the warmth of his breath feathering against the moisture left on her skin.

"I doubt they are talking about us."

"They might be," she said, leaning back a little to look into his face.

"Would you mind?" he asked.

"Tonight, *mi corazón,*" she said, leaning forward again to press her lips against the scar that marred his cheek, "I shall mind nothing except the dawn."

"Why are you smiling?" he asked, using his thumb to brush a sweat-damped strand of hair away from her cheek.

She lay curved against his body, her own sated and fulfilled in ways she had not dreamed possible. At his question, her lips tilted.

"I knew all about horses," she said.

"Horses?"

"My father's passion, besides my mother and his country, was to produce the finest Barbs in all of Spain, no small feat, since that is a horse which has been bred there for thousands of years. Since he refused to marry again after my mother's death, he knew I would eventually be his heir. Everything on the estate would one day be my responsibility. He wanted me to be prepared to carry on the bloodlines he had begun."

"So..."

"He made me watch."

"The breeding?"

Although he had attempted to control it, she could hear a hint of shock in his voice. Perhaps no well brought up English girl would have been allowed to do that. Her father, however, had insisted upon it.

And because he had considered it merely another necessary aspect of her education, she had found nothing shocking about the experience. Not even the first time.

Despite her expectations, however, all she knew about the breeding of horses had *not* prepared her for tonight. The fury with which her father's stallions had mounted his mares bore no resemblance to the slow, deliberate seduction with which her husband had taken her.

"That surprises you," she said, tracing the fullness of his lower lip with her finger.

"I think it intimidates me," he said, smiling at her.

She could feel the movement of his lips beneath the tip of her finger. Another unfamiliar sensation to add to a night that had already been full of them.

"I had thought..." She moved her head a little from side to side, thinking how foolish she had been. "I had prepared myself for something like that."

"And you're disappointed?" he asked, his tone mocking.

"You know I'm not."

He did know. She could see that in his eyes. An arrogance that rivaled his brother's.

In this case, with just cause, she acknowledged.

"Horses *mate,*" he said. "They know nothing of making love."

And that, of course, was what Sebastian had done tonight. Through these long dark hours he had made love to her.

"If you are interested, however, in a more—"

"No," she denied quickly.

"No?" he said, lifting his upper body so that he could look down into her eyes.

Propped on his left elbow, he cupped his right hand under the fullness of her breast. Then he lowered his head, his tongue lightly rimming the nipple until again it began to tighten and then harden, almost aching with pleasure.

She had believed her body so sated it could not possibly respond. Not as it had before. As he began to touch her, however, that same slow heat began to coil, drifting like smoke into every emptiness she had ever felt. The warmth of its tendrils curled lightly around each nerve. Caressing. Beginning once more that spiraling descent into sheer mindlessness he had created before.

His hand deserted her breast, leaving its worship to his lips and tongue. The callused palm flattened, sliding downward, its roughness slightly abrasive over the smoothness of her skin. Another sensation, one she found as sensual as his lips against her breast.

His hand continued to move. Unhurried. Seemingly without direction.

Sunburned fingers spread to encompass the small, convex rise of her stomach. There where she would carry his children, she realized.

When she did, he would touch her exactly like this. With this love. And with joy.

And to the slow seduction of those physical caresses was added the more powerful aphrodisiac of mental images. Her belly filled with his seed, growing rounder and rounder until even the spread of his long fingers could no longer enclose it. The small rosebud mouth of their child, suckling her breasts as he did now.

With that thought, the waiting tinder of her body caught spark. What was happening within it was no longer smoke, but fire.

Then, as his fingers found the destination she had known they would ultimately seek, flame began to spread like a long, slow fuse through her lower body. Flickering along each quivering nerve and then leaping like wildfire to the next, it ignited everything in its path, gradually building into an uncontrollable conflagration.

Like the Phoenix, feelings she had believed must lie dormant awakened into life. Her pulse began to race and her breathing quickened, anticipating. She, who had learned the lessons of control at the hands of cruelty, was being taught the sweetness of release at the hands of love.

She drew breath, allowing her mind to float on the hot wind that was beginning to soar within the heart of the flame. Her body writhed against the tangled sheets, not to retreat from the demanding pressure of his stroking fingers, but to seek it.

It happened more quickly this time than before.

Her body, it seemed, was learning this new and difficult art.

Or perhaps each time he carried her there, to this place she could never have imagined, her love for him grew. Like the mythical grail, it replenished itself each time something was taken from it, growing stronger and more vital with each use.

If it did, she thought, her hips arching in response to what he was doing, eventually she would die. As then, just as she wondered if this ecstasy had already reached that point, Sebastian shifted his body so that his was over hers.

In a heartbeat, his fingers were replaced by the hard strength of his erection, pushing into her with that same sure, mindless domination of the stallions she had watched as a child. No less powerful.

She flinched away as he filled her beyond the physical limits of what she was, thrusting ever deeper until he touched the very walls of her soul. Claiming them. Making them, too, his own.

This was a man who had fought countless battles. Ruthless in war and in the defense of those he loved. From the first, she had believed in his strength. In his purpose. In his promises.

And he had never disappointed her. He didn't in this. Almost before she had time to be aware of the pain of his entry, it was only a fading echo. The reality of it, if there had been one, drowned out by the clamor of her senses.

His mouth opened over hers. His tongue mimicked the controlled lift and fall of his hips. His skin slid hot and damp over hers.

Suddenly, more quickly than before, so quickly she sensed it took him by surprise as well, her body began to arch wildly under his. Her nails scored his back, marking his body. Adding to the scars it already bore in her name.

Her last coherent thought was shock that the hoarse, inarticulate cry she heard came from her own throat. And then her consciousness, too, was consumed by the fire that had raged through her body, turning everything that had gone before—loss and grief and bitterness—to ash.

Slowly, so slowly, the shuddering eruption resolved into a trembling exhaustion, and then, after an eternity, the movement of their bodies ceased. Nerve endings flickered once and then stilled.

Their bodies joined, Sebastian lifted onto his elbows to look down again into her face. Eyes closed, she was reluctant to face him after her unbridled responses, feeling that somehow there must be something wrong with a woman taking as much pleasure in this as a man.

"Look at me," he commanded.

Only then did she open her eyes. Their lids seemed weighted, drugged with passion's aftermath, almost too heavy to lift.

When she had, she saw that he was smiling at her. There was no shock in the blue eyes—only love and joy. And in the undisguised pleasure of his smile, she forgot whatever silly embarrassment she had felt.

This was her husband. A man who knew her body intimately. Her body and her soul, she realized.

She did not regret making those revelations. How could she? The trust they represented were as much a part of this union as the simple vows that had joined them.

"Mi corazón," he said softly.

She was. And because—like that of her own parents—it seemed Sinclair marriages were magical, she knew she always would be his heart. Just as he, her so beloved husband, would always be hers.

"Mi corazón."

* * * * *

If you have enjoyed the adventures of the 19th century Sinclairs, please look for the continuation of the family line in my upcoming Intrigue, RAFE SINCLAIR'S REVENGE, which will be available in November of 2002. The hero of that book, Rafael Sinclair, bears the name of Pilar's father, and carries on the tradition of duty and service to country in the modern day world. And of course, he, too, finds his own Sinclair bride in the course of that story. I hope you'll watch for it!

Gayle Wilson